Princess in Waiting

Katherine of Aragon is best known as the first of Henry VIII's wives, whose scandalous divorce involved, among other things, the toppling of the Church of Rome in Britain. Little has been written about her life before becoming Queen of England, and it is that lack which this absorbing novel remedies.

Not much more than a child, the Princess of Aragon is betrothed to Prince Arthur, heir apparent to the English throne, and arrives in Plymouth with her small retinue of ladies. Tudor England comes alive with the story of their marriage, their brief, happy life together at Ludlow Castle, Prince Arthur's tragic death and Katherine's sad seven years of widowhood. Then follows marriage to the youthful Henry VIII . . .

Judith Saxton, author of *The bright day is done*, writes with verve, expertise and vivid detail of the unknown life of this fascinating historical figure.

Also by Judith Saxton

The bright day is done:
The story of Amy Robsart
(1974)

JUDITH SAXTON

Princess in Waiting

Constable London

First published in Great Britain 1976
by Constable and Company Ltd
10 Orange Street, London WC2H 7EG
Copyright © 1976 by Judith Saxton

ISBN 0 09 460970 5

Set in Intertype Plantin
Printed in Great Britain by
The Anchor Press Ltd
and bound by Wm Brendon & Son Ltd
both of Tiptree, Essex

For Alan, with love

Acknowledgements

I should like to thank the staff of the Wrexham Branch library and Prestatyn Branch library for their help, and in particular I must express my gratitude to the County Archivist of Shropshire and the staff of the Shrewsbury reference library whose longsuffering searchings for tiny fragments of fact made it possible for me to write of Katherine's journey to Ludlow, and her life at the castle.

Contents

1　Granada

The full heat of the summer afternoon lay on the land, and
the streets of Granada were deserted, save for an occasional
cat which strolled languidly across the thick, white dust.
In the shadows cast by buildings, beggars sprawled, content
to sleep, for almsgivers slept also, rich and poor alike being
as hungry for the cool spots in which to rest as they were
for bread.

Above and beyond the slumbering city, the Sierra Nevada
mountains hung in the burning blue sky, thrusting their
snow-clad peaks towards the brassy sun. They made a
backdrop of severe splendour for the huddled rooftops and
crumbling walls of the old city, enhancing even the rose-red
walls of the Alhambra Palace.

In the shadow of a small church something stirred, then
a monk came slowly out of the black cave of the doorway,
knuckling his eyes and biting on a yawn. He looked up to the
line of distant mountains, finding a deep and incredulous
pleasure in their beauty today as every day, though he had
lived in Granada now for the best part of ten years. He
dropped his gaze from the mountain tops to the Alhambra,
and patted the roll of parchment he had thrust into his
girdle. It was a message to the palace regarding the building
– or conversion, rather – of a convent in the city. He would
take it to the Alhambra, where even now clerks and scribes
would be stirring, and then he could conduct his business
in the cool of the Salon de Embajadores. By the time he had

finished, he reasoned, the worst of the day's heat would be over. He set off across the square, the soft dust rising chokingly around his sandalled feet and clouding the hem of his rough brown robe.

As he neared the palace, cupped in its orchards and woods, he mused on its perfection. The building had been conceived and carried out by heathen Moors, yet it had an almost spiritual beauty. From a distance it seemed to hover amidst its groves, a cluster of symmetrical walls and towers roofed with gleaming, blue-green tiles, encrusted here and there with golden lichen. For over two hundred years it had sheltered the Moslem princes with their wives, concubines, slaves and nobles. They had built it, beautified it, and lived in it to the full. But it had fallen before the crusading fury of the Spanish armies, and now it sheltered the royal family of Spain. In the courtyards where doe-eyed harem girls had danced for their masters, the Infantas Isabel, Juana, Maria and Catalina had played with their brother, the Infante Juan.

But now marriage, and death, had changed the family pattern, and only the youngest Infanta was left to sport with her ladies in the orange groves, and walk amidst the fountains and marble pillars in the Patio de los Leones. Only Catalina, the youngest of Queen Isabella's children, was still unmarried. The others had married and left, even Juan, though Juan's body had not left Spain. For the heir to the thrones of Castile and Aragon, the beloved only son of Queen Isabella and King Ferdinand, had died some months previously.

The monk emerged from the shade of the trees, and crossed the short stretch of baked earth as the palace walls loomed up before him. He entered by a side door, glad to be within the shelter of the thick walls. The palace was a maze of patios, rooms and corridors, but to one who knew it, it presented few problems, and the lanky man passed through the patios with pleasure in their familiar beauty his only emotion.

He was crossing a small, flower-filled courtyard deep in the palace, where a tinkling fountain played into a marble bowl, when an exclamation from above his head made him look up.

Poised in an open window embrasure, and leaning out at what seemed a very dangerous angle, was Catalina. Her loose hair was falling across her face, and she was scanning the courtyard below with anxious eyes.

'Brother Leofric! Is Pepe down there? My little dog, you know. He saw a cat crossing the patio, and I had my work cut out to stop him leaping from the window and perhaps breaking his legs.' She turned and spoke to some-one behind her, then resumed anxiously, 'When I would not let him jump, he turned and scuttled out of the doorway before I could stop him. Ah, there he is!'

As she spoke a small, ginger dog streaked past the monk's dusty robe, and dived triumphantly into a huge cluster of scarlet peonies. Brother Leofric crossed the paving stones in a couple of strides, seized Pepe by his quivering hind-quarters. 'Out with you,' he commanded, pulling the madly excited dog backwards out of the foliage. 'There's no cat in there now, you foolish fellow. You must go back to your mistress.'

He picked the dog up, and turned in the direction of the curved stone staircase which led up to the first floor apart-ments, but even as he placed a sandalled foot on the first step, there was a quick pattering sound and the Infanta arrived, breathless, holding out her arms for her dog.

'Thank you, Brother,' she said sweetly. 'He can be a ter-rible trial, can't you, Pepe, but I love him very much.'

The dog turned in her arms and licked her chin wildly,

whilst his tail almost blurred with the speed of its wagging.

'Quiet, you rascal,' she admonished. 'You wanted that cat so badly that you ran away from me – what a way to behave! Now we must go back to Margot, or she will think me very rude indeed. Goodbye, Brother Leofric.'

She had both arms tightly round Pepe, restraining his efforts to escape, but she smiled with as much charm and dignity as though she were giving a royal audience, instead of struggling to control a little dog.

Leofric, admiring the child, raised a hand, half in blessing, half in farewell, and continued towards the Salon de Embajadores.

Margot, he mused, entering the dark shade of the palace once more; that would be the Princess Margaret of Austria who had married their Prince Juan. She was his widow now, and the mother of his dead child, for she had borne him a babe, months after Juan himself was dead. The girl would be company for Catalina, he reflected, though she was some years the elder; but such companionship would not be of long duration for she was the child of the Emperor Maximilian, and he would want her to marry again so that he could use the new marriage to ally himself to another powerful throne in Europe. The Spanish connection was already bought, for Philip of Burgundy, Margaret's handsome, fun-loving brother, was married to Juan's sister, Juana.

So many different strands to so many different webs they wove, these monarchs, he thought. To protect their kingdoms, to enlarge their domains, they sold their dearly loved children into loveless marriages without a second thought, or a single pang of conscience. A girl-child would be placed in the arms of one's enemy, if by so doing one could ensure that the enemy would not move against one, for a while at any rate. Why, Catalina herself had been betrothed when she was only three, to a little princeling; Arthur of England, was it not? She might marry him, or she might not, but she would marry someone, and soon, he reflected. He admired and loved Queen Isabella for her fierce religious convictions, for her occasional heartwarming kindness, even for her ruthlessness, and he believed Ferdinand to be an efficient and brave king. But he knew that their daughter Catalina could make them allies, and that she was fast approaching marriageable age. She would not be lonely long, to play in the halls and gardens of the Alhambra.

He reached the ornate archway leading into the Salon de Embajadores, and remembering his errand, forgot the trials and tribulations of the Spanish royal family. His eyes flickered across the faces of the men and women who crowded the apartment, and found the man he sought. His hand went to the parchment roll, and he set off purposefully across the mosaic floor, the words he would use already crowding to his tongue. In matters of state, the convent might be a small problem, and it was his business to see that it was not treated lightly. He caught at the heavy silken sleeve of the dignitary who dealt with building problems, and began his carefully rehearsed speech.

'I found him, Margot. Or rather, Brother Leofric did. He was digging in a bed of peonies, still searching for the cat. Look, there's dirt on his face.' Catalina brushed earth off her pet's nose, and dumped him down on the tiles. Then she settled herself on a cushion and picked up her embroidery once more.

'I take it, child, that you mean to say your dog was digging in a flower bed, and not Brother Leofric?'

The deep, musical voice with its hint of laughter came from Margot's mouth with perfect seriousness, but Catalina knew she was being teased, and smiled obediently.

13

'Yes, I meant Pepe,' she said. 'Brother Leofric was merely passing through the palace to see an official, I imagine.'

'I see,' Margot said. 'Now, Catalina, we were conversing in French, were we not, when Pepe staged his untimely interruption? Shall we continue?'

Catalina sighed, but said laboriously, in French, 'I am not clever, like you, Margot. When you came to Spain you could not speak a word of our language, but now you chatter away fluently, without the trace of an accent. You have a gift, but I have to learn the hard way.'

'I learned French from an early age,' Margot reminded her. 'And as for Spanish, I had a very good teacher.'

She bent her gaze to the work in her lap and Catalina, watching, thought that she saw a tear form in the dark eye. If Margot wept, reflected the younger girl, it was no wonder. She had been betrothed to Charles of France from an early age, had been brought up in the French court and called 'Madame la Reine'. But then the King – or more likely, his ministers – had decided that the rich heiress of Brittany was the more important match for France, and little Margot had been sent away, shamed and puzzled.

After that, she had been married once more, by proxy, to Juan, heir to the throne of Spain. She and her retinue had suffered an appalling sea voyage to reach Santander, where no one had expected her, for Laredo had been the supposed port of arrival. During the crossing of the Bay of Biscay, when such storms had blown up that all hope had seemed lost, Margot had written herself a little epitaph, with a wry humour which still puzzled Catalina.

Here lies Margot, the willing bride,
Twice married – but a virgin when she died.

But she had not died, of course. She had fallen in love, instead. She had taken one look at Juan – who might so easily have been a pompous, self-righteous young man – and had seen at a glance his charm, his easy good-humour, his naturalness. It had not been difficult for Juan to love Margot in return, and their marriage had been perfect, with Margot quickening with child, and Spain in ecstasies over their new Infanta.

But within five months of the marriage day, Juan lay dead. And Margot's unhappiness had brought about the birth of the child prematurely. The baby had been dead, also.

So now she waited in the Alhambra, for the message to come, telling her to take ship once more, to marry some other Prince, or King, who could assist her father in his ambitious scheming.

And she wept. Catalina watched the tear, and wondered. For Margot had been the very model of bravery when Juan had died. She, Catalina, had not cried, for 'A Spanish Infanta does not give way,' she had told her nurse stiffly, and she had locked her hurt away in her heart, and envied her sister Maria the easy, painless tears.

Does Margot grieve for the baby? Catalina wondered. But how could one weep for a child that one had never known? At the age of twelve, Catalina found babies boring, and could not imagine why women made such a fuss over the creatures, though the love which she gave so freely to Pepe must, she imagined, have its source in the same feelings of protectiveness for one smaller than oneself.

Margot looked up from her work, and patted her face with the edge of her handkerchief. The perspiration which dewed her brow and upper lip was whisked away – and so was the tear, if it had been a tear.

'Yes, Juan was a good teacher,' she said quietly, as though

15

there had been no pause in their conversation. 'But I am doing my best, Catalina, to teach you to speak good French. Come, you must try hard, you know, or you'll go to England and be unable to converse with your new husband!'

'I believe the English speak Spanish,' protested Catalina. 'Or at least, some of them do. When the English ambassadors came to sue for my hand at Medina del Campo, they spoke Spanish well enough.'

'Catalina, you were *three*,' protested Margot. 'You cannot possibly remember Medina del Campo, let alone the English ambassadors.'

Catalina compressed her lips and sewed virtuously away at her work. Very well, if Margot did not believe her, then she would make no effort to convince. But she *did* remember that day. It had been the day of her first bullfight.

The crowds, the smell of sweat and death, blood and glory, were stamped indelibly on her mind, and though she had seen many bullfights since, they only served to awaken the memory of that first occasion. She had been carried away by the colour and the excitement, so that when, during a lull in the spectacle, strange men who spoke Spanish with stilted accents had come to talk to her mother, she had scarcely noticed. But then Isabella had lifted her up in her arms, crushing the stiff gown richly sewn with jewels, and she had come out of her awed amazement over the bull and the matadors to find herself the centre of an admiring throng. One, by one, the pale-faced strangers had kissed her hand, and for the first time, she heard herself addressed as the Princess of Wales.

'Ambassadors to Spain speak the language of course,' Margot told her, when she remained silent. 'But you will find that few of the nobles and ladies of the court can understand a word of your tongue. Yet most people speak French. Have you ever tried to learn English, Catalina?'

'No,' said the Infanta, and as she spoke, a little cold wind of apprehension blew round her heart. Margot had been jilted by France, as Margot's father, Maximilian, had been jilted by Brittany. Did her mother fear that Catalina, too, might be tossed aside by Arthur of England for some other bride? Was that why she had never been asked to learn English?

But Margot was laughing, speaking again. 'You will have a sore sea voyage to undertake, Catalina, to reach your new country,' she was saying. 'You too, will write yourself an epitaph before you reach England's shores.'

Catalina, compressing her lips again, hoped that she would be courageous in the face of danger, as Margot had been. But she knew she would never make up cheeky and irreverent rhymes. She would pray, she told herself sternly. God would be more pleased with prayers than with poems. Then the thought of all the prayers God must have to listen to set her wondering whether Margot's rhyme might have been quite a welcome change, especially as prayers said by the desperately afraid are apt to be monotonous. She caught the thought guiltily and tried to banish it from her mind. She had never been so quick to see the funny side of a situation before Margot came, and thinking it over, she was not sure that this was a good thing. She knew the kingdom of heaven, as taught by Isabella, to be a serious place. No one could enter with a joke on their lips, and a beaming smile.

She voiced the thought to Margot, who said blandly, 'Where is Juan now, then?'

The question brought Catalina up short. Of course, whenever she thought of her brother she saw him laughing, joking. Yet it was incredible that there could be a heaven without Juan.

'Would you laugh in the face of death, then?' she asked incredulously.

'Better than to weep, surely, if you believe that heaven is a better place than earth,' said Margot, twinkling at her solemn young sister-in-law.

But Catalina was shocked again. If she believed heaven to be a better place than this earth? *If?* How did Margot dare say such things? She glanced at the older girl and thought that Margot was laughing at her.

'You'd better not let my mother hear you say things like that,' Catalina said warningly, her cheeks hot.

'Why not? If your mother can't hear me, God certainly can. I'm not afraid of *His* wrath. Why should I fear your mother?'

Catalina opened her mouth to reply 'because mother is nearer,' and realized that the words would be blasphemy. So she gave an outraged gasp and waited for heaven to strike Margot dead – or if not dead, dumb, so that her tongue could make no more terrible remarks.

Nothing happened. Margot continued to smile and stitch, dropping small remarks into the silence like pebbles into a pool.

In her turn, now, she studied her sister-in-law. A small girl still, though there was time enough for her to grow, and sturdily built. Catalina's skin was milk and roses, and her hair had the rich glow of ripe corn, but though she had inherited Queen Isabella's colouring she had, in some way, not quite inherited her mother's unusual beauty. Yet her features were good, her eyes wide and blue, with an appealing innocence.

Margot wondered about Catalina's upbringing. She had been dragged around Spain in the wake of an army whilst her mother fought the heathen Moors and drove them from the land; she had been born, indeed, during a break in the

18

campaign when her parents had hurried to Alcala de Henares, so that Isabella might give birth in the castle there, instead of in a draughty tent pressed close against a mountain.

Peace had not come to Spain until Catalina was six, and then it was an unsettled peace, with the two monarchs having to journey constantly across their realm to quell rebellion and keep their subjects as happy as possible.

And amidst all the bustle and uncertainty of the court at war, Catalina had been brought up. She had been in her tent before the walls of Granada when a random shot had set fire to the canvas, and she and her sisters had rushed out into the flame-lapped darkness, half asleep, wholly bewildered and terrified. It was Pepe, Catalina boasted, who had woken her as she lay on her straw pallet. He had barked, and pulled at her shift until she had tumbled from her blankets, to hear the roar of the flames, the shouts of the soldiery and the cries of her sisters as they were hurried away from the danger.

And from the violence and suffering of war, she had been brought to the garden of the Alhambra, where fountains played in patio and courtyard, and even in the tiled and beautiful rooms.

All this had affected the child, Margot believed, so that now, her nature itself was divided. She knew and understood the frenzy of religious zeal which drove her mother to fight against the Moors, though some might have questioned her right to drive them from the country they had occupied for hundreds of years. She understood, also, the love of beauty and of peace which had led to the building of the Alhambra, with its fountains and gardens, its fish swimming lazily in its marble basins, its poems and its gilded statuary.

And what would become of her, in England? Would the English try to understand her strong and stubborn loyalties which had been born as she struggled to keep up with her parents as they roved Spain with their armies? Would her self-sufficiency be resented by a people used to more sheltered and conventional royalty? Or would they see and understand the vulnerable child, who had been forced by circumstance to grow a shell of independence and who was convinced that God was on her side, because she had been brought up to believe Him a Spaniard?

Margot sighed, then smiled. After all, the Tudors had not held the throne of England for so very long, themselves. Henry VII had won it in the year of Catalina's birth, so perhaps this son to whom Catalina was to go as bride would be a fitting match for the Infanta, who tried to make the world believe her as severe and self-righteous as she pretended.

Margot bent once more over her work. She should be wondering about her own fate, she scolded herself, rather than worrying about Catalina. After all, of the two of them, her own future was the more uncertain. At least Catalina *was* betrothed; she was merely a widow. She paraded the eligible princes in Europe through her mind, discarding them one by one. None could compare favourably with what she had known of Juan. Then she remembered her dismay when she had been told that Spain was her destiny; she, who had been Queen of France but for fate – and Anne of Brittany. Yet she knew now that no marriage could have been better or happier for her than that with Juan, though their time together had been so brief. Digging her needle into her work, she resolved that she would make the best of whatever match her father had in mind – and that she would not leave Spain until she had to.

2 For King and Country

The royal retinue of the court of Spain had crowded onto
the quayside, and seldom had Corunna known a more elegant throng or a more exciting occasion, for when Juana
had gone to wed Philip of Burgundy, the mighty fleet of
ships had sailed from Laredo.

But this time, it was the last of the Infantas who was
leaving her country for a new husband, and this time she
had travelled the long and dusty miles from Granada alone
– unless you counted the court, of course. For Catalina, who
had accompanied her sisters to their marriages as far as the
borders of Spain, could not expect her mother or father to
go with her, though they had intended it. The deceitful
Moors had chosen the very moment of her journey to rise in
revolt against their Spanish overlords, and it was, plainly,
the duty of the King and Queen to quell rebellion rather than
to bid farewell to their youngest daughter.

So Catalina stood on the cobbles, smelling the fish and
the salt sea and the tar, and said her farewells in the stiff
and formal language of the court to the nobles and ladies
she had known all her life. The members of her suite, who
would travel with her, fidgeted whilst she delivered the last
messages for her mother, reminded them of various small
duties, and finally, accepted the bows and sweeping curtsies
with the appropriate responses.

But though the expression of solemn duty carved on her
countenance never altered, inwardly Catalina was a ferment
of excitement. She remembered the farewells of her sister

Juana, of the way Ferdinand had clasped his daughter to his breast, so that when Juana boarded her ship she still had the pattern of her father's waistcoat on one cheek; how on that occasion Juan had called jokes and encouragement to his sister, making her laugh and choke so that Isabella had admonished her ebullient son. Of course, she missed the family, the feeling of having to leave her loved ones, but on the other hand, she felt doubly adventurous. For had she not already been weeks on her journey, crossing the choking plains and resting in every suitable castle that they passed? She felt that now, she was grown-up indeed.

When the solemn farewells were over, she and her maids of honour went aboard the flagship, the *Vera Cruz*, and together they clustered at the ship's rail and watched the sailors preparing to cast off.

'Isn't it exciting? To be sailing at last, I mean,' Maria de Rojas exclaimed.

'It is not a matter for excitement, Maria. It is a solemn moment, when our Infanta bids farewell to her homeland.'

The speaker drew her long countenance into a forbidding frown, and turned to the Infanta with a solicitous expression. 'My child, would you like to retire to your cabin, now? There is little point in your standing about on the deck, and you might be in the way. Come below, and you can rest.'

Catalina smiled, but shook her head. 'No thank you, Elvira,' she said politely. 'I, too, find this an exciting experience. I am not tired, and would prefer to remain on deck.'

The older woman clucked beneath her breath, hesitated, then set off across the deck to the stairs which led to the cabins.

'Dona Elvira is a very good woman,' Maria said doubtfully, 'but she is very strong-willed, is she not? I do hope that she doesn't mean to keep us *very* quiet and subdued, all the way to England.'

Catalina had moved off, and was conversing with an older woman, so the three young girls put their heads together.

'Queen Isabella said that Dona Elvira was more than a chaperon, she was to stand in place of a mother to the Infanta,' Inez de Vinegas reminded her friends. 'So it will be difficult for any of us, even Catalina, to stand against her.'

'She is a terrible old woman,' Francesca de Carceres said roundly. Her eyes seemed to snap with annoyance as she gazed darkly in the direction taken by their duenna. 'She will make us all do just as she pleases until the Infanta is wed to Prince Arthur. Then, perhaps, life will be easier.'

'We are very young,' Maria said peaceably. 'Indeed, Francesca, you are the youngest of us all, for you have not yet attained thirteen, have you? Perhaps we need guidance, and Dona Elvira will be happy to give it.'

Francesca groaned and stamped on the deck, making a passing sailor turn and stare. 'I am in the charge of the Infanta,' she said haughtily. 'I will not have to obey Dona Elvira.' Then, as her friends stared, she wilted. 'Oh, well, I suppose I shall obey her,' she admitted. 'But not willingly, or for very long.'

Catalina rejoined the group, attracted by their laughter. 'What is so amusing?' she asked.

Maria said naughtily, 'It is Francesca, Infanta. She is telling us of her devotion to Dona Elvira and her determination to do as the duenna bids her.'

Catalina did not join in the laughter. 'The Queen bade us obey Elvira as we would obey her,' she said solemnly. 'So we can do no less.'

It was Francesca the irrepressible who broke the uncomfortable silence. 'The sailors have cast off,' she cried. 'Look, oh look, Infanta, the land is moving away from us!'

'Why, we are moving quite quickly now that the wind has

caught our sails,' agreed Catalina, too excited to tell Francesca that the land was unlikely to have moved an inch. 'See how small the people on the quay seem! Wave, my friends, wave goodbye to our motherland!'

'*Adios, Espagna!*' Francesca shouted, and Catalina forgot her royal dignity for long enough to press against the creaking ship's side and strain her eyes to pick out the faces of her courtiers on the quay.

Just for a moment, with everyone's attention on the land they were leaving behind, an onlooker would have been unable to tell which of the young women was a future queen, so bright-eyed and eager did they all look.

Four days later, the small convoy of ships struggled back into Laredo harbour for refitting. Storm-battered and seasick, the young girls clinging to the heaving planks looked very different from the carefree creatures who had sailed out of Corunna with such high hopes.

'Back to Spain,' Catalina said, trying to sound disheartened. But somehow, the excitement had gone out of the voyage. All they wanted now was to feel land – any land – beneath their feet once more.

Francesca was the only one with spirit enough left to call out, '*Hola, Espagna!*' as the ship drew alongside the quay.

A month passed before the *Vera Cruz* and her convoy sailed once more, but when they did, they were heartened by the arrival of a famous Devonshire pilot, Stephen Brett, who had been sent by the English king to guide them safely across the oceans.

'We shall soon see these white cliffs of Dover,' Catalina

told her ladies, and it seemed at first as though her faith in God's guidance, aided by that of Stephen Brett, would be rewarded. But when they rounded Ushant the autumn sun hid his face and a wind came moaning over the ocean, churning the calm blue sea into great waves, upon which the ships were tossed like corks.

Without exception, the Infanta and her women were ill, and believed that they would undoubtedly die of their malady before ever reaching land.

In their cabin, the maids of honour suffered from agonies as first they were constantly seasick, and then gnawing pains attacked their empty bellies with cramps and yet those same bellies rejected all food and drink.

'Shall we ever reach England?' gasped Maria, lying limp across the bed she shared with Francesca. 'Or is it to be our fate to feed the fishes?'

'We've been feeding the fishes ever since we rounded Ushant and the storm attacked us,' reminded Francesca practically. She had suffered less than the others, due perhaps to her youth and consequent resilience.

Maria shuddered at this crude reminder of her inner torments. 'I shall never eat anything again, I'm sure about *that*,' she said quickly. 'Even our Infanta seems to have lost her determination never to rail against fate. She says the terrible gales augur ill for the English match.'

'It is good to hear that she believes we'll survive to reach England,' said Francesca. 'I don't think we'll ever make harbour. We'll continue on our way like a ghost ship until our food runs out, or we die of sheer exhaustion. Woe, Maria, not even a Christian burial, two nameless corpses afloat on the tossing ocean!'

'You are a dreadful child, with an evil mind,' Maria moaned, clasping herself round the waist. 'I don't want to hear your foolishness.'

'I've always imagined my corpse, pale and lovely, lying on a pall of black velvet, with the mourners weeping because I died so young,' Francesca continued remorselessly. 'Now it looks as though no one will know who I am, and even if I do get cast ashore, I expect the body will be unrecognizable. Swollen with sea water, battered by the rocks . . .'

'Francesca de Carceres, you're the most ghoulish girl alive,' shouted Maria, clasping first her palpitating heart and then her churning stomach. 'You're cruel to talk about death and drowned corpses, with the ship tossing and creaking and all our lives in danger. I'll tell Dona Elvira you're a bad, wicked girl who jokes about a terrible fate for the Infanta.'

'Oh, phoo, who cares about Dona Elvira? She has been more ill than any of us and once Catalina is married, *she* will be our chaperon and Elvira will be just another lady in waiting. If we drown . . .'

'Francesca, be quiet!' shrieked Maria. 'I'm going to the Infanta, to see what I can do for her.'

Francesca caught the elder girl by the shoulders and turned her towards the small window. 'Look, foolish one. See over there? That's land – England at last, Maria. With this wind, we shall make for the nearest port, for the captain won't risk making for Gravesend, even though we are expected there, with such a precious cargo. If you hadn't been feeling so sorry for yourself, you could have seen the cliffs half an hour since.'

'Oh, sweet Jesu, thanks,' gasped Maria. 'I wonder which port is nearest? Let us go to Catalina, she will know, I'm sure. The pilot, Stephen Brett, will have sent a signal to our captain, and he will have told the Infanta.'

The two girls hurried to the Infanta's cabin where they found her calmly ordering her dresses to be laid out, so that she could choose which one to wear to go ashore. The faithful Inez, a little wan but obviously cheered by her task, was scuttling about the cabin with her arms full of silks and satins.

'Hello, my friends,' Catalina greeted them. 'The pilot, Brett, says we'll be in Plymouth tomorrow if the wind stays in its present quarter. How glad I shall be to touch English soil, after the horrors we have undergone on the sea!'

'It will be good to be on firm ground,' agreed Maria; and Francesca said, 'But the English will think all high-born Spanish ladies have pale green complexions, Catalina, if we leave the *Vera Cruz* as soon as she anchors.'

'I don't really mind what people think,' Catalina said firmly. 'I have been more ill and miserable than I dreamed possible during these past few days, and I want only to hurry ashore, so that I can give thanks to God for our deliverance.'

'You are so sensible, Catalina,' said a weak voice from the bed. Dona Elvira sat on the coverlet, her face yellow and her eyes half shut. Even when the ships had cruised through calm waters the duenna had not been her usual self, but once the rough weather had started even Francesca, who heartily disliked the duenna, had to pity her.

Their relentless guardian had seemed at first about to die of seasickness. Several times, after a bout of particular fierceness, she had lost consciousness, alarming her husband, the attentive Don Pedro Manrique, and even causing her son Inigo to express some concern.

But Dona Elvira's new meekness and humility were to be shortlived. The ship anchored, and within moments of arriving safely upon English soil, Elvira had begun to take command once more, issuing her orders as though she had forgotten her recent indisposition.

Catalina and her ladies stepped onto the quayside with a certain caution, for to their dismay the homely cobbles seemed as inclined to tip and tilt as the wooden deck had been. The Infanta was handed into a litter, and sank back on the cushions, trying to deny the similarity of her lurching progress to that of a small barque on a rough sea.

She had asked that she be taken straight to the church, and she had little time in the short journey between quay and the nearest place of worship to take stock of her surroundings, but from thence they were taken to the house of a notable Plymouth citizen, and Catalina began to sit up and take notice.

'She'm stayin' wi' we,' muttered a bystander. 'Mister Paynter, he's got a fine new house, so she'm stayin' there. Pretty l'il wench, ain't she?'

Envious friends gazed at the fortunate fellow who would wait on this small, richly-dressed young lady, who had undertaken such a terrible journey across the seas to wed their own Prince Arthur.

'Her be pretty, right enough, but why do she hide beneath that veil?' asked an elderly lady with a widow's barbe, its softly pleated linen folds completely hiding her chin and neck from the eyes of passers-by.

'A foreign custom, likely,' suggested the first speaker. 'Why, the Spaniards live cheek by jowl with Arabs and Africans, they may ha' picked up some strange habits.'

The words were totally lost on Catalina, but the tone of proprietorial pride warmed her heart. They were friendly towards her already, these people. And so well dressed were the peasants in the streets that she thought them all the retainers of nobles.

Mr Paynter's new house was admired, and they lodged their very comfortably, impressed by all they saw and experienced.

'Such soft beds,' enthused Fancesca, well used, as the

youngest, to being given the hardest of resting places. 'And ample food, though strange to our palates, perhaps.'

'They were not expecting us, yet we have had a warm welcome,' Catalina said, her eyes shining. 'Log fires in our bedrooms, warm water to wash ourselves, cool wine and wafer biscuits to refresh us. And this is only the house of a humble knight!'

The following day, Catalina was glad enough to spend the time quietly, becoming used to her surroundings, sleeping, and sorting out her wardrobe, but the day after that she was very glad to hear that her fellow countryman, Don Pedro de Ayala, envoy of the Spanish monarchs, was waiting below, hoping for an audience.

Ayala had been in England for some time, though he was in truth ambassador to Scotland, so his command of the language was excellent and he was able to interpret for the Infanta as well as to amuse her with his lively and informed conversation.

Catalina greeted Ayala as an old friend, for she had known him well in her childhood and had always admired and liked the handsome and sophisticated churchman.

'Don Pedro, you are the very man to settle my doubts and explain the habits of the people to me,' she said. 'We haven't seen much of England yet, but in this corner of it, certainly, life seems much softer and pleasanter than the life of a similar community back at home in Spain.'

'I would agree with you, Infanta. Life is more placid here, as indeed, are the people. But it has not always been so and even today, the north of the country is wild and barren, and the people suspicious and quick to draw their knives. However, there will be no reason for you to visit the north, and you will find the people here friendly and welcoming. They love the Tudors, you see, and even those who do not, welcome the prosperity which has come with the peace that Henry brought with him. Now tell me, do you wish to see something of Plymouth, before you set out on your journey to the capital?'

'Why, most certainly,' said Catalina eagerly. 'I've seen practically nothing of the town, and it is my landing place, after all.'

So the two of them set out, though Catalina insisted that she would prefer to walk rather than ride in the litter which Mr Paynter offered her. She found that her first impression of the town had been misleading, for she had not once glanced backwards, towards the sea, and this was the heart of Plymouth.

'What a great bay!' she exclaimed. 'What is the little island called? And the river? Oh, there are *two* rivers. Who lives in the castle on the hill beside the harbour?'

'What a number of questions, Infanta,' exclaimed Ayala, laughing. 'Let us answer the easiest first. The island is the Isle of St Nicholas, and it is privately owned though the castle you can see on it is uninhabited and largely ruined, I believe. The river there,' he waved a hand, 'is the Tamar, which divides Devon and Cornwall, and the other river which flows into the bay is the Plym. Oddly enough, the eastern half of the bay into which the Plym flows is known locally as Cattewater, and the western half is called the Hamoaze.'

Catalina, blinking a little, suggested that they might stroll on the green common overlooking the sound.

'Yes, indeed, you should not go to London without walking on the Hoe,' agreed Ayala. 'The chapel that stands on it should interest you, as it is dedicated to your patron saint, Catherine.'

So the two of them strolled on the Hoe, smiling at the cottagers who came running out to greet them. De Ayala, for his part, congratulated himself on spending the previous evening pumping good Master Paynter for local news and information, as well as for his foresight in riding hell-for-leather down to Plymouth as soon as news of the landing of a Spanish fleet had filtered through to his ears. Catalina merely enjoyed the sensation of being in a country whose mellow beauty and friendly people seemed like an answer to a prayer. I could never be unhappy here, she thought, enjoying the golden October sunshine and the pleasant warmth of the land breeze, scented with gorse and thyme.

The idyll in Plymouth had to end, of course, but as they journeyed slowly through the autumn countryside, seeing the fruitful orchards being harvested, and the gleaning of the last of the golden stubble, Catalina could not but believe she had come to a land flowing with milk and honey, a veritable paradise.

'Everyone is so *friendly*,' she emphasized to Don Pedro de Ayala, as they rode, side by side, along the broad highway leading into Exeter. 'Peasants, knights, nobles, all welcome me as though they knew me well already.'

'They think you beautiful,' Ayala told her. 'They see a likeness to your great-grandfather, John of Gaunt. His daughter, Katherine, had golden hair as had Gaunt, I believe. And the charm of your being a foreign princess is thus combined with traditional English looks.' He laughed as Catalina shook her head protestingly. 'Yes, yes, Infanta. You may think yourself Spanish through and through, but the English will point to your blue eyes and fair skin and tell themselves that Blood Will Out! You must realize that to these insular people, to be English is everything.'

Catalina looked around her. Overhead, the trees hung low across their path, heavy with their burden of red and gold. Beside the road, pink dusted, the rich red loam showed between the clumps of vivid, brittle bracken. And in between the tough bracken stems, a tiny stream chattered and sang as it plunged over its rocky bed. 'To be English could be everything for me, too,' Catalina murmured. 'Why was I told that I was bound for a foggy little island full of uncouth and rough people? Surely, those who speak thus do so out of jealousy? Why, you yourself are ambassador to Scotland, yet you prefer to be here, amongst the English.'

'Ah, yes, Scotland,' said Ayala. He drew out his handkerchief and trumpeted into it whilst he collected his thoughts. 'I am, indeed, ambassador to King James of Scotland. And that country, too, is different from Spain. A cold, wild, beautiful land, but barren, and mountainous. To be truthful, Infanta, I left Scotland gladly enough, for the English court. There is much that I can give to life in England, which would not be appreciated in Scotland for the people, Infanta, are not like the English at all. They are proud, quarrelsome, haughty and self-righteous, and they lack any spirit of gentleness or conciliation. Indeed, they would think such things merely a sign of weakness. They have no use for diplomacy, preferring to take what they want, or do without. Aye, King James is welcome to his glens and his dagger-swift lords!'

'Yet you keep Scottish retainers,' said Catalina naughtily, and was rewarded by his look of astonishment.

'I may not speak English, but I have been well tutored in Latin,' she reminded him. 'I asked one of the nobles why some of your men spoke with a strange tongue, and he looked as though he'd bitten into a lemon instead of an orange, and said your men were Scots.'

Ayala recovered his poise, saying urbanely. 'Aye, they are excellent servants and come gladly enough into the rich lowlands of England. They are quarrelsome though, and I have my work cut out to make them abide by the law, but they are very good fighters.'

'Then why do they always seem to lose their battles

against the English?' asked Catalina frankly, and was grati-
fied to see the self-confident Ayala look confused. But he
changed the subject with such dexterity that she took pity
on him, and referred no more to his wild Scots.

The reception which awaited them in Exeter would have
made Catalina forget Ayala's very existence had he wished
it, let alone his Scottish affairs. The King had sent his
steward, Lord Willoughby de Broke, to see that his son's
betrothed had everything that she desired, and many nobles
of the English court had journeyed down with de Broke to
join their entourage. A banquet was held in her honour, and
Catalina sat wide-eyed at the table as course followed course
in rapid succession. The heat from the great fires, the light
from the smoky torches fixed to the walls, the uninhibited
talk and laughter as the wine sank in the goblets, suddenly
made the Infanta think wildly that this was more orgy than
feast; she had never seen so much food, nor such hearty
appetites. She saw peacocks roasted and garnished and then
made gay once more with their own plumage, swans treated
likewise, dishes of smaller birds, and then the procession of
meats, the herb salads, the plates piled high with saffron
yellow rice, with mushrooms, and always, the great jugs
of wine, from pale rose to darkest ruby red.

Around her were the townspeople, come to see their
Arthur's betrothed. They, too, ate of the food, and Catalina
guessed that those who served at table would easily find
several meals from the viands sent back from the banquet.

'The English eat full hearty, do they not, Infanta?'
Francesca whispered. 'See the roasted boar with an orange
in its mouth? It reminds me strongly of that knight over
there; see, he's guffawing over something said by his
friend.'

Catalina frowned reprovingly, but the similarity between
the two faces, both piggy yet fierce, was too much for her

gravity. She gave a muffled giggle, but said, 'I wonder whether anyone has noticed that I don't eat very much? Do you suppose it offends them?'

'They're too busy eating to notice much else,' said Maria, glancing up and down the table. 'But they'll suppose that your veil makes eating difficult, Infanta. I've seen several of them glancing at it with curiosity, though they obviously respect your desire to remain unseen until after your wedding, even if they don't understand it. Oh, Infanta, suppose you were to try to eat *that* through your veil?'

Catalina eyed the dish of sticky preserved peaches and clotted yellow cream and choked on another laugh. She could imagine all too clearly how fatal it would be if her veil were to fall when she was taking a spoonful of the concoction to her mouth.

Now that sweetmeats were replacing the meat dishes, the atmosphere was becoming both warmer and smokier. Bowls of nuts and fruit appeared and the faces of their hosts, shining with grease and perspiration, grew flushed as the wine sank in the jugs. Servants began unobtrusively to escort from the table those who were becoming noticeably the worse for drink, and one or two of the townspeople actually seemed to be sleeping, nodding over their plates and mugs.

Catalina took her courage in both hands, and caught the eyes of her ladies. They rose, and as though a great gust of wind had blown along the table, everyone else rose also. The Infanta's face, seen through her veil, was smiling, mouthing pleasantries, as she left the hall of her lodgings. She left the English to their reflections – and the rest of the wine.

34

3 The Meeting

As day followed golden day, it seemed as though the very heavens were conspiring to captivate the Infanta, for who would not fall in love with a countryside bathed in soft autumn sunshine, and caressed only by the gentlest of breezes? Catalina certainly did so, as the sun shone from a clear blue sky upon her train of Spaniards, and upon the English nobles who joined their ranks as they moved nearer to London.

The pleasure of the maids of honour, however, was tempered by their dismay at the behaviour of Dona Elvira.

'She will scarcely allow us to exchange a civil greeting with the Englishmen,' Maria grumbled, as they rode along a wide country road. 'The journey itself is the pleasantest part of our time in England, for despite soft beds and an abundance of rich food, when Elvira has us under a roof, she begins her scoldings.'

'We are within twenty leagues of London now,' comforted Inez. 'When we reach the city, Catalina is to be married, and then *she* will be our chaperon. Elvira will not watch us so closely then.'

'The duenna has not watched us so closely since Dr Puebla joined us at Ambresbury,' Francesca reminded them. 'She has been too intent on belittling the ambassador, for fear he will lessen her authority with the Infanta.'

Dr Puebla was the Spanish ambassador to the English court; indeed, it was he who had drawn up Catalina's marriage treaty. A small, ingratiating man with intelligence shining from his sharp eyes, he had done his best to make himself useful to the royal party. But Dona Elvira disliked him and did not shrink from showing it, and the aristocratic Don Pedro de Ayala was equally scornful of his compatriot.

'He's a Jew, turned Christian from convenience rather than conviction, when Queen Isabella gave the Jews four months to be baptized or to take their faith into Islam,' he told Catalina, his airy tone underlaid by a vein of venom. 'Many Jews went, but the ones to whom money and position meant more than their faith stayed, and were baptized.'

'It must be hard, to make the choice between your faith and the country where your ancestors have lived for centuries,' Francesca had said, but to Catalina the decision had seemed inevitable.

'I came to England because it was my duty to do so,' she said, her very tone a rebuke. 'Duty must come before desires. Why, for my faith, I'd do more.'

'Aye, and so I would myself, for the blood royal flows in your veins as it flows, to a lesser extent, in mine,' Ayala said with a touch of complacency. 'De Puebla is a commoner, and knows no call of duty as we do.'

Francesca had remained silent, realizing that argument was fruitless. But she had felt sympathy, if nothing else, for the ugly little man.

So now she said, looking hard at Ayala's back as he rode beside the Infanta's litter, 'For all he is a bishop, Don Pedro Ayala is no saint. There were stories enough told in Spain, but to hear him talking to our Catalina, one would scarcely take him for a man of the church!'

'Ayala is all right,' Maria said goodnaturedly. 'And so is Puebla, in his way. But they're like oil and water, they simply won't mix, and nothing will make them. It is a pity that Catalina has taken her lead from Ayala in despising the ambassador, but once she is married and Ayala returns to Spain, she will learn to value Puebla for his good qualities, I'm sure.'

'I wonder . . .' began Francesca, then stopped abruptly. 'Don't say the good weather is changing at last,' she said. 'I declare I felt a drop of rain on my face!'

The girls looked at the sky. Whilst they talked it had clouded over, and now it looked anything but promising.

'Perhaps we're in for a shower,' Maria said, unwilling to believe that the English weather could ever be unpleasant.

But such hopes were soon dashed. The rain fell heavily, ceaselessly, and a nipping wind got up and blew gusts almost horizontally so that even in her closely curtained litter, the Infanta began to feel the rigours of the weather.

'The clouds are heavy,' gasped an Englishman in uncertain Spanish, approaching the three young women as they rode their steeds close to the Infanta's litter. 'It would seem wise to ride straight for the Bishop's Palace – Dogmersfield – and not to linger for a meal.'

Before they could reply, he had moved ahead once more, his horse speedily carrying him beyond their range of vision, blurred as it was by the driving rain. So they arrived at Dogmersfield earlier than they had planned, but very wet, and hungry, too. It was an imposing building, but no one was much interested in the towers and windows, nor did they waste time in trying to gauge the extent of the parkland surrounding it. Thoughts of warm fires, dry clothes and a good hot meal filled everyone's mind.

Seeing the state of his guests, their host cut short his planned speech of welcome and sped the royal party on their way upstairs, to where they would find hot water for washing, and a large part of their baggage already awaiting them. On their return to the great hall, they found most lavish hospitality in the form of a table groaning beneath the weight of food upon it, minstrels up in the gallery playing and singing, and servants hovering, quick to obey a command or a gesture.

Refreshed, but still weary, they gathered when they had eaten in a smaller chamber, to brush their clothes, play a game of cards perhaps, and talk, before making their way to bed. It was here that the messenger found them. Soaked through, mired and breathless, he dropped on one knee to deliver his message. King Henry and his son Arthur could not bear to wait until the Infanta reached Lambeth the following day. They were on their way to Dogmersfield even now, to see Catalina.

The words fell into the sudden silence with a dreadful clarity, and Catalina could see consternation on the faces of several of her suite.

'How can this be?' Maria said. 'It is not the custom for a bridegroom to see the face of his bride until after the marriage ceremony has been performed.'

'That is a Spanish custom,' Catalina said doubtfully. 'Might it be different in England?' She turned to Ayala who had accompanied the messenger, raising her brows.

His nod confirmed her suspicion. 'Aye, Infanta, in England it is not thought necessary to hide the bride's face from her future husband. Where would you like to receive your betrothed, and the King?'

Dona Elvira suddenly surged to her feet in a flurry of crackling black taffeta. 'Go to the King,' she commanded Ayala. 'Tell him that our Infanta has her parents' orders. She is to behave as becomes an Infanta of Spain and will see no one unveiled until after her marriage.'

Catalina said doubtfully, 'Dona Elvira, would it not be wiser to see the King? After all, we are in his country, where, as Don Pedro Ayala has made plain, such is not the practice. If we do not wish to offend . . .'

Dona Elvira cut across the Infanta's speech impatiently. 'Certainly not. We are subjects of Spain and until you

38

are married to this Prince we will abide by the orders given by your parents.'

'I think the Infanta is right,' Ayala said smoothly, but was overruled by the redoubtable duenna.

'The Infanta Catalina is young. Naturally, she wishes to please and fears to offend. But her first duty must still be to her parents, and they expressed the wish to me personally, that she should behave as she would if she were in her own country, until she is wed. Do not waste further time in argument, therefore, but take my message to the King.'

So Don Pedro de Ayala went with the messenger, though Catalina thought she could guess by the set of his shoulders what he thought of a woman who spoke as Dona Elvira had done. She looked at her women. They were gazing at Dona Elvira with unmistakable dislike.

'So we shan't get a glimpse of this Prince, who is said to have hair like gold, until the formal meeting, tomorrow,' sighed Francesca. 'I wonder, though? Kings are not usually content to be ordered about by old women, and this King hasn't yet met Dona Elvira or tried the sharpness of her tongue. I wonder!'

'They'll never come; they'll think it is Catalina who orders them away,' sighed Maria, and sat down with the Infanta to ply her needle. But Inez followed Francesca to the chamber they had been given for the night.

'I'll back a Tudor who fought to get the crown, and fights to keep the crown, against an obstinate Manuel, however blue her blood,' Francesca said, unpinning her dark hair and beginning to ply her brush vigorously. 'If the King arrives here despite Dona Elvira, I shall not be unprepared.'

'Judging by Ayala's expression, he will not try to persuade the King to abandon the visit,' Inez agreed. She rummaged in her jewel box, and drawing out a necklace of glittering

39

gems, exchanged them for the plain gold beads which she had worn round her throat.

The two girls took their time brushing their gowns, rubbing their cheeks to give themselves a healthy flush and scenting their headdresses and the hems of their skirts so that when they moved, a pleasant aroma filled the air. Then they returned to the parlour and settled down to play cards, their absence unremarked.

Francesca had been almost on the point of conceding Dona Elvira the victory, when the door burst open and one of Catalina's pages burst in, his eyes bulging in his pink young face.

'The King, Infanta, he's here! He says he'll see you even if you are abed, for in his realm, he alone may command his subjects.'

The King followed so closely on the heels of the young page that Catalina had barely time to scramble to her feet before her future father-in-law was striding across the room, followed by a slim young man who she guessed must be the Prince of Wales. The King stopped, and waited. No one spoke, Catalina was frozen in mid-movement by the surprise of their sudden arrival. The silence crystallized and held the three main actors suspended for a moment, like flies in amber. Then the King held out his hand, speaking quickly, with an authoritative yet pleasant ring to his voice, and Catalina slowly lifted the veil which she had lowered, and smiled timidly at the two men.

The interpreter began to chatter, and Catalina understood that the King was complimenting her on her charming looks, apologizing for his rain-soaked clothing and for the haste with which he had entered her chamber.

Catalina smiled composedly, intent now on hiding her confusion and surprise. She thought the King of England was a bold man who made his own conventions, and would not appreciate any signs of faintheartedness from his son's betrothed. She studied him as the interpreter spoke, noting the thick gold hair streaked with grey, the lean countenance, the cold blue of his hooded eyes. His cloak was dark with rain and liberally splashed with mud, and the smell of horse and wet saddlery hung about him, yet something in his bearing, perhaps his very carelessness, showed him to be very much the King.

Presently, when Catalina's conventional reply to his opening remarks had been translated first into Latin and then into English, it was considered time to introduce the Prince of Wales.

The boy stepped forward, his hat with its long curled feather in one hand, raindrops sparkling in the curls on his head, and Catalina glanced instinctively towards Dona Elvira. But the duenna, her face set as marble with frustrated ill-humour, turned her shoulder on the company, making it plain to the Infanta at least, that her behaviour in greeting the King and the Prince with a degree of complacency was thoroughly disapproved of in one quarter. Catalina, no whit impressed by this display of annoyance, took the opportunity of staring as frankly at Arthur as he was staring at her.

He was like his father, with the subtle difference that his smile was warm, with a warmth that reached his eyes, and his mouth was gentle, the lips full and soft.

He was shy, as well. When he spoke his voice shook and the colour came and went in his face.

His words were translated for Catalina and she nodded, answering, but to her his tone spoke more clearly than the conventional greeting. His eyes looked into hers, warm with admiration, and abruptly he said, 'You are fair, Katherine.'

'*Gracias*. Katherine ees Catalina?'

The boy laughed delightedly. 'Yes, yes, Princess. You

have spoken English already, you see? You will soon learn to speak our language.'

Once again the translator got to work and Katherine nodded, suddenly grave. She would have to learn English now, to please this charming young man with the laughing eyes. She remembered that this was to be a dynastic marriage, where choice did not enter into the bargain, and thought how lucky she was. So easily he might have been ugly, or vicious. He might have been disappointed in her slight figure, her fair colouring. Instead, they talked through the interpreter of her white bird which chattered in Spanish, and of the horse he had ridden to reach her side. But always their eyes told a different, warmer story.

Then the King spoke to his son, and Katherine felt the atmosphere change; the lightheartedness seemed to go out of the Prince, as though the recollection of his father's presence had been enough to dampen his spirits. Hastily, she suggested that the men might like to eat, and refresh themselves. 'Then we could dance,' she suggested, and was rewarded by the swift pleasure which chased across the boy's expressive features.

In the brief interval whilst King and Prince ate, Katherine tried to assure Dona Elvira that no harm could possibly have been done by acceding to the King's harmless request for an audience, but the duenna proved adamant.

'Request? Hah! A royal command which he'd no right to give,' Elvira said viciously, then folded her long upper lip tightly over her long front teeth, and became immersed in reading her Bible. Katherine decided, with an inward shrug, that since Elvira seemed to be sulking, she would have to proceed as she thought best. So when the King and Arthur joined them, she ordered her minstrels to play a Spanish tune which she knew well. She danced with Francesca first, the two girls forgetting their illustrious audience in the

42

pleasures of the quick, graceful movements, so that they danced beautifully and naturally.

'Now, Maria, let us dance the base dance,' Katherine said as they swirled to a halt with the applause of the Spaniards and the English ringing in their ears. 'Francesca must be tired.'

Francesca was not tired, thought resentfully that she could never be tired of dancing. But she admitted nevertheless that Katherine was one of the best dancers amongst them, and whether partnered by Maria or herself, she excelled.

After the second dance, it needed little encouragement for Arthur to take the floor to show the Spaniards an English dance. His partner, Lady Guilford, was a good performer too, though in deference to her wishes they measured a stately rather than a gay step.

In the excitement of dancing, Katherine had almost forgotten the duenna, but as soon as the King and his son had taken their departure, Dona Elvira began to loose the thunderbolts of her wrath at Katherine's head. The Infanta, protected by her royal status and by her mother in particular, had never received such a set-down. But Katherine was beginning to feel the threads of dependence loosening, and she spoke firmly to the duenna.

'Thank you for your advice, Elvira,' she said pleasantly. 'But I'm sure your fears for my reputation are unfounded. To show my future husband the dances of my country, to speak with him and his father with so many honourable people looking on, can surely not be called light conduct. I'm tired now, but I won't trouble you to help me disrobe. My women will do all that is necessary.'

She left the room quickly, eager to hear what her friends thought of Prince Arthur.

'He has a charm which I find lacking in King Henry,'

43

Maria said. 'Did you notice his chin, Catalina? Gentler than his father's, less aggressive. And when he smiles, a dimple comes.'

'You must call me Katherine, now,' Katherine said, smiling. 'He seems a friendly youth, does he not? I think I am very fortunate. Very fortunate indeed.'

Riding through the downpour to their lodgings, father and son were silent, both thinking of the girl they had left behind. But once warmly clad and with a cup of wine before him, Henry said cautiously, 'Well, son? What do you think of your little wife, eh?'

'She's fair; yes, comely enough. Small, too. I like small wenches. I had thought she'd be dark, but I find auburn locks pleasing. Aye, she's well enough.'

Arthur answered offhandedly because he did not want his father to know how much the maid had meant to him. He had dreaded this meeting, imagining a stiff, self-possessed young woman who would be more sophisticated than he, and would hold him in contempt for his lack of assurance. Instead, he'd seen a small, slender girl, whose skin glowed golden in the candlelight. She had been shy, her gaze often cast down, but when she had looked at him, her eyes had shown an admiration which she was unable to voice.

Arthur looked at his father through his thick, fair lashes. A brooding considering look. He wished he dared say, 'But marrying an innocent virgin is work I'm ill-equipped for, because you hedge me so about with restrictions and advisers that I am ill at ease with women'.

The words remained unsaid, as they always had. He had heard other boys of his own age boasting of their experiences; the hand under the table whilst they ate, squeezing the thigh of a likely wench, the swift, hot embrace in a

44

secluded corner. Most of the lads were familiar with the bodies of maidens, who giggled and protested but were themselves stimulated by curiosity into all but the final act. And some of the pages and attendants, he knew, had experienced their first woman. The stories varied, but were, essentially, the same. A plump little chambermaid who came to draw back the young master's bedcurtains, and found herself the not unwilling bedsharer. The pretty farm wench, minding her father's pigs or geese, giving herself cheerfully on a fine summer day to the lusty young lad fresh from service at court.

But for a prince of the blood, none of these things were possible. He was too closely watched for that. Some might have rebelled, managed to steal away, but Arthur was in any case a little in awe of young women. His sisters were different, of course; he was fond of Margaret, though she was backward in learning and spent most of her time at her lessons, and Mary was only just emerging from babyhood.

So though Arthur's friends talked freely before him, and boasted freely too, it was understood that King Henry had no intention of allowing his son to enter into even the lightest liaison with any female. I'm as pure as any nun – purer than most – he thought savagely, and it is my father's fault. He's a cold creature, and doesn't need women. Our mother receives no more than his lukewarm affection, tardily given. And he was not asked to wed at fifteen, to a little maid without a word of English. If I knew more, had some experience to guide me, words would surely not be necessary.

He thought again of Katherine. Her smallness, the pure oval of her face, the strange foreign gown she wore which hid her shape completely. English fashions tell more, he thought guiltily. Our women's gowns are low-cut, revealing the top of their plump white breasts, and the skirts flow softly,

45

somehow, so that the shape of their legs shows when they walk.

I shall not see her shape until our wedding night, he thought, and the imagined scene brought the colour rising to his forehead. What would it be like – to possess her? To touch her naked body and caress her unbound hair? To know the delights of the flesh which others had hinted at?

He swallowed, aware of his father's cynical eyes on him and cursing the fair skin which flushed so easily, revealing his thoughts. He tried to think of other things, and began to talk of the Welsh marches where he had lately been, and of the coming procession into London. But always, his thoughts returned to Katherine. He vowed, clenching his teeth, that he would teach her to love him. He would protect her from his father, too, see that she was not made to feel foolish, or kept short because of Henry's confounded meanness over personal expenditure.

Margaret will befriend her, Arthur thought hopefully. Although she was not clever, even at twelve Margaret was very much the young lady, eager to see her favourite brother's new wife. Henry, Duke of York, his only brother now living, was ten, too young to care whether the bride was beautiful or plain. He was a happy little boy, intelligent enough to keep pace with his studies but already preferring sports and music to his books.

Arthur thought, with a pang of envy, how different Henry's life would be to his own. As a second son he was not expected to excel at everything he did. He was without personal doubts and fears, too, never worrying about what sort of impression he made on others, only determined to *make* an impression. He loved fine clothes, and crowds, and delighted in the interest and admiration of all about him. Henry would not shiver in his shoes at the thought of bedding any girl, be she peasant or princess. He would not worry that he might hurt her, or prove inadequate. He would simply make sure he was the centre of attraction and then boast endlessly of his prowess. Arthur caught at a mental picture of Henry as he had last seen him, clapping his hands and crowing with mirth because he had beaten Margaret at chess. The recollection of the child's outright pleasure made him laugh aloud. Young Hal, married! It was impossible to imagine. He was nothing more nor less than a happy, self-satisfied little dumpling.

'What amuses you?' asked Henry immediately.

Inwardly, Arthur fumed, he would read my thoughts, if he could, but aloud he said evenly, 'I was thinking of Hal, father. Such a placid young knave. But he will enjoy the pageantry of the wedding.'

He did not hear his father's answer, as the King talked of the masque in which the children would play major roles. His mind had flown back once again to his Spanish bride.

4 Marriage

'Sister, why don't you raise your veil so that the people may see your face?'

The piercing whisper reached Katherine's ears despite the noise from the crowds pressing close to the roadway to see her pass. She glanced sideways, amused, at the inquisitive face of the young Duke of York who rode beside her, escorting her into the City of London.

'Because I have an eye in the middle of my head,' she

whispered back teasingly, enjoying the puzzled look on the cherubic face. But the remark was lost on Hal, whose Latin was sufficient to ask the question but not yet up to the standard of exchanging lighthearted banter. Katherine, laughing, tried her faltering French.

'*Parce que j'ai l'oeil dans ma tête – là!*' She pointed dramatically to her smooth forehead, mistily seen through the veiling.

Young Hal said, 'Have you? Does my father know?' then, as she laughed again, a frown descended on his angelic brow and his mouth pursed indignantly.

He does not like being teased, thought Katherine. Spoilt, probably. She remembered the teasing that had gone on in the family at home, with Queen Isabella telling her daughter Maria that should a terrible Turk ever force his way into their home, one reproving look from Maria would send him packing. 'This is my mother-in-law, treat her soberly and with respect,' she would tell people who came to visit the royal family, and even solemn Maria had smiled, and taken in good part all the teasing that came her way. Even quick-witted, mercurial Juana had been teased, told she was surely of gipsy blood for her gaiety and her dark beauty, and she had never sulked or grown surly, as it seemed likely that the young Duke of York might.

However, if Henry could not take teasing it could not be all his fault, so Katherine, comfortably ensconced in her Spanish saddle which made falling off almost an impossibility, decided to humour her betrothed's brother.

'The crowd cheer more for you than they do for me,' she remarked. 'Perhaps they realize I am a little nervous. In Spain, our people are smaller, less robust. Here, even the peasants are broad and burly.'

The cleric who rode beside her mule leaned forward and began to translate the remark, and the Duke of York replied immediately, his face lighting with pleasure, his annoyance forgotten.

'The people are pleased to see you, sister, but they are proud of me. I'm big for my age, and I'm *never* afraid of the common folk, even when I'm on foot and they crowd close and breathe garlic and sour cheese into my face.'

Katherine pretended to shudder, not wanting to hurt the lad's feelings by telling him of her childhood spent shoulder to shoulder with the soldiery and their women, who sometimes smelt of things far worse than garlic or cheese.

'Why does that old lady wear black, droopy things beside her cheeks?' enquired the Duke of York presently. 'She puts me in mind of a bloodhound, because of her headdress which looks like the dog's ears, and her own face, which is so long and solemn. Yes, a bloodhound, and one who has lost the scent, also. Who is she?'

Katherine laughed outright at the translation. 'She is a very important person, for she takes the place of my mother until my marriage, and I should do as she bids me. Her name is Dona Elvira Manuel, for in Spain we do not change our names when we marry. So Dona Elvira is still a Manuel as her father was, though her son and her husband bear the name Manrique.'

Young Henry heard the translation but his thoughts had already strayed to London Bridge, which lay ahead of them. It always brought a most satisfactory response from foreigners, impressed by its size and the buildings which narrowed the roadway so that a procession across it was a slow business. He watched Katherine's face eagerly for signs of amazement, longing to hear her words of praise and astonishment.

'Eight hundred feet long and thirty feet wide,' droned the translator, whilst Katherine's eyes widened as she saw, not only the enormous proportions of the bridge, but the extraordinary beauty of the river with swans clustered thick as lilies on the water, and overhead, the scavenging red kites wheeling and mewing.

'The river is not as busy as it usually is,' young Henry told his new sister regretfully. 'Usually, one can scarcely see the water for boats, both plying for hire and going up and down about their business.'

'The boatmen charge extra to shoot the bridge,' informed the translator, and Katherine, eyeing the way in which the mighty force of the river was channelled into narrow, fast and obviously dangerous currents by the bridge supports, thought to herself that the boatmen earned their money – and so did their passengers, in a manner of speaking!

'Don't your women look odd?' young Henry suddenly exclaimed. 'Not in themselves, but in the way they are riding alongside the English women.'

Katherine agreed, laughing, that they did indeed present an unusual picture. Because of the different saddle design, the Spanish faced one way on their horses and the English the other, so that it looked as though the pairs of riders had quarrelled and were not speaking; and indeed, they were not, because their position made speech as impossible as the lack of a common language.

'We shall have to take to English saddles as well as English customs, and I'm sure both will suit us admirably,' Katherine said, and as the translator did his work she gazed eagerly ahead at the spires and towers of the great palaces which lined the river. One of them, she knew, was the Bishop's Palace of St Paul's, and it was there that she would stay until the day of her wedding.

The great chamber was full of scurrying figures. Servants hurried about on mysterious errands, noblewomen moved more majestically across the floor. The figure of the Princess alone stood quiet and still.

It was her wedding day, and her marriage robe was heavy about her shoulders, her hair loose to her knees. She had looked at her reflection in the mirror of polished metal, and had scarcely known herself. The white silk gown encrusted with gemstones and scattered with lustrous pearls was beautiful, the mantilla on her head echoing the white and gold of the hem and sleeve edgings; and with her hair brushed until it shone as though it, too, was made of precious gold and copper, she looked, not like Infanta Catalina nor even like Princess Katherine, but like some fair damsel from the far off days of that other Arthur who had ruled in England, once.

Will *he* find me fair? she wondered. She moistened her lips nervously, and drew herself up as the door of the chamber swung open. Young Hal, as she had learned to call Arthur's brother, and some other gentlemen entered, for it was Hal's task to accompany her to St Paul's cathedral. Smiling, she held out her hand to him, her long sleeve-point almost touching the ground, and took a tentative step in his direction, but the weight of the heavily ruched and embroidered satin train held her back and she had to wait, smiling at her young escort, until her women had carefully lifted and arranged the whispering folds. Then they left the room together, the Princess in dazzling white, the Duke of York in scarlet and blue, their hands joined and despite the difference in their ages, his head already only an inch or so short of hers.

They entered the hush of the cathedral from the roar of the streets outside, plunging into the dark calm from the noisy bluster of voice and wind. Now, Queen Elizabeth's sister Cecily carried the train, calm and beautiful in blue, with her sad, knowledge-shadowed eyes fixed on the ground at her feet. Before them, in the centre of the aisle, a circular stage had been erected, covered in red velvet with steps all round it. Arthur waited at the foot of the stairs, clad in satin as white as his face, the only colour the gems in his sword hilt, and the gold of his hair.

Katherine knew that the raised box with its latticed window hid the King and Queen, for she had been told that they would watch from such a place, and she caught a glimpse of them as she passed below it, the King and Queen grave, the Countess of Richmond, who sat between them, weeping copiously and mopping her eyes with the heavy black mourning veils she always wore.

Then she was mounting the steps, steadily, knowing that behind her, the train was being anxiously arranged so that its weight should not unbalance her. Arthur climbed the steps from the opposite side, and they reached the top simultaneously and stood before the Archbishop of Canterbury.

For the rest of the service, Katherine was conscious only of the feet of the various dignitaries who mounted the dais, for her eyes were lowered, and anyway, the mantilla restricted her range of vision. But she could feel Arthur's hand in hers, warm, a little damp from nervousness, but always vastly reassuring. The familiar, sonorous Latin words rolled and echoed round her head, up into the faraway timbers of the roof, bounced off the coloured tiles beneath the feet of the illustrious congregation. She made the appropriate responses, her voice small but firm, hearing them from afar, as though another person spoke; and Arthur's voice, too, seemed remote and faint, though he stood so close that when he turned to her, she could feel his breath on her cheek.

Then it was over. She was descending the steps, stumbling so that she made the dais rock, being seized by young Hal who stood nearby, waiting to resume his protective role as escort to this new sister.

Outside, the roar of the crowds met them, lifting them out of seriousness into a wild joy. Hal's cheeks turned pink and his eyes shone as he lifted his hand and beamed at the press of people, and Katherine smiled and nodded also, pushing her mantilla aside so that her face could be plainly seen. Out of the corner of her eye she could see Arthur, the colour in his cheeks now, his smile one of genuine pleasure when the people called his name and wished him a happy life.

The procession wound its slow way to the Bishop's palace where the marriage feast would be held. They passed a conduit which ran with wine, and the very streets were bedecked with tapestries, pageants, cloth of gold arras, to make the bridal procession glorious indeed. Hal's eyes were wide, and he babbled constantly to the quiet girl at his side, though she could not concentrate on his chatter, could not, in any case, understand a word of it, for in his excitement the boy spoke in English. But she smiled, and nodded, following his pointing finger, appearing to gaze as eagerly as he wished.

They swept into the great hall, and Katherine saw the tables laden with food and wine, the top table with dishes of solid gold, the chair she would presently occupy. Her knees felt shaky and she longed for peace and quiet, but she was a royal princess, and knew that she would be the last person to be left alone that day; indeed, when the time came to set aside this magnificence, she would not be alone. She would never be alone again.

The bridal chamber was strewn with sweet-smelling herbs and fresh green rushes, and in the hearth burned a bright log fire. As they entered, the sweet, spicy scent of burning

53

wood met them, but it was lost almost immediately in the incense in the burners carried by the priests.

Katherine knew that her face was pale from fatigue, and that her eyes by now were shadowed, but glancing at Arthur she saw that he, too, was fighting against weariness. As their eyes met, his face softened, and the smile which brought the dimple out near his mouth, brightened his face.

Queen Elizabeth and King Henry had accompanied them, as had Katherine's women and the grooms of the chamber, who served the Prince of Wales. Now, as the churchmen began to chant, the Princess was swept into one corner of the room and Francesca, Inez, and Maria began removing the stiff and formal gown, the loops of the farthingale, the shifts and chemises, from her tired young body.

Arthur, being undressed by his gentlemen, caught a glimpse of his bride, and smiled to himself. So many layers! It's like peeling an onion, he thought, amused. Layer after layer, until you get to the heart.

The last garment fluttered from her body and her women left her, taking their flickering torches with them so that only the light from the fire and a glimmer from the cressets still beside the door illumined the scene. Katherine stood quietly waiting, the gleaming silk of her gold and copper hair falling like a cloak about her, so that Arthur could only see the tender backs of her knees, her calves, and her bare feet.

Then one of the old men beckoned him to kneel and pray beside her, and he approached softly, giving her one quick glance as he knelt but seeing little beside the flush on her cheek and a rounded shoulder gleaming softly through the thickness of that glorious hair.

Soon enough, now, we shall be left alone, Arthur thought. Two people, married in sight of God and the law, would gaze on each other's nakedness, as long ago Adam and Eve had done. It was supposed to be the custom this night to spend the hours of darkness in prayer, but he knew that few men and women actually did so.

The priests bade them rise. Slowly, solemnly, they were blessed, and so was the bed. They were sprinkled with holy water, and so was the bed. Prayers were said that the marriage might be fruitful. More incense swung, scenting the air so that for a moment it filled his head, and faces loomed crazily, frighteningly, as he longed for the heady perfume to leave his nostrils.

Then the priests made their signs of the cross, and shuffled out, chanting. The last two attendants to leave took the torches from beside the door, and as the door swung slowly shut, they were alone at last, in the flickering firelight.

Arthur raised his eyes from gazing respectfully at the floor and looked speculatively at his bride. She gazed back, her eyes wide and unafraid. She seemed more interested than apprehensive, he noted with amusement. Slowly, he put his hands on her shoulders and ran his fingers down her arms to the elbows. Her skin was soft and warm, like velvet to touch. Then he looked deliberately at her body. She shivered a little, making him catch his breath. The firelight painted her small breasts gold, gilded the pink nipples, and stroked a delicate paintbrush of rose across the curve of her stomach. The shadows of her were dark blue. Tenderly, he moved his hands over her smoothness, enjoying the feel of skin so soft that it made his fingers feel rough and coarse, noticing almost with detachment that this simple act was making her breathe more quickly, so that her breasts rose and fell and her lips parted.

With an effort, he raised his gaze to her face and saw her eyes half covered by the lids, an expression in them of awakening desire. Her tongue nervously moistened her lips, and suddenly he was afraid. She was waiting for him to make the next move in this suddenly adult game, yet she was mature, ripe. She needed a man, not a nervous boy. How could he satisfy her?

He wanted to talk to her, to explain that he had never possessed a woman; that he was afraid of hurting her, afraid of making a fool of himself. But how could he express such thoughts in Latin? His hands dropped from her body and he saw the look of sleepy pleasure fade from her face, to be replaced by bewilderment, the expression of a child who has done wrong without meaning to. Quickly, before fear could unman him again, he pushed her onto the bed and sprawled on top of her, horribly aware that he was doing everything wrong and that her eyes were now frightened as well as bewildered.

Desperately, he squeezed her breast and she gave a little muffled cry of pain and tried to push him away. Then she paused, her hand still on his chest. He saw the sudden understanding fill her eyes and she smiled, with gentleness and fellow-feeling. Under her hand his heart thundered out its message of fear, and against his arm he could feel within the softness of her breast, the rapid heartbeats, in time with his own. He slid off her, aware now that he was not failing her in any way, that she understood and sympathized with his fear, even knew the echo of it within her own young body.

'Tonight, we will sleep,' he whispered, miming the action of slumber with cheek laid on folded hands.

'Tonight, sleep,' she repeated obediently. 'An' tomorrow?'

'We will wait until tomorrow, before we worry about tomorrow,' he said confusedly, his head already longing for the pillow, and for oblivion. He put his arms about her, and felt her lips nuzzle briefly at his chin and then almost at once relax, as sleep took her.

He lay wakeful for a few moments longer, as the fire sank

in the grate and her breathing deepened. He felt a glow of complete contentment at her trust as she slept in his arms. They had no common language except Latin, and yet they had understood each other and would continue to do so. A touch, a glance exchanged between them, and their marriage would be consummated without the need for discussion. Their moment of love, when it came, would be the deeper for the understanding that had saved them from struggling to conform to the standards they had believed were expected of them.

Where there is trust, love may follow without fear or pain, he thought, as he plunged thankfully into a deep and dreamless sleep.

5 Celebrations

Katherine and Arthur sat on a cushioned seat in the royal barge, huddled cosily beneath a fur lap-rug, whilst the oarsmen, dressed in Tudor white and green, pulled strong and smooth with their long blades, their breath hanging on the still air like puffs of thistledown.

Katherine moved her hand beneath the protection of the warm russet mantle, and felt Arthur's fingers clasp her own. She wondered what he was thinking, sitting beside her, his blue velvet cap cocked at an angle on his yellow hair. All that was strange and beautiful to her must be familiar to him. The soft clop and swish of the oars, the great white swans gliding inquisitively towards their craft, the tall buildings standing close to the river. If only I could speak English, she thought wistfully, I could ask my husband the names of the palaces as we pass them. We could discuss the people in boats, who gaze so curiously at the royal barge; who are they, what do they do for a living? As it was, they could only exchange smiles, their fingers entwined beneath the mantle warm and friendly, the closest they could come to an embrace.

Henry VII was talking in a low voice to Elizabeth of York. Katherine thought that few women could be as lovely as her mother-in-law. She was past her first youth, being quite thirty-five, yet her skin was white and smooth, her pale gold hair untouched by grey, her eyes wide and clear. She had been as kind to Katherine as she knew how to be, talking to her through an interpreter, apologizing because she could not speak Spanish. Katherine, watching, noticed that the Queen deferred to the King in all things, and that his attitude to her was coolly polite, lacking all the warmth of strong feeling which Katherine had seen between her own parents.

The children were well-loved, that was evident. Henry had stayed with his tutor, but would be at Baynard's Castle to greet them, so only Arthur's sisters were in the barge. Margaret, tall as Katherine and full-figured, sat by her mother, her goodlooking face marred, this morning, by her peevish expression. The hair beneath her coif was uncompromisingly red, reminding Katherine of the popular belief that redhaired women were wanton. She smiled at the girl, and received no more than the blankest of stares in return.

Little Mary would be about five, thought Katherine. An enchanting child, her auburn curls caught up with white ribbon, her pale blue woollen cloak pushed back so that she could gesture as she talked. Her hat, white and warm, swung carelessly from one hand, and her smile as she glanced towards Katherine was friendly.

It seemed as though of all the royal children, Mary was the most fortunate. The King and Queen poured affection over their baby daughter, seldom chastising her, whilst the older children spoilt her and made much of her.

The barge drew alongside the water-steps of the Castle, and for a moment, speculation about her new family was at an end. Katherine was bustled into the apartments which were to be hers, and to her dismay saw that during the festivities at any rate, she was to live once more with her maidens, for beside her own bed was a truckle cot for an attendant, and access to her room could only be gained by going through that of her women.

But it would have been thought strange had she complained, so she endured mutely, as she endured all the entertainments which had been arranged for her pleasure. And mutely most of these pleasures were taken, too. She was surrounded by the royal family, all determined that she should be surprised, excited and over-awed by their father's generous displays. The King, she soon realized, did not talk much. But his wife and the younger children never seemed able to stop their tongues from wagging – and all their chatter was in English. Of all that bright company, King Henry, Prince Arthur, and his bride were the only people who did not keep up a constant flow of talk. But the King watched her closely, Katherine knew.

'Anyone would think I was a brood-mare,' she said irritably to Maria one night as they lay in their beds. 'The King is studying my points for breeding, and does not bother to hide his interest. I am only thankful that he has not, as yet, tried to examine my teeth!'

'He is a strange man, but I believe he means well,' Maria said comfortably. 'He has not been rude, even if he stares somewhat.'

'Just because I cannot converse in English, that does not

mean I can understand nothing,' Katherine said indignantly. 'I know he was complaining about our Spanish fashions to one of his councillors the other day, and I *know* that he said I might have no hips and no breasts, because of the way they eyed me.'

Maria laughed. 'The ladies of the English court do not scruple to show their breasts and the shape of their hips to an observer,' she pointed out. 'But I am told there is some disagreement over whether you should go to Ludlow with Arthur when he returns there in a few days. They say that the King thought you might prefer to stay with the court for the winter months, because apparently this Wales is a wild, cold place, unfitted for one of your rank and gentle nature.'

'Stay here with *them*? Never!' Katherine declared. 'As for cold, do they imagine it is always sunny in Spain? They should live in the Pyrenees in winter as I have done, in a tent torn and rocked by the howling wind, with icicles a foot long hanging from the rocks.'

'No doubt you will be asked which you prefer,' Maria said. 'After all, you and Arthur are married now. They cannot keep you apart if it is your wish to remain together. I hear they're arguing about the consummation of the marriage – whether it should be allowed to go forward, or whether it would be wiser if you continued to sleep apart.'

'I am unlikely to have babies if I sleep apart from my husband,' Katherine said. She moved restlessly, rustling the bedcovers, and heard Maria turn also, on her creaking straw mattress. 'Why am *I* not consulted? Why does everyone behave as though I were a child just because I cannot speak their language?'

'Don Pedro says,' Maria said frankly, 'that it is because Arthur is a stripling, still. They remember your brother, Princess. Many said that had Juan not bedded Margaret of Austria before his full strength was on him, he would be alive today. Many members of our Spanish suite have remarked that there is a great physical resemblance between your husband and the Infante Juan.'

Katherine nodded in the dark. Yes, she had seen the likeness between dead Juan and Arthur Tudor. Both blondhaired and fair-skinned, both with strong, straight young bodies, both blue-eyed. She swallowed, aware of rising panic. Suppose they said that she might not stay with Arthur. She liked him much better than any other member of his family and felt it would not be long before love flourished between them. But was it right to risk his health by accompanying him to Ludlow so that they might live as man and wife? She thought of waving goodbye to her husband and settling down to life at the English court, and the panic strengthened. Arthur was the only one who understood her, she thought wildly. The only one who really cared about her. She could not see him leave her without a struggle.

She turned restlessly in bed, and found herself wishing that Arthur was beside her so that they could discuss this new development. It was so difficult to speak to him, for they were seldom left alone and always, always, the interpreter hovered near. If only they would realize, Katherine thought desperately, that we *can* exchange ideas and thoughts, when we are undisturbed. They could not converse, except in difficult, stilted Latin, but they could understand each other well enough in their own way.

She decided, before she slept, that the following day she would find the opportunity of having a talk with either her husband or the King. She would do her best to persuade them that she would be happier in Ludlow than parted from Arthur.

But next morning, she awoke with a great drum of pain beating within her head, throbbing through her body so that she groaned when she moved. They were at Windsor, and she found the castle cold and draughty. Good manners forbade her to wrap her warm cloaks and mantles around her shoulders, so she wore her stately dresses with aplomb, trying to forget the fact that her wooden farthingale held her skirts so far from her legs that they were always cold.

And now, they said, she had an ague. Motherly women brewed possets and brought her hot bricks to keep the bed warm. The fire blazed up in her chamber, and Katherine cuddled thankfully under the blankets, warm for the first time for several days.

On the second day of her illness, however, the King himself came to see her, with the interpreter hovering close, and though he was polite enough, it was abundantly clear to Katherine where his true concern lay.

'I *must* get up,' she told her women tearfully the following morning, struggling into her clothes. 'King Henry will take my illness as an excuse for keeping me from Ludlow Castle. He may even say that any children I bear will be sickly, like their mother. I'm going down to the great hall for dinner.'

And go down she did, though her knees trembled and the sight of the rich food made her stomach turn over.

After dinner, the King, the Queen, the nobles of the Spanish suite, and members of the Council met with the young couple themselves to discuss the vexed question of whether Arthur and Katherine should go to Ludlow as a married couple, or whether Katherine should stay at court until the weather was more clement.

Dona Elvira was shrilly insistent that Queen Isabella was a devoutly religious woman who would not dream of keeping a man from his wife.

'Whom God hath joined together, let no man put asunder,' she said dreadfully, scowling at King Henry.

The King sighed, but asked what others felt. Some thought the young people should live together, but others, particularly the more sober members of the Spanish suite, remembered Juan and urged separate establishments, for a time at least.

The King's face, carefully devoid of expression, was turned to Katherine for her opinion and she said gently, in French, 'I would like to accompany my husband, if that is what he wishes, also.'

Prince Arthur fidgeted and reddened. 'The final decision must lie with my father,' he said stiffly, and Katherine saw him give the King a significant glance.

Henry bowed his head for a moment, considering. Then he said, 'The young people should be together for the begetting of heirs. The Welsh marches for both of them, eh, my dear?'

Queen Elizabeth smiled, and agreed. Dona Elvira smiled also, her triumph all-important to her. But some of the other faces were grave, and Katherine knew that they thought of Juan.

'You will have to sit for your portrait before you leave us, my love,' said Elizabeth of York. 'We may not have your presence amongst us, but we will be able to gaze upon your likeness.'

'That would be delightful,' Katherine said cautiously, after the translation. 'But who will paint such a portrait?'

'There is a Spanish painter in London at present; Miguel Sittow. His work is good. Have you heard of him?'

'Why yes. He has painted me before, though long ago when I was only a child. I'd like him to paint the portrait, and it would be nice to be able talk to him in my own language,' Katherine said composedly.

But inwardly she felt far from cool. She did indeed know Miguel; he had, she supposed, painted portraits in most of the courts of Europe. A dark intense young man with a passion for his work, he had expressed an ardent desire to paint her the year before, when they had met in the Alhambra. He had been painting a picture of a beautiful young lady of the court, to send to her betrothed, and the youngest Infanta had watched, fascinated, as the picture grew upon the canvas both in beauty and accuracy.

He had talked to her, aware when he came out of the abstraction that his art brought upon him, that the girl was lonely and happy to have his attention occasionally.

'I would like to paint you,' he told her one warm, still afternoon when he was preparing a new canvas for another portrait. 'You have a quality of untouched innocence which is rare enough in an Infanta. You do not think yourself beautiful, do you, little one?'

'No, for I am not beautiful,' Katherine had said frankly. 'Juana is very lovely, is she not, and my sister Isabella was beautiful, too. I am not tall, and my eyelashes are light brown instead of glossy black, as they should be.'

She had sighed enviously, thinking of Juana's lustrous black eyes, and the enchanting little face set amidst cloudy night-dark hair.

'You are fair,' Sittow had acknowledged, 'and beautiful, also. Just because you are not tall, and your breasts are slight, as yet, that does not make you plain.' He turned his eyes upon her, seeing her flush as his glance bored through her formal gown to the frame beneath. 'You have a body that will give joy some day,' he said.

Katherine was shocked. Of course she was, she told herself fiercely. Yet she did not complain to Queen Isabella. For she found that she enjoyed being in the painter's company even more now that he had said he admired her. She watched him whenever she could, seeing the dark head bent over his work, or watching his anxious care as he mixed his colours, the little tablets of what looked like dark earth and mounds of clay turning into the vivid shades he loved.

Right up until the moment that he finished the last of his commissions and left, his mule laden with the tools of his trade, he did not appear to notice the youngest Infanta particularly. But as he rode out of the courtyard, he had called out, apparently to no one in particular, 'A body that will give joy, one day; remember!'

She had run into the fig orchard then, to be alone. To press her hands to her burning cheeks and feel guilty pleasure because a man had had the courage to find her beautiful, and to tell her so.

And it had been a turning point in her life. She realized that, now. From that moment, she had ceased to find her fair skin distasteful and her blue eyes insipid. The hair which she had despised because it was not black, she realized joyfully *was* beautiful. It was coloured the rich glow of corn, intermingled with the richer shade of well-polished copper. A shifting, changing cloak which clothed her to the knee, it was something now to be proud of, and whenever she brushed its lustrous length she thanked Sittow for opening her eyes to the beauty inherent in the silky tresses.

But now! She wondered with a sudden thump of the heart if he would remember her. She no longer bloomed in the Alhambra, pink and gold amongst the dark Spaniards. Here, there were women fairer of skin than herself, and because of her married state her hair would be covered. She knew a stab of disappointment that her main beauty was hidden away for none but her women to see. Then she scolded herself. She was a woman now, a married woman. Or was she? The colour rose in her cheeks as the problem presented itself. Did the fact that she had promised to lie with Arthur make a woman of her, or was it the physical actuality of losing her virginity? She shrewdly suspected that it was the latter.

She thought regretfully that it would not have mattered that her hair was covered, had she been able to meet the painter this time a married woman in very truth. She had tried to speak to Arthur apart, but always, someone was listening. Sometimes it was merely clerics, ambassadors, or officials, but often it was his sister, Margaret. Arthur was very fond of Margaret and Katherine was shocked at her own inability to like the younger girl. Margaret wore English fashions well, but Katherine thought her bold. She was only twelve, yet already she challenged men with suggestive glances from her bright blue eyes. She made less effort to be nice to Katherine than any other member of the Royal family, and Katherine thought the girl was jealous of the affection given to his bride by Arthur. After all, they were the eldest children and together they bore the brunt of parental wrath when wrongdoing was discovered.

Then a piece of gossip related by young Hal confirmed Katherine's faint distaste for her sister-in-law. They were huddled close to the fire one cold afternoon, desultorily playing chess and watching Margaret, apparently impervious to the cold, peacocking up and down the presence chamber in a green gown embroidered all over with white and red roses.

'Margaret thinks herself so fine,' Hal said resentfully as his sister's train brushed against their board, sending two of his pieces clattering to the floor. 'She is always telling me what to do, and running to my tutor with tales of my bad behaviour, but for all that, she lets him put his hand down her dress when he is correcting her French exercises. I saw him.'

They were conversing in the usual polygot mixture of

Latin, French and English and Katherine, thinking that she had misunderstood, said carefully, 'Did you say that Mr Skelton put his hand in your sister's dress, Hal? Surely I misunderstood you?'

'Why?' said Hal scornfully, pushing a pawn at random across the board. 'You can't have been here all this time without noticing that my tutor has a fondness for the wenches, or that Margaret makes sheep's eyes at all the men?'

'I hardly know Mr Skelton,' protested Katherine. 'And why should he want to do such a thing, Hal? Are you sure you are not mistaken?'

'Sure? Of course I'm sure,' said Hal with the cheerful callousness of a ten-year old. 'He's always chasing the wenches. But Margaret likes him feeling her breasts. The colour came up until her face was red as a beet, and she sat as still as anything.' He grinned widely at Katherine's obvious horror. 'I think it's silly,' he said frankly. 'I shan't go round putting *my* hand . . . '

'Oh stop it, Hal,' Katherine cried, amusement struggling with dismay. 'I'm sure if you did see such a thing you should have told no one. Now be a good boy, and promise me you won't say anything to anyone else.'

'I promise I won't tell anyone else,' said Hal cheerfully, picking up two walnuts and cracking them. He handed the kernels to his sister-in-law. 'Why should I tell anyone, when most of the court know that Margaret likes being cuddled?'

Katherine sighed, laughed, and gave up. What a way they behaved, these young English girls! But she was glad, on the whole, that Hal had told her the story. It would be a lesson to her to behave with the utmost tact and propriety when she sat for her portrait. She would be careful to show nothing but cool politeness to Master Miguel Sittow.

In the chamber set aside for his work, Miguel Sittow was getting ready for his royal visitor. He had chosen a low and comfortable stool for a seat, well cushioned so that the royal behind should not get stiff too quickly. Arranging his paints, he cursed softly beneath his breath at the confounded arrogance of the aristocracy. Surely they could have told him which member of the royal family he was to paint this time? He liked to think himself into the right mood before he began work, even on his preliminary sketches, and besides, there were his colours. Women showed more skin surface than men, and suppose it was one of the children? Or all four of them?

He paled. A touch of the Tudor dramatics, their tendency to insist on their rights, had attended the last portrait he had painted of the family. Coloured it, you might say. Hal had appeared with an arrogant scowl, Margaret had somehow managed to resemble both an outraged reigning monarch and a lecherous porker, and Arthur had looked pale and insignificant. Mary was always easy to paint, but nevertheless King Henry had not been pleased with his picture. He had paid all right, but grudgingly, and Miguel had feared he would get no more royal patronage.

And then, only a few months later, he had been summoned to paint Margaret on her own, to send, he imagined, to James IV of Scotland, who was her betrothed. After half a dozen sittings he had felt quite sorry for James. That a young creature, not then twelve, could have run circles round him, Miguel Sittow, was unthinkable. But she had done so, despite the chaperon who was with them constantly. James of Scotland had a reputation as a ladies' man, but would he have the energy to keep pace with Margaret Tudor? Miguel doubted it.

But despite the fact that several times only the presence of her women had prevented him from upending her across his knee and administering a spanking in the usual area, the painting had been a good one. Because of the importance of the eventual owner of the portrait, Margaret had worn her favourite gown, had rubbed her cheeks into roses, and had refrained from sulking when Miguel snubbed her. He had conveyed the look of demanding invitation in the bold blue eyes without altogether meaning to, but such a look was just what a King should wish to see in his prospective bride, he had told himself with an inward grin. If she was like that at eleven . . . well, he pitied James.

Once more he moved the draperies behind the model's stool, eyeing them through half-closed lids. Black had been the obvious choice but it occurred to him that the Countess of Richmond, the King's mother, might be his sitter. A fearsome old dame, autocratic, self-satisfied and a prig, yet so superstitious that at time of great joy she would weep and wail and tear her hair like any eastern idol-worshipper, in case the narrow and bigoted God in whom she believed grudged her joy and punished her. And since she dressed always in black, as though in mourning for life itself, the thought of setting her against the heavy black velvet background made him wince.

Panic-stricken, he jumped onto the dais and began pulling the velvet down. If it *was* the Richmond witch she would refuse to let him change the backing, and the thought of that severe, uncompromising countenance unrelieved by any colour made the artist in him shudder.

But scarcely had he pulled down the first fold when the door opened. He glanced over his shoulder, then froze with amazement. Coming slowly into the room, richly dressed in the Spanish fashion, was Catalina, the youngest of Queen Isabella's children.

'Now what is my fair Spaniard doing in this cold land?' he said softly, and was rewarded by the swift flood of colour

69

that rose to her brow and the quick lowering of her lids.

The girl beside her, a typical Spanish beauty with white skin and eyes like sloes, looked bewildered, gazing from her mistress to the painter. He smiled at her, then helped his sitter onto the dais.

Why was it the demure, the unapproachable, which attracted him most? he wondered. He had not forgotten the slim young Infanta with the glorious copper-gold hair rippling down her back, dancing and singing around the awe-inspiring halls of the Alhambra.

He refixed the black velvet and glancing at the Princess's backview, saw with sadness that a headdress now hid the glorious hair and the shape of her shoulders. But we all grow up, he reflected, and are none the worse for that.

'You are now the Princess of Wales, yes?' he said, walking over to his drawing board. He selected a pencil and began to draw with quick, light strokes. 'Katherine of Aragon, Princess of Wales, bride of the heir to the kingdom, Prince Arthur?'

She nodded, and glanced down at the gold necklet she wore. The letter K was alternated with the red and white roses of Lancaster and York.

'You find married life to your liking, Princess?'

'Very much, *señor*.'

Bad liars, these fair-skinned girls. He noticed the way the colour had flown to her face at his words, and thought he would be making a shrewd guess from her flush and downcast eyes that, as yet, Arthur had not laid a hand on her. He thought scornfully that the young Tudor sprig mould be no match for this Spanish rose when it came to a bedding. She was young and innocent, but there was a promise of passion in the soft fullness of her lower lip, and the little round chin spoke of determination. His sketch was taking shape; before him on the page, the oval face, the steady gaze, the mouth with its interesting and definite curves. He worked on, his pencil rapid, sketching face and shoulders from various angles to find the position which pleased him best.

A restless stirring from the other girl made him look up. She said rather crossly, 'We've been here two hours, *señor*, and my mistress hasn't moved. But she must be getting stiff and tired. I think she should retire now.'

He was all contrition, though a part of his mind knew that had he been interrupted before he had found the correct pose, he would have felt less sympathy for his sitter.

Katherine stood up, her knees trembling from holding the pose, but her mind at peace after the long silence.

'Thank you, *señor*. At the same time, tomorrow?'

'If you please, Princess. You are not overtired?'

'Not at all, *señor*. Goodbye.'

She held out her hand and he bent over it, kissing not the back as she had expected, but turning it over so that his lips fitted briefly into her rosy little palm. He felt her instinctive withdrawal and mentally saluted Arthur. He may not have possessed his wife as yet, but he had certainly aroused feelings in her. The Infanta he had known in Spain would have blushed and smiled at his action, but it would have held no significance for her.

I would make a good secret service agent, he thought, not displeased with himself, as he bowed the two young ladies out of the apartment.

'The portrait is an excellent likeness,' exclaimed Elizabeth of York. 'When you are far away on the Welsh border with Arthur we shall still enjoy looking at your pretty face. Sittow is a master painter; he has captured an expression of thoughtfulness which you often wear, a serious yet contented expression. I've often noticed you looking just like that, haven't you, my lord?'

King Henry jerked his head, as though his thoughts had been far away, and said, 'To be sure, my dear, to be sure.' But Katherine, eyeing him shrewdly, thought that he had agreed without even hearing the question.

A strange man, this Henry of England. Sometimes he seemed so cold and indifferent that she wondered whether he thought about his wife at all; at other times he seemed as concerned about his children as was the Queen. And today she was feeling unhappy herself, because those of her friends who had come to England merely to see her married were leaving for Spain once more.

When the time came for their departure, she said her farewells with outward cheerfulness, giving messages for her parents and some close friends. But when the sounds of their horses and mules had faded into the distance, she gave way to despair. Spain seemed so far away, and her own future so uncertain. She was to leave for Ludlow shortly, another unknown place full of strangers. And the English court had closed up again after her friends had left, as though they had felt the Spaniards as an intrusion; guests whose presence had been enjoyable enough, but whose departure once more left the family complete.

Feeling abandoned by all Katherine went to her chamber, but a messenger came knocking at the door, asking that she and her women go to the King's study, for he had something to show her. With a little lift of interest, Katherine complied. She wondered what Henry meant; was it a letter, perhaps, from her mother?

But when she entered the room, the King was standing behind a table upon which gems glittered frostily in the light from the window. Seeing her puzzled glance, he said genially, 'Choose which you prefer, daughter. Do they please you?'

'They are very beautiful,' Katherine said hesitantly. 'But . . . for me? Why, when you have given me so many pleasant things?'

'You grieve for your departing friends,' the King said simply.

So Katherine bent over the table and examined the jewels, but she could not help wondering why this extravagant gesture? It had not taken her long to realize that Henry did not enjoy parting with money. His pageants and shows after the wedding feast had largely been paid for by the city fathers, and those for which he *had* paid were used over and over again, in different guises, so that his money went as far as possible.

The Queen was a good and provident wife and worked industriously with her needle, but new clothes were a rarity in the royal nursery, and Mary wore many a gown which Margaret had worn years before. Cloaks had thin and frayed edges trimmed off and were hemmed again, and gowns were treated likewise, whilst the small economy of mending hose again and again could not have been easy for the Queen, especially as Hal grew so fast that he could not wear the same clothes for more than a few weeks without alterations having to be made. Katherine had watched with awe as her mother-in-law patiently added material to Hal's hose, so that he might still wear a pair that he had outgrown.

Yet it seemed that today, Henry was disposed to be generous. Katherine chose first, a girdle of chased gold set with pearls and rubies in the form of red and white roses, and then, at the King's insistence, a brooch which had taken her fancy. A pendant carved on ivory caught her eye – a diamond-studded St George was slaying with a long, emerald-tipped sword, a red-enamelled dragon.

73

She would have drawn back then, content with the pieces which she had chosen, but Henry lunged across the table, picked almost at random a ring set with a great diamond, and gestured her to try it on. When she demurred, he came round the table, put his arm about her shoulders, and tried the ring on each of her fingers in turn, smiling teasingly at her. Katherine endeavoured to look pleasant and unself-conscious, and wished very hard that the King would return to his usual demeanour, because this joviality seemed so false as to be almost frightening.

He had captured her hand and held it firmly, pushing the gold circlets one by one onto her fingers, turning her hand to the light so that the gems caught fire from the pale sunshine. He squeezed her fingers, telling her that jewels became her, that she should wear more rings, and then he caught at a necklace of sapphires and insisted on putting it round her neck, saying, 'This you must have, daughter! It matches your eyes.'

It was the first time the King had made a personal remark to her, of whatever nature, and Katherine felt supremely uncomfortable, as though this was all a charade played for some purpose which she was too young and foolish to understand. Henry took her little chin between his finger and thumb and made her look into his eyes, told her to smile, just for him, to show that she did not dislike being left in his care.

Katherine was flushed, a lifetime of the rigid etiquette of the Spanish court telling her that King or no, he had no right to treat her like a kitchenmaid, squeezing her shoulders, fumbling with her neck and hair as he adjusted necklaces.

Then Arthur came in – and stopped short on the threshold. King Henry quickly let go of Katherine and stepped back, saying in his most cold and bored voice, 'Have you chosen enough, daughter? Then the rest shall be divided amongst your women.'

But Katherine noticed that he made no attempt to chuck even the prettiest of her maidens under the chin, nor did he press the rings on their fingers. He exchanged a few words with Arthur, too quick and low for Katherine to follow, and left the room as though he had no further interest in the proceedings.

For long afterwards, however, Katherine remembered the incident with a little murmur of fear and uncertainty, and she knew that Arthur, too, had been puzzled by his father's behaviour. But soon they would leave for Ludlow, and soon she would be a long way from Henry and the English court.

6   Journey

'Why can you not ride pillion behind me, instead of behind your Master of Horse?' Arthur asked impatiently. 'My charger is strong, and we are both light. We would make better speed.'

They had set out on their journey at last, and were on the road to Oxford, where they would spend Christmas.

Katherine's understanding of the English language was improving, but she still felt diffidence over speaking it in public, so she said in Spanish, 'Your parents thought it better that you should ride out from London alone, waving to the crowds. Tomorrow, perhaps, if we are travelling through quiet and unfrequented parts, I might ride with you.'

There was a pause for translation and Katherine thought desperately, 'I *must* learn English. Just a little, each day. How can Arthur and I ever learn true love if we have to rely on an interpreter all the time?'

'Tonight, we will stay at Abingdon,' Arthur said instructively, and Katherine said brightly, 'Tonight, we weel stay Abeengdon, yes?' She smiled at his pleasure, but wished that she could ask him whether they would share a room once more, or whether she would sleep with her women. If they had been alone, the question would not have been impossible, but riding along with the courtiers crowding close, she could only sigh impatiently for the night, and possess her curiosity as best she might.

That evening, she and Arthur and most of her suite were lodged in a fine new house, built of stone, and Katherine's cooks made a meal in the Spanish style for their master and mistress, though they suffered somewhat from lack of familiar vegetables. They shared a room once again, and after the meal was over their attendants undressed them and they were left in the wide new chamber smelling of sawdust and mortar still. They looked at each other doubtfully, both wearing their shifts against the cold, though the bed had been provided with hot bricks and a fire burned on the hearth.

'Let us get into bed, it will be warmer between the sheets,' Arthur said, and as they climbed onto the high feather mattress, they caught each other's eye and both burst into simultaneous laughter.

'Do not worry, Katherine, we have time enough to learn about each other during the journey to Ludlow,' Arthur said. 'We can choose the moment ourselves, when we shall become truly man and wife.'

They lay talking quietly for a while, Arthur trying to teach Katherine some simple English words and Katherine repeating his pronunciation as best she could, though her accent was still heavy. Then they grew drowsy and rolled towards each other in the middle of the big bed, curling close for warmth, as two puppies will curl into a ball against the cold.

Slowly, they were growing to know one another. They were becoming at ease in each other's company. The most difficult barrier, that of understanding, had been surmounted, and beside that, language was of little account. So they slept without guilt, waiting for the fulfilment which would come at the right moment.

It was a cold morning. During the night there had been light flurries of snow, and frost had be-furred the trees so that they stood out against the sky, their whiteness making the clouds look grey. The sun was up, however, and the clouds were dispersing in the early morning mist. It was going to be a fine day.

Arthur had insisted that today Katherine should travel in the litter so that she should be warmer, for the previous day's journey had not been pleasant. Sleet had whipped across the flat Oxfordshire meadows, stinging their faces and blotting out any beauty that the landscape might have to offer, and everyone had been thoroughly exhausted by the time they stopped for the night.

But now, jogging along the road in the horse-drawn litter, wrapped in fur rugs so that only her face was visible, Katherine looked bright and healthy, with her cheeks rosily glowing from the warmth of her coverings and the sharp nip of the morning air. Around her mouth, a halo of her breath hung, and she puffed more misty vapour, enjoying the strangeness of seeing her own breathing as a child would.

'We've almost reached Oxford,' Arthur called down to

her, leaning nearer. 'See those spires in the distance? The ancient city of Oxford, where we will stay over the Christmas season. You will enjoy yourself there, for it is a great centre of learning.'

She nodded and smiled, understanding more from his tone than from the actual words.

Arthur himself was aware that the first thrill of their early departure was wearing off. He had felt warm after a good breakfast and his servants had made sure that he was warmly clad. But every time he sucked a breath of the icy air it made him want to cough, and his numbed fingers could scarcely hold onto the ornate leather reins. He rode a mettlesome steed to impress the students of the university, but he thought ruefully that on such a day he would have preferred an easier, quieter mount. The road was rutted and uneven, and he had to keep Black Prince very much in check in case the stallion slipped and injured himself.

'This horse has been fed oats,' he said accusingly to his Master of Horse. 'What he wants is a good gallop to get the fidgets out of his legs, and I dare not even let him break into a trot on this surface.'

'Will you approach Magdalen College across the fields of Christchurch, Sire, instead of through the town?' suggested the man. 'The sun will be well up by then, and you could perhaps let the horse canter.'

Arthur frowned. 'No, the route is planned. The good citizens of Oxford will be watching for us over Folly Bridge, up St Aldates and then along Fish Street. We will follow that road.'

'Perhaps you would like to change your mount?' enquired the man diffidently, and showed no surprise when Arthur shook his head.

Arthur reflected that he was glad Christmas was to be spent at Oxford. He liked the town and felt at home there, but more than that, the advantages for Katherine would be overwhelming. She would be in the company of learned men, many of whom spoke her language, which would be better for her by far than being shut away for the twelve days of Christmas in the home of some country squire, with whom she would be able to exchange no more than smiles and nods.

She would lodge at Woodstock, he knew, a comfortable little palace with plenty of room for her suite and his gentlemen as well. It would be pleasant for all of them, to relax for a while without having to worry over different lodgings. The Spaniards could cook for themselves if they wished to do so, but it was more likely that they would prefer to try English cooking over the festive season. He hoped so; he did not altogether like the food which had been served to him by Katherine's cooks.

Black Prince cocked up his ears and coquetted to one side, slipping on a patch of ice and blowing indignantly down his nostrils. He had seen ahead of them the crowds waiting to welcome the Prince of Wales and his bride. Arthur gathered up the reins and chafed his hands together in a vain attempt to bring warmth and feeling flooding back. Then he straightened his back and rode towards the cheering which swelled and burgeoned at their approach.

'Princess Katherine, do you remember me? How well you look, and how happy! It is plain that English life agrees with you.'

Katherine held out her hands to the tall, sparse-haired man who had spoken, her smile spontaneous.

'Richard Mayew! It is good to see you, and I shall look forward to seeing your university and the city of Oxford.'

Katherine had grown fond of Mayew, President of Magdalen College, when he had ridden beside her mount on the journey from Plymouth to London, for his command of the Spanish tongue was excellent, and he had interpreted for her on several occasions.

'I only hope my students behave themselves with decorum,' Mayew remarked as they began to cross Folly Bridge. 'This river, Princess, is the mighty Thames, the same river which flows through London. Oxford is surrounded by water, for the Thames here forms many streams and rivulets, and another river, the Cherwell, also loops itself about the city.'

'Yes, I can see that the situation is low, being cupped in the hollow of the land just here,' Katherine replied.

'And unhealthy, as you have doubtless heard. Why every summer, for almost fifty years, the plague has stalked through the streets of Oxford.'

'The plague seems hot everywhere,' Katherine said. 'The reason my mother couldn't send me to England last year was because plague had broken out in Spain.'

'Aye, so I heard. But Oxford is unhealthily situated, there can be no doubt of that. Why, at one time it was feared that there would be no university left, so many of the scholars died.'

Katherine nodded her understanding. She looked over the flat meadows and was glad that she and Arthur were going to live at Ludlow, for she had been told that the town was in mountainous country, and healthy.

'Is that the cathedral I can see?' she asked presently. 'Across the meadows – are they Christchurch meadows? – over to my right?'

Mayew nodded. 'Yes, and we are riding up St Aldates. At the cross you and your ladies will continue to travel straight ahead, up Cornmarket, whilst the Prince will turn to the right and go in royal progress down Fish Street, to my own college.'

'Yes, I see. Arthur had promised to show me the city,' Katherine said a trifle wistfully, 'but I suppose we may have the opportunity of seeing it once again, before we continue on towards Ludlow?'

She understood that this was essentially a man's city, a place of great learning, but nevertheless she thought she would not like her mother to be told that Katherine had allowed herself to be shepherded straight through Oxford without meeting or conversing with any of the divines and scholars who worked there.

Richard Mayew, correctly reading the expression on the Princess's face, said soothingly. 'You shall see Oxford, indeed you shall. Have you read what Erasmus said of Oxford? He called it the dirtiest city and the unhealthiest which he had visited in all his travels. You must have a chance to disagree with him.'

'I expect you have arranged for the city to be cleaned, knowing that Arthur and I were coming to visit you,' said Katherine immediately, and was rewarded by his guilty smile of acknowledgement.

'Perhaps, Princess. Would you like to hear some of the history of our city? The building on your right, for instance. That is the Abbey of the blessed St Frideswide of sacred memory, the patron saint of Oxford. She was a princess like yourself, the daughter of King Didanus of ancient times. It is said that a suitor came to woo her, and overcome by her beauty and piety, tried to force her to become his wife. God struck him blind as a punishment for his various sins, but because of her stainless purity he gave the virgin Princess the power to perform miraculous cures. She gave her suitor back his sight of course, provided that he troubled her no further, and after sundry other deeds of a similar nature, she founded the great Priory which you see before you.'

Katherine looked with new interest at the pile of grey stone buildings, crouching in the lush watermeadows. In summer, she thought, they would barely be visible from the road, so surrounded were they by great trees and the long, reeded grass.

'It is a beautiful place,' she said respectfully. 'Do many people come to the saint's Priory now, hoping for cures?'

Mayew shrugged. 'The blessed St Frideswide, though doubtless a virgin of remarkable purity and piety, did not know much about architecture,' he explained. 'The site is always damp and when the rivers flood, as they do fairly frequently, the occupants of the Priory are the ones who pray for miracles.'

But Katherine's attention had been caught by another building which she could see in the distance.

'Is that your college of Magdalen?' she exclaimed, pointing.

Mayew sniffed. 'That? Why, that's only Merton. It is one of the oldest colleges but the only thing of importance about it would be its bell tower. Magdalen has the highest tower in Oxford – higher than Carfax, which we will pass, presently.'

They had to pause, then, to hear an oration delivered by a group of scholars, their faces wreathed in smiles and bearing boughs of holly, thickly berried. Katherine watched the group with interest, noticing that though some of the young men were warmly dressed and seemed well-fed, there were others, no less happy, certainly, but thinly clad and with that look about them which experience had told her meant they often knew hunger.

She mentioned the fact to her mentor, in a whisper, and he nodded. 'Aye, sure enough. Some lads are sent by their parents or guardians to get an education and they pick a bright, intelligent boy to accompany their sons who will also benefit from the teaching. But Oxford does not close its doors to the poor, who would learn. And some of the greatest scholars began here, in rags.'

'Yet you do not take women into your colleges?'

Mayew smiled. 'No, Spain has certainly done better than us, there, for a woman lectures in Madrid, I know. Here is the cross, Princess, and there is Carfax tower. A pageant is being performed for you now, by the townsfolk this time.'

As the actors began nervously to pace and pontificate upon the raised wooden stage, Katherine said quietly, 'The scholars and the citizens seem to mix well enough today, sir. I have, however, heard stories that it is quite otherwise, at times.'

Mayew looked down into the round and innocent eyes turned up to his, and sighed. Heaven knows, he thought, boys can be mischievous enough. But women – be praised the gods that no women were taught in Oxford nor ever would be – women were worse. He could imagine the sort of stories which would have been whispered gleefully around the Spanish courts, and thought resentfully that the Spaniards were too self-satisfied, and behaved always as though they never had upheavals or disturbances. Queen Isabella's right to the crown of Castile was not as strong as that of her cousin, whom she had deposed on a flimsy charge of bastardy. Then he smiled, remembering the Tudor claim to the throne also rested on a strange relationship, and that perhaps the strongest right both for Isabella and Henry Seven was that both had won the crown by conquest.

But Katherine's wide eyes were still fixed enquiringly on his; he could not dismiss the troubles between town and gown as lightly as he would have wished.

'There have been incidents, blown up by the evil-minded to appear important,' he admitted. The blue eyes continued to stare with a kitten's innocent puzzlement, and he continued almost despite himself. 'Why, the worst incident took place three hundred years ago, when a couple of scholars were hanged by the townspeople because they killed an Oxford girl. It was an accident of course, and the two fellows were not in any way involved with the girl's death; they roomed with the scholar who had got himself entangled with her, certainly, but that was all. It was murder, of course, but they were lawless days.' He sighed, and around him courtiers muttered one to another as the pageant took its laborious course. 'Oxford memories are long, however, and about thirty years after the girl and the two scholars had died, when you would have thought that all ill-feeling must have died too, there was another affray. Though that was partly the fault of the Church.' He glanced covertly round him for the figure of a friar but though there were many in the throng, Mayew was in the centre of the Princess's suite and safe enough from prying ears.

'Some members of the university tried to present a petition to Cardinal Otho, who was staying at Osney Abbey. Tradition has handed down the story, but does not mention what the university were petitioning for. The Cardinal, an impudent fellow, gave orders that they weren't to be allowed in and understandably, they tried to kick the door down. Things got a bit out of hand, and the scholars must have been a trifle noisy, but that was no excuse for what happened. The Cardinal's cook – who was the man's own brother, mark you; shows what sort of a churchman *he* was – threw a cauldron of boiling soup into the face of a university man. The fellow was annoyed, and who can blame him? A nasty thing to have in the face at the best of times, and I understand from a reliable source that it was not even a good soup, but greasy and unpalatable.'

He did not hear Katherine's involuntary gurgle of amusement. He was back in the thirteenth century, firmly on the side of the outraged university men.

'Well, the scholar was Irish, and they're a fiery crowd, the Irish. And his friend, who happened to be a Welshman – they're even more easily upset than the Irish, my dear – took offence at his friend's treatment, and shot the cook.'

He smiled reminiscently, as though he himself had been one of the indignant and insulted young men, besieging Osney Abbey.

'The battle went on for days, with neither side willing to give in, and half of them, no doubt, quite in the dark as to why they were fighting. They had to bring troops in from Abingdon in the end, or no doubt the two factions – or their descendants – would be fighting still.'

He dragged his mind back from his story, where the scholars of long ago had fought so gloriously, and pointed out that the pageant was at last coming to an end, and soon Katherine and Arthur would have to say their goodbyes.

As he had hoped, this took Katherine's thoughts off town and gown and she began to look around at the strange mixture which was Oxford. The rich merchants, the bustle of shop, guild, and household, and the colleges and the scholars; at odds they might be, yet they made a curiously pleasant whole, and never more so when they stood together as they did now, to welcome royalty in their several fashions.

The procession began to move forward once more, and to Mayew's relief, Katherine passed Swyndlestock Tavern, where the most recent riot had started, without more than a casual glance. Grateful for her absentmindedness, Mayew began to talk of the house to which she went, the little palace of Woodstock, for he had no desire to remind her of the scandal which had rocked Oxford in the not-too-distant past. The riot of St Scholastica's Day, when scholars had complained that the ale at the Swyndlestock Tavern was bad, and when town and gown had fought for three days and nights. There had been sixty scholars dead or missing at the end of the battle, and countless townsfolk also.

But Katherine cared nothing for riots, now. She was saying her stilted Latin farewells to Arthur, assuring him that she would be happy at Woodstock and would look forward to his arrival there. Yet all the time, her eyes spoke the eloquent words which her lips could not.

Arthur raised his hand, and wheeled his horse round. They could see its polished hindquarters disappearing down Fish Street, and then the crowds blocked their view. Mayew saw tears in the Princess's eyes and began, hastily, to talk of Woodstock.

'It's a pleasant enough little place, and was a hunting lodge I believe,' he told her. 'It was built by the man they say founded the university of Oxford, Henry Second. And of course, there is the legend that he built it so that he could steal away down a secret path to the bower of his mistress, the Fair Rosamund.'

'Was she beautiful?' asked Katherine wistfully.

'Very beautiful. But one day, Queen Eleanor found out that she was being deceived. Some say she poisoned her rival, others that Rosamund swore an oath to take refuge from the King's passionate love in a nunnery. But whatever the truth may be, you should take a trip to see Fair Rosamund's tomb, at Godstow, before you leave us.'

'Oh, yes,' breathed Katherine, forgetting for the moment

that she had parted from Arthur with only stiff words of Latin passing between them.

They passed down Cornmarket, crowded with burghers and merchants, passed the lovely old church of St Michael, and left the town by the North Gate across the track leading over St Giles meadow, called after the little church of St Giles which stood outside the city walls.

'Oxford is a city of churches,' Katherine remarked dreamily. The sun was high overhead now, and though it was still frosty, she felt too warm in her litter piled with furs. She wondered how Arthur was getting on, and whether it was much further to Woodstock, for she had a healthy appetite and breakfast seemed a long time ago.

Fortunately, the President had arranged that she should honour the lord of a small manor at Binsey by eating beneath his roof, and Katherine was only too glad to agree.

'After you have rested, Princess, perhaps you would like to see the Holy Well at Binsey,' Mayew suggested. 'St Frideswide took refuge there for a while during the building of her abbey, and it was she who brought the well into being. Many pilgrims come to pray here. For health, or for love, or for a child.'

He glanced curiously at the rosy face below his shoulder but the faint, interested smile still curved her lips. I'll wager she's virgin still, he thought, and was shocked by his own crudeness. What did it matter, anyway, whether the young people had consummated their marriage yet, or not? They had all their lives before them, and Arthur, besides, was young for his years. Kept like that by his father, no doubt with the best of intentions, but time and proximity would work the miracle between them, he had little doubt. Affection and trust they shared already; he had seen both in the glances they had exchanged when they parted.

She was a daughter of Isabella, this fair young creature, and would know her duties as wife to the heir to the throne well enough. Mayew knew that the good Queen had given her new daughter-in-law a holy relic, a girdle that she could wear in childbirth to give her an easy bearing. Soon enough, she would need her mother-in-law's gift.

Soon enough, in truth, he thought, suddenly compassionate. So young, with the bloom of innocence there for all to see, and yet in a year she might be screaming and biting through her lower lip, whilst her swollen belly gave forth its fruit. Being of royal blood, wearing the holy relic even, would not spare her one jot of the agony of childbirth which is the lot of a woman.

He looked away quickly, drawing her attention to the beauties of the countryside, not wanting to think of her smooth flesh torn and marred by childbirth.

'Here is Binsey Manor, sir,' said a voice at his elbow, and he was caught up once more in the whirl of introductions and interpretations, whilst Katherine smiled and smiled until her cheeks were stiff.

But as she welcomed all these kind and cheerful people, gave them her hand to kiss and exchanged curtsies with their wives, her thoughts were not unlike Richard Mayew's. Everyone knew that St Frideswide had a special weakness for brides, particularly those who wanted children. It was her duty to bear Arthur sons. She must have a word in the Saint's ear, before she left Oxford.

7 A New Home

Katherine enjoyed her stay at Woodstock. The palace itself was a pleasant, mellow building but the gardens were a joy and must, she imagined, be very lovely in summertime. Even in the winter, pale sunshine on frosted cobwebs sparkling like spun sugar, and the thick clumps of holly trees with their dark green foliage and massed scarlet berries, made the garden colourful and charming.

Katherine and her maids of honour dreamed around the leafless walks, searching for Fair Rosamund's bower, content to enjoy their fantasies of Henry II's intriguing love.

They visited Oxford, though only twice, for Katherine contracted a heavy cold and feared to go into the city more often than was necessary when weakened by her illness, in case she sickened with one of the more deadly diseases common to Oxford.

But she visited Fair Rosamund's tomb, and prayed to St Frideswide, and before they began their journey once more, she had seen most of the colleges with her guide, Richard Mayew.

'Magdalen looks its best when approached gradually,' he told her proudly, so she and her women rode slowly up to the college, pausing to gaze at the fairytale picture the building presented, with its golden stones rimed with frost, and all the little pinnacles and turrets tinkling with icicles. It stood proudly outlined against the pale blue sky, with the river behind it flung like a loving arm in a half-circle round the green water meadows. The Spaniards thought it more like a palace than Woodstock, and Katherine even ventured inside the big hall, where the hordes of scholars warming their feet in the rushes gave her a cheer, and laughed at her bright confusion.

In the evenings they stayed close to the fire in the great hall of their little palace, and told stories of Fair Rosamund, and Queen Eleanor, and the great men of Oxford, whilst the tapestries moved in the draught so that now one scene, now another, would be thrown into prominence and then quietly withdrawn.

Christmas came, and with it the miracle plays, the gifts, the carol singing, and the festive food. Katherine watched, enchanted, as the baby Jesus was born again, in another land and another tongue, yet as familiar and dear to her as though she was once more within the rose-red walls of the Alhambra with her own family about her. An added delight to her was the Child, for the scholars had acquired from somewhere a real, live baby, which lay squalling most realistically in the cradle, instead of the more conventional stiffly jointed – and silent – wooden doll.

'But you must not be sad that our visit to Oxford is ended,' Arthur said to her, as they rode out of the city for the last time. 'For every day now brings us nearer to Ludlow Castle, where a great deal of our married lives will be spent. You will like the castle, Katherine; nay, you will love it, as I do. It is a *real* castle, you know, built to withstand a long siege. Yet it is my home, and I love it.'

'I loved Oxford,' Katherine replied when the translator had finished. 'I loved Woodstock too. So no doubt I shall love our new home most of all.'

Arthur smiled. 'And there is my new house at Bewdley,' he said. 'It is stone-built, on a hill, and warm. But I must not tell you, for you will soon see it yourself. You *should* like it, for when it was being made good inside I thought of you all the time. Strange, that I had never even seen you, then.'

The interpreter gabbled swiftly and efficiently, and Katherine nodded, smiling. She was on horseback once again, riding pillion. And the journey, in some extraordinary way, seemed to be getting easier the further they travelled, instead of more and more tiring and exacting. She supposed it was because of the increasing affection she felt for the people of England, and the increasing affection between Arthur and herself. Sometimes she hardly needed to listen to the interpreter, and sometimes as the liquid Spanish words poured from her lips and her hands fluttered expressively, she felt that Arthur understood her completely.

They did not have much time to spare, to spend at Bewdley. Only one night, in fact. They arrived at the house as dusk was falling, spreading its soft blue cloak round the new knot garden and old yew trees alike, and they left the next morning as the sun was coming up, glittering blood-red on the window panes so that when Katherine looked back, it was as though a fire burned in the house. A clear flame from the reflected sunrise.

'It is a very fine mansion,' Katherine murmured, to excuse the backward glance, and smiled at Arthur. He smiled too, and raised his golden brows with such a meaningful look that Katherine laughed aloud, and blushed.

For at Bewdley, they had begun to move towards eventual intimacy.

A good meal had been prepared for them, by servants who had arrived early, and Arthur had shown her over his house with considerable pride. In the fine bedchamber, he had pointed out that the tapestries were his Aunt Cecily's work, and the bedcurtains, violet and purple with silver thread, had been made by Queen Elizabeth especially for her eldest son. The room was warm and firelit, scented by bowls of rose pot-pourri and the lavender sprigs between the sheets.

At ease with one another, they lay in the big bed, enjoying the comfort of the well-stuffed feather mattress, and the sound of misty rain tapping on the windowpanes only heightened their enjoyment of warmth and shelter. It had been a simple matter to pull the bedcurtains close, whilst commenting on the lovely work done by the Queen, and to roll over and touch very gently as they shared the middle of the bed. In the dark behind the curtains, Arthur had smoothed Katherine's long, long hair, and kissed her ear, her neck, her mouth. The kisses, puppyish at first, became more assured, more searching, and then he pulled her close to him, and it seemed suddenly that he acted with assurance, no longer afraid that his caresses would hurt or offend.

Afterwards, as the hot blood cooled, Arthur pulled back the bedcurtains so that he could see her in the firelight's last glow.

She lay quiescent, her wonderful hair spread out on the pillows, her body still flushed from his touch. He smiled, and she smiled back without resentment, her eyes dreamy.

As he gazed, the last little flame flickered and died, and the logs settled down into their bed of hot white ash. Darkness came back, save for a lightening near the windows where the shutters did not quite meet. In the friendly, secret dark, they clung together again and at last slept, enfolded in each other's arms.

When dawn broke the light roused them, and they straightened the bed and put on their shifts, then lay down again and slumbered once more, until Dona Elvira woke them, to send Arthur off to his gentlemen for dressing, and to superintend Katherine's ablutions herself.

Katherine had washed sketchily and dressed quickly,

hugging to herself the beautiful secret that she and Arthur
were, at last, beginning to be easy together.

And now they were leaving Bewdley behind and drawing every moment closer to their new home.

'There, Katherine! Can you see it? It is a happy chance
that the sun is shining, for I can tell you, Ludlow Castle
looks grim with storm clouds hanging over its head.'

Arthur gestured ahead, and Katherine sat up straighter
to stare. Stark and black against the blue hills of Wales the
castle frowned down on the surrounding land of the marches.
Even from this distance, they could see the trees which
grew close to the grim, grey walls, and the shape of the
tall towers. It seemed to Katherine that Ludlow was an awe-
some place, a lone citadel against whatever threats those
innocent-seeming hills might hold. But she straightened her
shoulders, and smiled ahead, for surely Ludlow Castle
would be a place of destiny, for her? The challenges it
would hold – a new language, a new way of life – were
such that she should be proud to face them.

As they neared the castle, the murmurs from her suite
grew louder. The town was on a hill, as Arthur had told
her, and the huddle of shops and houses within the curve
of the town walls, the rush of the river Teme as it hurried,
rain-swollen, through its gorge, were all strange to the
Spaniards, and less inviting than anything they had seen
in England so far.

But to Katherine, it was beautiful. Partly because Arthur
loved it, and partly because it pleased her senses. The procession passed under the arch of the walls and began to
climb the hill, crowned by the castle. Once more, they were
being welcomed by a people who had not had a chance to
see their Spanish Princess of Wales. Narrow streets

crowded with people, voices calling, dogs barking, children crying. Yet the subtle difference was there, and it was a difference which warmed Katherine's heart. For these folk, welcoming though they were, were used to royalty. Arthur had lived amongst them for several years, and now they welcomed him home, greeting his new wife with interest, certainly. But Katherine had the idea that when the procession had passed, the housewife would return to her baking or her washtub, the children would squabble over a top spinning crazily on the cobbles, and the stout butcher would go back to his shop and his yard. They were looking her over now, and bidding her welcome, knowing that they would be seeing her around their town for many, many months.

She could hear the exclamations on every side, and though their accents rendered it impossible that she could understand, she caught the gist of their meaning.

'A bonny child!' said the redfaced housewife. 'A match for our bonny prince.'

'Aye, come from good Plantagenet stock, ye can tell that,' chuckled the butcher, eyeing the strand of hair which had escaped from her hood.

'A real Spanish Princess!' called the children, one to another. 'Will she dance and play the games of her country, up in the castle?'

Then the procession left the narrow streets, passed the church where a small knot of monks stood tiptoe to see, and they were before the castle.

There was a narrow bridge over the moat and the blue January sky was reflected in the water. Close to the banks, broad lily pads spread their cushioned leaves and amidst the reeds, a pair of stately swans sailed, ignoring the clamour.

The cosy familiarity of birds on water dispelled the recollection that the moat had been built for purposes of defence rather than beauty. The horses clattered over the bridge and cheers came from the people waiting within the walls, thronging forward to call to friends in their train. Katherine heard Spanish, French, English, Latin even, being spoken, and she waved and smiled and stared as her horse carried her through the gates and into the big outer courtyard.

She dismounted, spoke to servants, smiled, and smiled again. The uproar seemed louder now, confined within these tall walls. She glanced over the heads of the people who crowded close to see her, and saw the nobles of the household, those who would actually serve her, were waiting at the door of the great hall. She wondered at their numbers, until Arthur whispered, 'Many of the Welsh have come in from the hills to greet you,' and then she understood.

Holding hands, they advanced towards their welcome. Huge hounds raced to meet them, and Katherine spread her fingers for their caresses, so that they would recognize her in future. Arthur proudly recited their names, fondling the great beasts as they pushed against him, flattening their ears and wagging their heavy tails in an ecstasy of reunion.

The hounds proved a respite, during which Arthur whispered, 'They only want to vow their allegiance, these wild Welsh, my love. Many of them can speak less English than you!'

So she stood straight, with his hand warm in hers, and walked beside him into the great hall. She got a confused glimpse of richly embroidered hangings and magnificent tapestries, of walls painted in gold, purple, scarlet, silver, and of slender arches in the warm grey stone. Then her husband's friends were pressing forward, eager to meet the Princess of Wales.

Katherine put on her best smile as determinedly as

though it had been a jewel. She held out her hand, and her eyes met those of the man who had bowed before her. 'You are at home now, Princess,' he said in her own tongue, and Katherine smiled and agreed.

She moved on to the next person, a woman this time, tall and elegantly pale. She was addressed in lisping English and bent her concentration towards giving an intelligible answer.

They were home indeed. And their duties had already begun.

8   Ludlow

High in the ice-blue sky above the town, a hawk wheeled and turned in the clean, cold air. Below, the river Teme was a slender snake of silver, rushing between steep snow-covered banks, and Ludlow Castle seemed no bigger than a snuffbox, though it stood proud and dark on the crest of the hill, dominating the crouched cottages, the snow-thatched houses, and the narrow streets of the march town.

The hawk was hungry, for the winter had been cruelly hard, so that he had gradually been driven by lack of prey from the craggy grandeur of the high mountains down to the gentle hills of the border country.

Swinging on the wind current, his sharp eyes saw the dog which slunk through the streets, searching for scraps in the kennels, and the tiny movement of a rat, bolder than its fellows, who ventured into the castle's cobbled court-yard. He watched the creature closely, his speed and hunger urging him to pounce, his fear of the high, enclosing walls of the castle making him hesitate.

Suddenly, the rat stopped short in its jerky, erratic run. From above, the hawk could not at first see the reason for the animal's sudden stillness; then he realized that it was eating. The thought of food decided him. He hovered a moment longer, concentrating completely on the arrowing of his deadly, downward flight. Then he fell out of the sky into his stoop, the wind which tore at his feathers unregarded, as he hurtled earthwards onto his unsuspecting prey.

From her window, Katherine had seen the hawk's leisurely flight, had seen it hanging in the air above, and had watched with amazement as its stoop brought it down into the courtyard below, to seize the rat in curved, predatory claws.

She saw the clean, golden-feathered body brace itself for the unexpected weight – it was a big, fat kitchen rat, she thought approvingly – and then the hawk was airborne again, beating its narrow wings rhythmically as it rose gradually above the towering walls. When it was level with her window, she looked almost straight into its cruel topaz eyes, and she could not help thinking, 'You are freer by far than I!' as the bird caught the wind and sideslipped over the height of the wall, to make its way in a great curving flight off to the distant hills.

It was very early in the morning; so early, in fact, that her women still lay in their beds and as yet, only the stable lads were stirring, and that half-heartedly. The snow still lay upon the ground and the bite of it was in the air, so that Katherine shivered, and pulled her bedgown close about her. Behind the bedcurtains, Arthur slumbered. She had not wanted to wake him when she slipped from between the sheets, but he was still fast; his lids had not even flickered as she tucked the blankets warmly round him again.

Standing in the window embrasure, watching the early light gradually soften into the blue of morning, she remembered the night before, and began to worry again. Arthur had come to her only four or five times since they had arrived at the castle, and each time he had grown more venturesome, easier with her. Remembering Juan, she hesitated to hurry his slow and careful essays into intimacy, yet she found it more and more difficult to restrain her own ardent feelings. So when she awoke first, rather than lie quiet in the bed to respond restrainedly to Arthur's kisses, she had risen, planning to be dressing with her women by the time he awoke. With a cautious glance at the bed, therefore, she padded to the door to call Maria, who would wait upon her that morning.

'You are up early, my little wife!'

The sound of his voice made her jump guiltily, and she put her hand to her throat, glancing back at the bed. He had pulled the bedcurtains back and watched her, smiling, his face clear and innocent of any deception, either of her own making or his.

She laughed too, glad to realize that her reason for leaving their bed had not dawned upon him.

'I was watching a hawk. It caught a rat in the courtyard,' she said, her voice still heavily accented, though her English had improved immensely.

'A hawk? In the courtyard? Who is flying a hawk before sunrise?' Arthur said lazily. He yawned hugely, and stretched, long, pale arms flying above his head, long, pale hair falling into his sleepy, mirth-creased eyes.

'No one. It was a wild bird.' Katherine explained. 'I watched it circling, thus,' her hand described an arc in the air. 'The courtyard was . . . was . . .' She stopped, defeated, then began again, heaving an exaggerated sigh. 'No persons was in the courtyard.'

Arthur laughed and yawned again, then said with his voice cracking, 'The courtyard was empty, you mean. No wonder, at this hour of the day. Why are you up so early, Katherine?'

'It is going to be a fine day,' Katherine said. 'I shall go to the chapel, and perhaps later, might venture outside the walls. The snow is melting, is it not?'

Arthur wriggled out of the sheets and reached for his shirt. He shrugged himself into it and shouted 'Ouch!' as his feet skidded on the rushes and found his cloak-brooch, where he had idly tossed it the night before.

Katherine giggled, and Arthur said 'Hussy!' affectionately, then tiptoed past her, giving her shoulders a brief squeeze as he did so. He would return to his own room now, she knew, and his gentlemen would dress him. No one would speak of the night he had spent, any more than her women would show curiosity as to how their mistress had spent the hours of darkness. But as she roused Maria, tipping the slumbering maiden out of her blankets and onto the rushes with a ruthless hand, she wondered whether her women knew that the Prince of Wales had shared her bed, the previous night.

'Did you sleep well, Princess?' Maria said, without any irony in her voice, and Katherine's smiling affirmative brought no speculative glance.

And nor it should, she thought now, standing upon one leg whilst Maria laboriously rolled up her new scarlet stocking. For I have been a married woman for a long time; quite four months. Not one of my women should wonder if I am virgin still. Only I may worry over such a question.

'What are you dreaming of, Princess,' Elvira said archly.

99

She bustled about, annoyed at having slept whilst the Princess was awake, and surveyed Katherine's glowing silk gown critically. 'It seems that the weather is changing for the better at last – the sky is as blue as your gown! Will you walk in the gardens after chapel?'

'Yes, I would enjoy that,' Katherine said decidedly, eyeing her reflection in the polished metal mirror. The air will do me good, she thought, for penned up here my skin has a sallow look. Perhaps the fresh air will bring back the colour to my cheeks, and the liveliness to my eyes.

The service in the chapel of St Mary Magdalene, read by a monk from the monastery at Goalford Gate, was the first moment of the day when the court began to assemble. Katherine sat with her women and smiled across at her friend, Margaret Plantagenet, where she knelt at the feet of one of the many saints in the chapel. Margaret held her new baby in her arms, for she was the wife of a marcher lord, Richard Pole, and they had three children living. The youngest, a lint-haired boy only a few weeks old, was swaddled still, but Katherine loved to play with him, and to bounce him on her knee.

Watching Margaret's bent head, she could not but wonder at the older woman's placidity, her bloom of contentment. For Margaret was the daughter of the Duke of Clarence, brother of the late Edward IV, and her brother Warwick had been put to death solely to assure Ferdinand of Aragon that his youngest daughter could safely wed a Tudor, without any fear that a true Plantagenet heir might one day claim the throne.

To safeguard himself and his heirs from Margaret and her children, Henry VII had married her to Richard Pole, a humble squire, who was now one of Arthur's gentlemen.

Yet Katherine was sure that their marriage was a happy one. Margaret Pole was not pretty; the beauty of the Plantagenets had passed her by, and likewise the colourful and boisterous personality which her father and King Edward had had in full measure. She was tall, with light brown hair and eyes as cool and clear as water. Yet her husband adored her, and his affection was most warmly returned. She had borne him children who were both beautiful and healthy, and she was popular with Welsh and English alike. What more could any man ask?

I hope Arthur and I have a marriage like that, Katherine thought longingly. She watched as the babe in Margaret's arms stirred and whimpered, pressing his face against his mother's breast, and she thought with quick pleasure how she would love to feel her own son nuzzling for her milk, how she too would hug him to her, as Margaret was hugging her baby now.

The monk gave the blessing, and the women began to leave the chapel. Katherine walked beside Margaret, touching the baby's cheek with her finger, feeling the softness of his thistledown hair against her skin. But the child wanted to be fed and turned his head, impatient with Katherine's caresses.

'I will feed you in my chamber now, and break my own fast later,' Margaret cooed softly, her very tone a caress, and the baby gurgled and smiled, his eyes only for his mother as hers were only for her son.

'When you have boys, you will discover they are as greedy as grown men, and never want to wait for a meal,' Margaret said to Katherine, excusing her own conduct with a teasing smile for the child in her arms. 'I know I should make him wait, but his shouts would take away your appetite, Princess.'

Katherine laughed and disclaimed, then went away with

her women. The day passed uneventfully, as days did in the castle when winter chained them to its walls. Katherine and Francesca worked with Dr Booth, Arthur's tutor, for most of the morning. Arthur was learning Welsh, and the women English, so since Katherine enjoyed her husband's company she usually joined him when he studied.

When evening came the weather had turned back to winter again, with a great gale hurling itself at the castle and howling round battlements and rooftops, so that voices had to be raised and gowns held tight against the swirling draughts.

In the hall, the wild Welsh from the hills played and sang wilder songs to the music of the harp, and told stories in their native tongue, whilst a monk translated for Katherine's benefit, and Arthur's brow furrowed with the effort of translating the words for himself.

After a while Katherine saw that her women were restive, and told Arthur that she would retire to her apartments. 'We will dance, before we seek our beds,' she said hopefully, for he had not danced with her at the castle, seeming to prefer to remain with the men who spoke of battles, and sad tales of war, in song and verse.

'We will dance together, one day,' Arthur said politely, but she could see that his mind was elsewhere, so she turned and left the room with the best grace she could muster.

Once in her apartment, Katherine ordered the fire to be piled high, and then she walked over to the shutters, and peered through a crack in the blistered wood. She was joined presently by Margaret, who had settled her babe for the night and now looked carefree and rather handsome, in a severely cut gown of blue-grey wool, with creamy lace at throat and wrist.

'I can hear wolves howling,' Katherine said presently.

'I can see their eyes shining out there in the darkness, like great yellow lamps. They grow bold tonight, do they not?'

'Once upon a time, the border barons paid tribute to their liege lords with wolves' heads,' Margaret remarked dreamily, leaning nearer the shutters and narrowing her eyes to peer into the blackness. The monk who translated for Katherine sat beside them, his voice so low and monotonous that the two young women sometimes forgot that a third person shared their talk. 'This castle had known others like yourself, Princess. Young men and women who would one day rule England have lived here.'

'Yes, I know. Your uncle Edward was brought up here, was he not? And thus your father?'

Margaret nodded. 'They both lived here; my cousins also – Prince Edward and his little brother, Richard. It was here that Edward heard of his father's death and of his own hopes. But it is best not spoken of.'

'I suppose you are right,' Katherine said. 'I love the history of the castle, though. Marion of the heath, who drew her lover up onto Pendover tower with a ladder of leather, and then died by her own hand when she found he had betrayed her merely to gain access into the castle. Poor wench! Love deceives, sometimes. Brother Joseph has told me many stories. About the ancient king, Caradoc, who lived and fought in these parts, and was betrayed, and taken to Rome, and sent home by the Emperor Claudius for his bravery, and his magnificent speeches.'

'Yes, there are many tales such as that one,' Margaret agreed. 'Have you heard of the boiling well of Ludlow, where eyes are cured by an infusion of the miraculous mud? Or the burning well, at Wenlock quite near to the Priory of that name?'

'I have heard of them and would dearly like to see them,

when spring arrives,' Katherine sighed. 'But will it be possible, Margaret?'

'The weather has kept even the men from hunting,' Margaret said cheerfully. 'When spring comes we will ride out of the castle; you mark my words.'

'Yes, but shall I be allowed to travel as far as Wenlock Priory?' urged Katherine. 'No one seems to take any notice of my desire to leave the castle, even for a short while.'

'You are a bride, Princess, and will soon persuade your husband,' Margaret said. 'He is a great lord here on the borders, though he is young, and can order us all if he so wishes.'

'Then I shall try to persuade him to take us to see Wenlock's burning well, when spring is here,' Katherine said decidedly. She turned from the window and held her hands out to the fire, shivering. 'Will spring *ever* arrive, Margaret?'

9 Wenlock

'The weather has remained pleasant, my lord, and we are almost at the Priory. It is a very large house, is it not?'

Katherine smiled up into Arthur's eyes as they rode side by side along the narrow, twisting street which led to the Priory. The sun was warm on their heads, and a brisk breeze blew softly into their faces, carrying on its breath the scent of wintersweet. Above the houses which leaned towards each other across the cobbles, they could see the roofs and tiles of the Priory, and they had already seen the

104

rich pastures and well tilled fields of the Priory farmland as they rode along through the pleasant countryside.

'It certainly looks big and flourishing,' Arthur conceded. His face coloured with a boy's pleasure as the villagers of Much Wenlock crowded close to the horses, pushing gifts at the royal couple, blowing kisses, and exclaiming over the beauty of their Prince and Princess.

'They be all white and gold,' a stout farmer shouted. 'And her gown be like a spring crocus. Aye, you can see the blood of Gaunt runs in her veins!'

Katherine smiled at the words, remembering that scene in Devon so long ago, it seemed, when de Ayala had said they would love her, the English people, because she looked English. She was learning the truth of that remark now, for herself.

The party had an air of holiday about it, as they rode under the big arch and into the Priory courtyard. Only the younger members of the royal suite had cared to come on such a journey so early in the year, and now they looked around them, rejoicing in their freedom from their elders, for the Poles were the oldest members of the court present.

The Prior stood ready to receive them, the wind tugging at his hooded cloak which he had thrown back in honour of the spring sunshine. Servants hovered, waiting to take the horses to the stables, eager to see for themselves the royal party.

The Prior began his speech of welcome, the Latin words rolling out sonorously, whilst around his head doves from the nearby dovecote fluttered, like scraps of torn manuscript paper against the blue.

'The doves know him for a man of peace, despite that nose,' whispered Arthur, and Katherine smiled, understanding the gist of the remark, if not the actual words, for the

Prior's strong face was dominated by a nose of truly majestic proportions.

'You and your lady wife will lodge in my house,' the Prior said, leading the procession into his dwelling. 'The chambers are not spacious, but I trust you will find them comfortable. The Princess will sleep here,' he indicated a low-ceilinged room whose window faced the chapel of the Priory. 'And the Prince will have the next room. I have placed screens for a body attendant, but I fear most of your suite will have to stay in the guest house, across the yard. There is another small room for your attendant, my lady, if you wish her to retire there.'

Katherine mumured her thanks and gestured to Inez, whose turn it was to attend her that night. When the Prior had gone off with Arthur to show him his chamber, she instructed Inez to pour her water for washing and then to lay out a clean shift and gown.

'And you may take your pallet into the adjoining room, for I do not think I shall be wakeful, after the journey,' she ended. 'We will go to the chapel to give thanks for our safe arrival, as soon as I have washed.'

Inez swung the heavy door shut, and immediately the Prior's deep, pleasant voice was silenced. Only through the open window could they hear the subdued murmur and the soft footfalls of the monks and the royal party going about their business.

'If you call, I shall not hear,' Inez said doubtfully. She pulled the pallet out from behind the screen and hesitated. 'Are you sure ... '

'If I need you, I will open the door and call,' Katherine assured her. 'Come now, Inez, help me off with my gown.'

He came to her that night, as she had known he would. When the stars pricked the dark skies outside her window, and she could hear the faint scuffle of the monks as they made their way to the chapel to say night office, he slipped into her room and made his way over to her bed.

She moved over, and put her warm arms round him, drawing him close. His feet were like ice from the stone-flagged floors, and she squeaked, trying to curl her own warm toes out of his way. Then she relented, because he was so chilled.

At first, his shivering shook the narrow bed but soon her warmth permeated his thin shirt and his tremors slowed and stopped. He stroked her hair, pressing his lips against her neck.

'I wish I could come to you with as little fuss at Ludlow,' he muttered. 'God, but this bed is narrow! Hard, too. I should think the mattress is stuffed with straw.'

'Horsehair, probably,' Katherine murmured. 'Are you warm now, my darling?'

As he grew warm again, so her closeness excited him. He cursed when his groping hands became entangled in her silken shift, and he tugged roughly at the material, cursing again when its soft strength would neither tear nor reveal an easy path to the tender flesh which it hid.

Katherine moved herself carefully away from him, and at once her shift became manageable. He pushed it away with impatient hands, so that at last their bodies touched with delicious intimacy. He pushed her shoulders flat on the bed so that she lay upon her back and then he was upon her, heavy on breasts, on stomach, on thighs. She felt his excitement mount, he was panting and triumphant. In the chapel, the monks' plainsong lifted, surged, and spilled over into a paean of praise; then it gradually sank into a calming hum of voices once more.

In the narrow bed, Katherine and Arthur lay still in each other's arms. As their sweat cooled, Arthur said in a voice as full of contentment as a cream-filled cat, 'At last we are one flesh, my little wife.'

Yet still Katherine doubted.

'The well is strange, indeed, Francesca, but you will surely see it, for though our company is large, there is plenty of room around the well, I understand,' Margaret Pole said comfortingly to Katherine's youngest maid of honour. They rode together, for today Katherine and Arthur seemed to need no one but each other. The glances they exchanged from time to time had the heavy, secret sweetness of lovers, and Margaret thought with amusement of the hard little bed she had helped Katherine to climb into the previous evening.

It was an open secret at the castle that Arthur was not encouraged to seek his bride's bed. Although he was almost of an age with Katherine, it was easy to see that he had not matured as fast as she. His voice had only lately broken, and only the faintest trace of down on lip and chin indicated a forthcoming beard. Yet Margaret thought that Arthur already loved his Spanish wife, and was equally certain that she loved him. Glances, a touch of the hand, a quick smile, could speak volumes. There were those in the castle who would vow that the couple were more like brother and sister than man and wife. Margaret knew they were wrong; knew even without having heard Inez's hushed words to Francesca whilst they were emptying Katherine's bathwater, that very morning.

'I was awoken by the monks' singing,' Inez had said. 'I thought I heard her stir, so I slipped into the room to see if she needed me. And Fran, they were lying together in that little bed, and she was calling him dear one, and heart's darling. I came out without a word, I can tell you.'

Francesca laughed, but Margaret said firmly, 'They are married, Inez. You must forget that you ever entered that room, for it is a sin to interfere in another's life.'

'But our duenna says that they are too young . . . ' Inez began, but Margaret hushed her.

'This is nothing to do with Elvira,' she said. She was tempted to say that two people in one bed did not necessarily mean what the girls obviously thought it meant. Instead she said, 'Forget all about it, both of you. Pretend you never went into the room, Inez – and indeed, you never should have.'

Liking Margaret, and anxious to please, Inez at once agreed to say nothing, and Francesca vowed that the matter was already forgotten, and with that, Margaret had to be content.

'Here is the well!' someone called. The company came to a halt and pages and grooms ran to the horses' heads. Katherine and Arthur dismounted and went forward, hand in hand, like two children.

'It is a miracle, or the devil's work,' Arthur said in a low voice. 'See, Katherine, how the water flames?'

'It cannot be water,' Katherine said incredulously. 'It must be spirit.'

'Dear God, there is curious,' gasped Master Rhys Thomas. 'I will taste, madam.'

He bent and scooped some of the water into his hand, despite the flames, choosing a spot which barely flickered with the blue and gold tongues.

'It *is* water, and sweet at that!' he exclaimed.

The fire burned on and around the water, which lay in a shallow depression, more like a basin than a well. Sometimes the flames leapt high, at other times they burned low. It seemed that mere chance ruled them.

The monk in charge of the well said that it was fed by a seepage of water which came in through the sides of the hollow. This was why the flames appeared to run up and down the banks. But when the weather was bad, the water sometimes burst forth from the earth in a fountain of flame, most curious to see.

For the amusement of his royal guests, the monk then speared a piece of meat on the point of his knife, and held it near and in the flames until it was well roasted, and the dripping juices made the fire hiss and sizzle. Then he offered it to the Prince and Princess. They laughed and exclaimed, but shook their heads, so the maids of honour accepted it and shared it with some of the young esquires, who pronounced it excellently cooked.

'It was strange, to see fire and water thus,' Arthur said as they rode homewards the next day, towards Ludlow once more. 'Jesu, but I am hot! We have had some real spring weather at last, Katherine, and you must be enjoying it after such a hard winter, for you are used to sunshine!'

Katherine smiled and refrained from telling her husband about the Pyrenees in winter; but she grew a little anxious when he insisted on taking off his cloak and hanging it beside his stirrup.

'Is it wise, when you are not used to the heat? You may catch a chill and then I should blame myself for begging to see Wenlock and the burning well.'

'We are nearly at the castle,' Arthur began. Then he smiled. 'To please you,' he added, and threw his cloak around his shoulders once more.

But presently he removed it again, for the horses were

climbing the steep street through the town of Ludlow which led to the castle, and sweat stood on his forehead.

'I am very hot,' he said apologetically, 'and my limbs feel heavy enough without the burden of my cloak. My head feels as though a band of iron were tight around it. I shall be glad to get home.'

Katherine was lifted off her horse in the courtyard of the castle, warm with the feeling that she had in very truth come home. Servants ran out to greet them, Dona Elvira and several of the older members of her suite came to ask how they had enjoyed their outing, and Arthur's hounds were everywhere, wagging their great tails, a welcome shining from their liquid eyes.

'We will go straight to the chapel . . . ' Arthur said.

Then Katherine saw the colour drain from his face, and he swayed uncertainly. As his knees buckled she started forward, but Richard Pole was there already.

'He is tired, and over-hot,' he said tersely to the shocked assembly. 'Go into the chapel, Princess, and give thanks that he got safely home to Ludlow before fainting. I will take the Prince to his room, and I am sure he will soon regain his senses.'

Katherine watched as Pole carried her husband easily in his arms, into the castle, Arthur's white face lay against the dark plum velvet of the man's sleeve, looking terribly vulnerable.

'Richard will take good care of your husband, my dear,' Margaret said. She drew Katherine into the chapel. 'Come and say your prayers, and doubtless we shall see the Prince looking fit and well, at dinner time.'

Katherine knelt in the cool dimness of the little chapel, with the bright afternoon sunlight diffused into jewel colours as it streamed through the high windows, and tried to pray for Arthur. But the words jumbled meaninglessly in her mind and she found that she was saying, 'Please let him be all right; oh, please, let him be all right,' over and over in her head.

She longed for the service to end, so that she might go to him, and ask him how he fared. But when she went to his apartments, she was refused admittance.

'We do not know exactly what is wrong with him,' Richard Pole told her, his eyes compassionate. 'But we cannot risk your health as well, Princess. The sickness may be contagious. He is getting the best treatment, and will soon be well again. Until then, I must be your messenger.'

But the next day, they had to tell her he was worse.

10 End of an Episode

Katherine had been sitting in the small, enclosed herb garden for the best part of an hour, with her embroidery in her lap. The sun beat down over the high wall of the castle, striking brilliance from the scarlet and green dragon she was working, sliding golden fingers across her bowed shoulders. Now and then a butterfly spread its wings for the sun's warmth, flattening itself humbly upon a scented flower, for only in that warm and sheltered garden could a butterfly have come from its chrysalis and lived when the spring was no more than well advanced.

And for the best part of twenty minutes, Katherine had not set a stitch. Her needle was threaded, and hung above her work like a scarlet dragonfly; but it did not descend, to plunge briskly into its place in the picture. Instead, the needle drooped in the hand which held it, whilst Katherine's blue eyes stared unseeingly at a clump of mint near her feet.

Margaret Pole, watching her, felt the first stirrings of unease. What could she be thinking of, that she sat so still, and noticed neither the butterfly nor the fact that her friend no longer spoke or read? Did she have some dreadful premonition about Arthur's illness? She had been kept from his side for fear of infection, and had hovered constantly outside the door of his chamber, stopping his attendants as they went in and out, to ask for news of her husband.

But today, she had agreed to go into the herb garden, with just Margaret for company. Does she wish to be alone with her thoughts, Margaret wondered. But her thoughts could not be pleasant, with her husband ill and herself in a foreign land, with only a few of her own countrymen around her.

She leaned forward, and touched Katherine gently on the knee.

'Would you like to go indoors now, my dear?' she asked gently.

Katherine shook her head and blinked. 'The sun is so warm and pleasant,' she said, frowning. 'Yet I feel heavy and lazy, as though I had toiled all day in the fields.'

Before she had finished speaking, Margaret was at her side, in time to anticipate Katherine's sudden slump sideways in her chair. She held the younger girl upright against her shoulder, and called frantically for help, feeling against her own side the slow, uneven heartbeats which stirred Katherine's rose-pink bodice.

Francesca, Maria, and Inez came running, with the black-clad figure of Dona Elvira not far behind, despite the fact that she was still dressed for midwinter and must have been sadly hampered by her clothing in the spring warmth.

'The Princess has fainted,' Margaret said breathlessly.

'Help me to lift her to her chamber, where she can be taken care of properly. And bring . . . '

Dona Elvira swept up and without further ado, cut across Margaret's speech with a volley of orders delivered in rapid-fire Spanish. The three girls, rather to Margaret's chagrin, scuttled to obey in a way which they had certainly not done when she herself had commanded.

Griffith Ap Rhys now came running, and took Katherine easily up in his arms. He was wearing a plum coloured doublet and Margaret saw, with a stab of superstitious fear, that the Princess's white face lay against the dark material exactly as Arthur's had lain against her husband's plum velvet coat.

'It is the sweating sickness,' she breathed, partly to herself, partly to Evan the page. The lad stood close to her, his lower lip trembling as he watched his mistress being carried into the castle.

Dona Elvira, though she spoke virtually no English, heard Margaret's words and nodded, then fired a command at her.

'She says, Katherine must see the best physicians, and at once, if you please,' Francesca interpreted. She smiled at Margaret. 'Will you see to it, my lady? I must go with my mistress.' She hesitated, her eyes suddenly swimming with tears. 'How is the Prince, my lady? This disease can kill, can it not, for already Evan's little companion, Lambert Prys, is dead.'

'The Princess will get the best possible attention, as indeed the Prince does,' Margaret said gently. 'The disease weakens, that is the worst fear. But we will pray for them both. They are young . . .'

She left the sentence unfinished, for had not Lambert Prys been young?

Once within the castle, Margaret ran along the stone-flagged passages and up the stairs to Arthur's apartments. She scratched on the door and slipped into the room. It had been divided by screens which formed a sort of ante-chamber near the door so that the sick lad would not be troubled by the movements and soft sounds of his attendants; but those who worked in the ante-chamber went quietly about their business, for fear of disturbing the Prince.

Yet the quiet in the room seemed more than the ordinary controlled calm. Attendants stood unnaturally still, the lack of urgency patent in the pot which boiled its scented brew untouched upon the fire. Sweet steam drifted across the room from the diffusing herbs, and the fire hissed and spat as the bubbles burst onto flaming wood. But no one moved to take the pot from the fire.

As Margaret paused, uncertain, the screens were pushed aside for a moment, and Richard Pole slipped through them, pushing back the lank hair which hung over his brow. He was pale and his eyes were red-rimmed through lack of sleep, and now he looked weary and dispirited to the bone. Margaret could have cried for him.

He saw her, and a pale smile touched his lips. Then he crossed the room and took her hands in his, squeezing her fingers. Margaret put her hand to his face, feeling the bristled skin where he had not shaved, sensing the despair in him.

'You should rest, my love,' she said without much conviction. 'How is the Prince?'

'Arthur is dead, Margaret,' Pole said wearily. 'We did all we could to save him, and at the end he rallied for a moment. But he was too weak to survive. He died just now, in my arms.'

Then he turned his head into her shoulder, and wept.

Katherine's sickroom was quiet. Outside the cruel sun, which had remained hidden for weeks so that they had been forced to stay within the castle, shone brightly. The Spanish women moved about their accustomed tasks and Margaret Pole sat close by the bed, a cloth wrung out in vinegar and water to hand, to bathe the sufferer's brow.

'She is young, and remarkably healthy,' the physician had told Margaret a day earlier. 'If we can break the fever fairly quickly it is my belief that she will live. Arthur's fever lasted too long, so that when it broke he was too weak to rally.'

So now she felt Katherine's brow anxiously; it still burned hot beneath her fingers.

Francesca moved across the room and stood beside her. She turned an enquiring face to Margaret, indicating the flush on Katherine's cheeks.

Carefully, she said, 'Our duenna would not give permission to remove the covers and bathe my mistress?'

Margaret shook her head ruefully. 'No. She said that if such treatment had not saved Arthur, then why should it save the Princess? Sometimes I think she would rather see Katherine die than take advice from an English physician. But I should not say such things.'

Francesca said excitedly, 'But you *should*, my lady! Elvira loves the Princess very much, in her own way. I will speak for you.'

Before Margaret could protest, Francesca had crossed the room and was speaking rapidly to Dona Elvira, her low voice accompanied as usual by eloquent gestures.

Margaret sighed, and reapplied the cloth to the Princess's face, smoothing away the sweat so that Katherine stilled her restless head movements for a moment. These Spaniards, she thought. They always spoke so vehemently that even a casual conversation sounded like a furious argument. Probably Francesca was merely giving Dona Elvira a watered-down account of her own words. Katherine moaned, and turned her head again, and Margaret stood up and reached for the cup of honey and water which stood close. If she could but moisten Katherine's lips . . .

Abruptly, she realized that Elvira was beside her. She looked angry, and hissed something at Margaret from between clenched teeth, her eyes snapping with annoyance. Francesca, her face wearing the first smile that Margaret had seen for days, seized the heavy bedclothes and began to pull them from the bed.

'She has agreed to try the bathing, but says if Katherine dies, ours will be the blame,' Francesca said. The three women pulled back the blankets, and Elvira shouted for attendants to bring cool water. Then they lifted Katherine from the bed and laid her upon a blanket, spread over the rushes on the floor.

The three women began bathing the Princess, whilst her other attendants stood around helplessly, watching the steam which arose from Katherine's hot and fevered body.

It was hard work, but for two hours no one even thought of resting, Margaret, sponging, bringing buckets of water, holding the cooling draught to Katherine's unresponsive lips, had long ceased to think of anything but the task on hand. Her back ached, her head throbbed, but still she toiled on, laying cool wet cloths on Katherine's body and taking them off, steaming.

'I think she is cooler,' Francesca whispered to Margaret, as they staggered back from the fire with yet another bucket of tepid water. 'I am sure she is cooler.'

'Pray God you're right,' Margaret said, reaching wearily for the honey draught. 'Come, my dear one, my sweeting, drink some of this.'

How many times she had held the cup to the Princess's

lips that afternoon, encouraging her with sweet words to drink! And how many times the honeyed water had trickled down Katherine's chin, unheeded. Yet now, the pale lips moved!

Margaret felt a pang of joy so keen that it was more like pain stabbing her breast. She pushed Elvira aside carelessly, and with her arm beneath Katherine's shoulders, raised her. She tipped the cup ruthlessly when she saw the girl's mouth move again, and the liquid splashed out, a great deal of it to run uselessly down Katherine's cheek and onto the already soaking floor rushes. But some went down her throat. Margaret distinctly heard the choked swallow.

'She took some of the drink!' she said in an awed whisper. 'Oh, Francesca, she took some of the drink!'

Almost as though she had heard the words, Katherine's head rolled weakly in the crook of Margaret's arms, and she said in a small, husky voice, 'Oh, how I want to drink! But how is Arthur? Am I ill, too?'

Within days, she was sitting up in her bed and drinking broth. The colour began to return faintly to her cheeks and her movements, though slow, showed signs of returning health. But no one dared tell her that her husband was dead. Even Elvira would not speak of it; Katherine was allowed to believe that Arthur was recovering slowly, like herself.

They knew they would have to tell her soon when the Earl of Surrey arrived, as chief mourner for the King, and with him the lords of Shrewsbury, Kent and Dorset. It was Katherine's first day out of bed, and she made her way unsteadily to the window-seat and sat watching the to-ing and fro-ing in the courtyard below.

'A great many people are coming to the castle,' she remarked presently. 'We seem to have more courtiers than ever. Surely Arthur is not well enough to see all these people?'

No one answered. Dona Elvira began to tell her beads, her head bent studiously to avoid the anxious glances of the other women.

'How dismal they look, in their black clothes,' Katherine said slowly. 'Now why should they come to see Arthur dressed in black?'

Once again, nobody spoke, and then they saw there would be no need of words. For tears formed in Katherine's eyes and spilled over, pouring unheeded down her cheeks, and Margaret ran across the room and caught the weeping girl in her arms, murmuring endearments.

Together, the Spanish Infanta and the Plantagenet daughter wept for the Tudor heir.

Time passed, and the weather turned again to the dismal, wintry clime they had known in the early days at Ludlow. Arthur's body lay in the church of St Lawrence, and on a foul day when the heavens opened and the streets were awash with rain, it was carried in procession to Worcester Cathedral, and buried in the choir there.

Katherine donned widow's weeds, and covered her neck and rounded chin with a barbe of finely pleated linen. The funeral was over, and the Spaniards grew restive, but still the King did not send for them.

'She wears widow's weeds who never was a wife, they say,' Francesca remarked to Margaret, her voice tinged with bitterness. 'At first, the King said we stayed here in case the Princess was with child. Now word had been sent to Spain – and to London also – that Katherine is as virgin as the day she left her mother's womb; yet still we linger.

And still she mourns Arthur. Who could doubt her love for him, even if they never were man and wife, when they see her shadowed eyes and sad mouth? She was so merry, when first we came here.'

'She will be merry again. And perhaps it is for the best that the marriage was never consummated, so that she can go to her new husband a virgin,' Margaret said, then regretted the words. Katherine had never said herself that she was a virgin. She had said nothing, hugging her grief to herself, shutting herself away even from her women, a distant and fragile figure who wanted none of them.

'How Ludlow has changed her,' Margaret remarked presently. 'She knows now that the world is a hard place, even for a princess. Being of royal blood cannot save one from sadness and death. She does not trust even us, her friends, as she used. Have you noticed, Francesca?'

'Yes, and at first I was hurt, because it seemed that she turned from me more than the others,' Francesca admitted. 'It is because I speak English, I think. Life here is so difficult now that we are neither guests nor hosts, yet if she sees me speak to a young esquire or a nobleman's son, she shows her displeasure immediately. She turns to Maria more and more – and to Dona Elvira.'

'Yes, I have noticed that she is meek with Elvira now,' Margaret said. 'She lets the old woman dictate to her, and never struggles to assert herself as she did when Arthur lived. But I am sure that when you return to London it will be different.'

'If she turns to Elvira, and does not ask for your advice or opinion, it is because she feels that the English King and Queen have pushed her aside,' Francesca said. 'We are a proud people, my lady, and sometimes our pride can be a barrier to friends and enemies alike. Now she feels she can best trust Elvira, who stands *in loco parentis* for Isabella, because they are both Spaniards, and because she no longer knows where she stands with the English people. When the Princess knows her future, whether it will be marriage to the little Duke of York or a return voyage to Spain, then she will be able to show us affection once more.'

11 London

The sunshine which streamed through the curtains of her litter warmed Katherine's winter-pale skin and the gentlest of breezes stirred her mourning veils, yet not even the lovely weather could dispel the gloom which hung over the small party.

Travelling by slow stages, staying at houses and abbeys where the welcome was warm and sincere, still the journey away from Ludlow seemed the end of all those bright hopes which Katherine had known only a few months earlier, when she had travelled with Arthur towards the Welsh mountains.

'Where shall we stay in London, Princess?' The girl who spoke, Maria de Rojas, did not have the same reservations about their journey as Katherine did. She was young, and she had hated the great, grim fortress perched high on its rock above the swirling Teme. Of Arthur she had known little, and the worries which plagued the Princess now that her status was in doubt seemed insignificant to Maria, with the sunshine beating down on her shoulders and the distant spires of the city clearly seen through the morning air.

Katherine parted the curtains of her litter and peered

ahead. Something of the fascination which the city held for the Spanish women sitting on their mules close to her, penetrated her mind, which had been numbed by sorrow and illness. Life, she reflected, had to go on. Arthur was dead, and her position as wife of the heir to the throne might be in the dust, but surely there would be a place for her somewhere in this great bustling world of royalty? She could not just be ignored because her marriage had ended in tragedy. Her elder sister Isabel had gone home to Spain when her husband, the King of Portugal, had died, but later she had remarried.

Despite herself, Katherine felt a little flutter of excitement beneath her ribs. To go home? Once, she had resigned herself never to seeing Spain or her parents again, but now it might be possible that she would tread once more the marble floors of the Alhambra, see the figs bursting ripe and purple against the white walls and the oranges glowing in their dark leaves, whilst the brilliant blue of the sky smiled down on everything. And even in London, life could not be as quiet as it had been in Ludlow.

Almost without realizing it, Katherine lifted her nose and sniffed the breeze. Delicately, the scents of warm grass, dust and mayblossom stirred her senses. There was a world out there, waiting for her! She could mourn Arthur sincerely enough, but she need no longer pretend that for her also, the world had finished. She turned to Maria, narrowing her eyes against the sunlight.

'We shall go to the court, Maria,' she said. 'And to Queen Elizabeth, who has promised to be a mother to me. And then, who knows? We are young.'

The other girl heard the hope and life springing in Katherine's voice, and smiled. So as they neared London, the Princess was coming out of her abstraction. A good thing, thought Maria severely. After all, her mistress had only known Arthur for five short months and since his death, Maria had lain sleepless for many nights, in the bed she had shared with Katherine knowing that her mistress sobbed dryly into her pillow, or lay wide-eyed, unable to find forgetfulness in sleep. She has mourned long enough, Maria thought now.

'A rider is approaching,' called Francesca. She, like her friends, was filled with pleasant anticipation as they approached the walls of London. How bored she had been at Ludlow, despite the interest and attention of the young esquires and the visitors to the castle. Now she would dance once more, she thought gleefully, and the men would pay court to her. It had not been too bad at Ludlow whilst the Prince lived, but with his death, the Spaniards had seemed little more than an embarrassment to their hosts. Francesca, proud of her worth, could not wait to get back to where she would be fully appreciated once more.

The rider approached, and drew rein beside Katherine's litter. He was a young man, dark-haired and shabbily dressed, but his manners, as he drew off his hat and bowed with a flourish, seemed excellent to the exiled Spaniards.

'Princess?' he said anxiously. 'Our good Queen, Elizabeth of York, has asked that you go to the Palace of Lambeth, where she will shortly visit you. I am Enrique, servant to Doctor de Puebla, and my master bids me welcome you.'

His horse moved ahead of the litter once more, and Katherine said acidly, 'I like the man better than I like the master. Who is Dr Puebla, to send messages on behalf of the Queen of England? I suppose de Ayala has gone back to Scotland, or back to Spain, perhaps.'

Maria, giving a noncommittal answer, thought, she is losing her remoteness, which is as well. But shall we now be plunged back into the violence of arguments between ambassadors, quarrels over the dowry, squabbles over precedent? She patted her mule and glanced at Katherine's profile. She liked what she saw. A mouth which drooped poignantly no longer, but which held its firm line, and eyes which glanced around with interest, instead of fixing dully on the canopy before her.

It will be all right once we get our orders, thought Maria.

'Time was, when the twelve days of Christmas seemed to pass in a flash, so full of enjoyment were they,' Maria sighed, pressing her nose to the windowpane. Inside Durham House, it was almost as cold as it was outside, and she breathed on the pane and drew a stiff little picture of icicles in the steam. 'Why have you come to visit us, Lady Margaret? Sometimes I wonder what we have done, to be cast into gloom here by ourselves, whilst the court makes merry, watches plays and pageants, and spares us not a thought.'

Margaret Plantagenet moved closer to Maria, so that the two women stood in the window embrasure, watching the dizzying fall of the white flakes outside.

Time has passed slowly, Margaret thought, for these Spaniards, since Richard and I lived side by side with them at Ludlow. They have watched the seasons merge from early summer to deepest winter, yet their lot has not changed for the better. England has been hard and unfriendly to them.

'Why, you have done nothing,' Margaret said softly. 'It is only that the King has many anxieties, and he is still displeased with King Ferdinand and Queen Isabella for not paying anything towards their daughter's expenses. It has been agreed, has it not, that the Princess is not our poor Arthur's widow? Therefore, she is not entitled to a third of the revenues of his estate, as she would have been.

And she is to be betrothed to Prince Henry, so the King feels merely that he has received one half of her dowry, and still awaits the final payment. I am sure that soon the Princess and her suite will return to court.'

Maria did not reply. She rubbed her hand slowly up and down the sleeves of her gown, trying to bring back warmth to her cold flesh. 'It is cold, this country,' she said suddenly. Her breath puffed out mist as she spoke, but she made no move to go nearer the fire, where a handful of women already huddled.

'It is, indeed,' Margaret said briskly. 'And that fire may be great enough for Spain, but it is not heaped high enough for England in December, my dear! You need a good fire and good food when *our* frosts bite, as Ludlow should have taught you.'

Maria shivered again. 'God, when I think how we grumbled at the cold there,' she said almost dreamily. 'Yet here, the cold reaches my very bones so that I am forever chilled, whether waking or sleeping.'

'Then why not ring for a servant to pile more fuel on those embers?'

Maria dropped her voice yet lower, though the women round the fire did not so much as glance towards the embrasure where she and Margaret stood. 'My lady, there *is* no more fuel. No more money with which to buy us logs, either,' she added miserably. 'The Princess does not complain, for she is sure that soon her parents will send money or the King will once more provide. But we . . . we are not so sure. The ways of the King are strange and though we see him but rarely, when the King does honour us, he looks at us coldly. With dislike, almost. And our food, too, has not been good or adequate enough to help us to resist the cold. The Princess has been ill again, she has had sores round her mouth, and I am sure these only come because of the cold and poor food. Could you not speak to Queen Elizabeth for us, lady?'

Margaret looked around the room with new eyes. The thin rushes on the floor, speckled with decay, the small fire smouldering on the hearth, the bare, uncurtained walls. She remembered Arthur's devotion to his little wife, the way he had striven always to stand between her and his father: surely Henry would not deliberately subject the child to such treatment? It must be ignorance on the King's part, and mismanagement on the part of the Princess and her servants.

'Maria, I am shocked to see you so ill provided for,' she said at last. 'But surely it is because the servants are misusing the money? Who takes the grant provided by King Henry and sees to its spending? Is it Katherine's treasurer? Surely we can arrange for someone who understands English money to deal with the Princess's revenues?'

'My lady, there *are* no revenues; Juan de Cuero, as treasurer, would be grateful for the administration of any sum, however paltry. You said yourself that the King did not feel obliged to pay any revenues since Katherine and Arthur never consummated their marriage. He makes the Princess no allowance, either. We have done our best with what little money we have ourselves, eked out by presents from the Queen and visiting Spanish gentlemen, but such money as we have has come to an end. Good management or bad, it makes no difference when there is no money to manage.'

Margaret was appalled. Katherine was a stranger in this land, but still she was a princess. And she was living in penury, depending on the charity of such fellow countrymen as heard of her plight, cut off from the very people who should have been her friends and comforters.

'I will speak to the Queen,' she said, after a moment. 'But

Maria, may I see the Princess? Is she well enough to speak to me for a little?'

'Yes, indeed. Try to cheer her, my lady! Tell her that you will see the Queen for her, and intercede on our behalf. No letters reach us, no news. The Princess would go mad with worry if it were not for Hernan Duque, who visits us and tells us what little he knows.'

'Duque? I should have thought de Puebla would have been more helpful. He is more than the resident Spanish ambassador at court, he is a good friend of King Henry's into the bargain.'

Maria shook her head. 'No, indeed. Margaret, you have been too long absent from our company. The Princess cannot bear the little doctor simply *because* he is a friend of the King's. She says he looks after Henry's interests instead of hers, and she regards him with scarcely veiled contempt. Truth to tell, she calls Duque a fool behind his back, but at least he is of good family, and tries to comfort her with tales of how she will doubtless sail for home when spring comes again.'

'She hates de Puebla? Calls Duque a fool? Surely she is no longer the sweet Princess we knew at Ludlow,' Margaret said sadly. 'May I see her now, Maria?'

The two young women walked together across the square of the hall, up the long, elegant staircase, and across the landing to where a bedroom door stood slightly ajar. Maria scratched on the panel and hearing a word in answer, motioned to Margaret to wait whilst she poked her head around the door and spoke in Spanish. Then she turned a smiling face to the other.

'She is overjoyed; go in now,' she said softly, and pushed Margaret into the room.

Katherine lay on a big fourposter bed, with the curtains drawn round it on three sides, so that she was sheltered from the draughts. Covers were piled on her, and she had soft pillows beneath her head, but the room, lit by candles, was cold and though the fire burned as brightly, Margaret guessed, as their fuel shortage would allow, the general atmosphere was depressing.

Three maids of honour sat by the bed, their chairs carefully sited so that they did not keep the warmth of the fire from their mistress. Margaret recognized Francesca and Inez – recognized even the musty black mourning gowns they wore – but the third maid was strange to her.

Before Margaret could greet Katherine however, a woman stepped out from the shadows, a bowl of gruel in her hands. It was Dona Elvira, Margaret realized. Elvira, who wore black from choice, looked no different from the way she had looked in Ludlow except now, if anything, she seemed more content. Certainly she was more in command, thought Margaret.

'Lady Margaret, how good to see you,' Elvira said graciously. Then her English obviously gave out, for she lapsed into Spanish, glancing sharply at Katherine.

'My friend, you are welcome,' Katherine said, her voice smaller than Margaret remembered it, and hoarse. 'Dona Elvira bids you welcome also, though she has not enough English to say it for herself. Come and sit by me, my friend, and tell me how you have fared since last we met.'

Margaret sat down on a corner of the bed, trying not to let her glance dwell too significantly on the half empty bowl of thin, grey gruel which Dona Elvira had placed on the table beside Katherine's book.

'I am well, Princess. My husband and children thrive, also. But you, my dear? How have you fared since your . . . since Arthur died? I believe,' she lowered her voice, 'I believe you are in a sorry state.'

'Only myself and my maids of honour speak English,

here,' Katherine said. 'My story, alas, is short. Nothing has happened! I am not Princess of Wales, nor am I yet betrothed to another. I have no revenues from my dowry; why, I know not. Neither do I have revenues from Wales, for I am *not* the widow of the late Prince of Wales. I am nothing.' She laughed shortly, without amusement.

Margaret, beginning to talk of how she was sure things would soon change for the better, and how she would personally speak to the Queen, took covert stock of Katherine. Gone was the open, childishly rosy countenance, the eyes that met one's gaze so confidingly and with such trust. Already, her changed fortunes had sharpened her features, and the ailment which thickened her throat and made her cough had wrought other changes besides the sores round her mouth.

She is growing up, becoming a woman, thought Margaret, and knew a dismay disproportionately large that the change should have come to Katherine unkindly, from hardship and unhappiness rather than in the course of nature. She wondered how much the Queen knew of her Spanish daughter, and was relieved to reflect that Elizabeth probably knew nothing. The Queen was pregnant, swelling with another child to secure the Tudors' hold on the succession. She had lost two sons now, little Edmund and poor Arthur. The children still living were strong enough, but Margaret was promised to King James of Scotland, and Henry was only one life on which to plant the hopes for the Tudor future. Mary was a sweet child to be sure; but a queen? No, England needed a king, and a strong king at that. Elizabeth must hope that her womb sheltered a sturdy boy child who could help young Hal to rule the kingdom that would be his, one day, if he lived.

'The Queen is with child, and must soon be delivered,' Katherine's voice cut across Margaret's thoughts with uncanny perspicacity. 'How can she think of me when even to mention my name will bring a frown to her husband's face?'

Margaret shifted uncomfortably. So Katherine, too, believed that Henry disliked her?

'I'll speak to the King, then,' she said with sudden decision. 'I cannot bear that you should have to live like this, in uncertainty and poverty. Believe me, my dear, your worries will soon be over.'

She stayed a while longer, telling Katherine of the court, and of the Welsh marches where she had been with her husband. Then she left, scarcely noticing the whirling snow until it was settling on her broad-brimmed hat, so determined was she to better Katherine's lot.

Left alone once more, Katherine motioned Francesca to continue reading aloud from the book of sermons with which she had been struggling when Margaret had entered the chamber. Yet even though the object of the exercise was to practise their English and to pick up each other's mistakes, she scarcely heard Francesca's stumbling, tortured voice. Margaret had looked so well and happy, she mused. How long it seemed since Katherine had felt either one or the other! And it was a delight to see a woman wearing colours again, for Margaret had long since shed her mourning black and she had worn her favourite russet wool, with the pretty colour close to her face accentuating the fairness of her complexion and the grey of her eyes. Katherine had smelt the freshness of snow and wind on her friend's skin, and seen the sparkle of health which lit her friend's eyes. Now, for the first time, she wondered whether she herself was wise to spend all her time in Durham House, never venturing into the city which lay so close to her walls. Few people would know her, she mused, for not only had few enough seen her even during the many processions she had taken part in during the wedding festivities, but fewer would recognize her today.

The thought of getting out once more, mixing with people other than the members of her suite, excited yet confused her. When I am better, she resolved, I shall go out myself, with Maria and Inez and perhaps even little Francesca, for she is so gay and lighthearted that she would make the adventure seem gay and lighthearted also.

Heartened by her decision, she turned her attention back to Francesca's spoken English, and pounced upon a fault in pronunciation. For if we are to go amongst the English people, then truly we must speak their language, she thought decidedly.

The court was at Richmond. Margaret had not gone straight from Durham House to the Queen, for the day had been too foul for travelling; instead she had gone to her own home, where she had nursed her babies and spoken more crossly than was her wont when she found their nurse down in the kitchen with the other servants, having left the children asleep upstairs, in their beds.

She moved across the room in the soft glow from the dying fire, straightening covers, moving a kitten from its nest in the rushes near the baby's cradle, firmly taking little Arthur's thumb out of his mouth, as she did every night. And as the child always did, she reflected ruefully, he would pop it back, sighing with noisy contentment as it soothed his mouth with its familiar presence.

Her sons were safely bestowed now, nurse noisily slapping up the stairs again with her mouth pursed into a button of annoyance at being scolded in front of the kitchenmaids.

Margaret slipped outside the door, saying in a whisper, 'You'd best get to bed yourself, Goodie; the little one may yet wake, for his teeth are coming, and he moved when I bent over the cradle. Rub his gums with the unguent if he needs soothing.'

'Yes'm. Will ye return tonight?'

'No, I think not. I shall stay at Richmond. But I shall be in tomorrow, to see my sons.'

Upon her arrival at the palace, Margaret went, not to the the great hall but upstairs, to the Queen's withdrawing chamber. Sure enough, Elizabeth of York sat before her mirror, whilst her maids buzzed around, the wind of their going making the candle flames bow and dip lazily. Margaret waited until Elizabeth got slowly and heavily to her feet, then sank into a deep curtsey.

'Margaret!'

The voice held genuine pleasure, and Margaret's eyes softened as she and the Queen smiled at one another. They were both pregnant, though Margaret's secret was not yet for all the world to see, for many months would pass before her hour came near, yet the sisterhood of childbearing was upon them, and they shared a common delight in the babe within them both.

'Your Grace.' Margaret said no more than that, yet Elizabeth's eyes flickered and she said, 'Lady Margaret will keep me company for a little. You may withdraw.'

Lifting trains to ease their steps, eyes incurious over their Queen but eager for the delights of dining in the hall still bright with Christmas cheer, the women jostled eagerly in the doorway, then were gone, and the Queen and her friend faced each other in the candles' glow.

'Your Grace, I have seen your daughter Katherine,' Margaret said without preamble. 'She is unhappy and alone, with very little money. Would it not be possible for her to come to court? I have promised I would intercede for her with the King, but judged it wisest to speak to you first.'

Elizabeth's gaze fell on her fine hands, and she twisted a great ruby ring round and round her finger, seemingly absorbed in making it catch the light of the nearest candle, so that it glowed like a fire.

'Ah, yes. Poor little Katherine. She has not been to court for many months, but I believe her to be unwell. It is this wretched climate. I am sure she will be welcomed to court again, when the weather is fine, and she has put off her mourning.'

Margaret looked meaningly at the finely pleated lawn collar, worn over a gown of deepest blue satin which matched the Queen's great eyes. The Queen looked down at her softly swelling bosom and said, in a voice which trembled a little, 'I know, Margaret; I know. Why should she mourn for a husband longer than I mourn for my son, when you can say with truth that he never was her husband, but will ever be my son? I cannot answer, my friend. Henry is a good man, but cold. He has taken the child in some dislike because her parents were – difficult – over the marriage, and now he says he, too, can be difficult. I would help her if I could, but until the child is born, I do not feel I can face the King's anger, which I should assuredly feel if I attempted to interfere.'

'But the Spaniards are hungry, your Grace. Cold, too. I found Katherine in bed, muffled in coverings and with only a bowl of the most unappetizing looking gruel to eat. The fire was small, and in the parlour when I spoke apart with her maid of honour, scarce a flame could be seen. They lack a few logs for a decent fire, madam.'

The Queen looked at Margaret uncertainly. 'Is it so? My husband cannot know of this. But do not fear, Margaret,

133

I will see that they have food, and wood for their fires.'
She glanced thoughtfully round the room. 'Hangings shall
be sent, and what little money I can spare, so that she can
buy fresh rushes and other necessaries. Does she have an
efficient housekeeper?'

'Most of her servants are Spanish,' Margaret told the
Queen. 'If she could employ an English staff, probably her
troubles would diminish.'

The Queen walked slowly towards the door, saying over
her shoulder, 'I will see that she has some money. As to the
rest, why, she should come to court to be near us. Be easy,
Margaret, and bid Katherine not to despair. I promise you
that whilst I live, my daughter shall not want. She shall be
sent for, as soon as her health permits, and as soon as my
child is born she may join my other daughters. She will be
company for Margaret, who misses her elder brother
sadly.'

The two women walked towards the sounds of gaiety and
music which came from the great hall where at this hour the
court sported, where very soon now the Queen would
watch the players perform their story of Christmas, with a
young lad playing the Virgin and a bundle of shawls, the
Baby.

She will keep her word, thought Margaret, well content.
While she lives, Katherine has the most important friend in
the kingdom.

'The Queen has given birth to a girl, Elvira, a baby girl!
Of course, she and the King had hoped for a boy, but the
child is alive and well, and so is Elizabeth of York, praise
be to God. They say she will be named Katherine, for the
Queen's sister, and for me, also. Perhaps I shall be a God-
mother!'

Katherine was up now, and in better health. Her black dress still did not – could not – become her, but she wore a hood fashioned from soft, lavender-coloured velvet, a gift from the Queen, and around her neck amethysts clustered, reflecting the lavender. With the sudden pleasure and enthusiasm brought about by the Queen's kindness, she had busied herself upon the yoke of her gown also, so that now the sombre black was enlivened a little by beautifully embroidered violets of white and purple.

Dona Elvira munched with her lips, eyeing the girl sharply.

'Named for you? Well, perhaps. But your position is still uncertain. Will you go to court again, before the Queen is up and about?'

'I should like to see the babe,' Katherine admitted. 'The Queen also, when it is permitted that I should visit her. Do you think I might go soon, Elvira?'

The older woman frowned, tapping her fingers on her girdle. Portentously, she moved her lips as though deeply worried by the rights and wrongs of the question. Then, slowly, she shook her head.

'Don't make any move, Princess, until the Queen asks for you,' she said triumphantly at last. 'Then if the King is minded to refuse you permission to visit his wife, he will be unable to do so, but if he wishes you to see the Queen, then the suggestion will come from him. Yes, I am sure that is the right thing to do.'

'But Dona Elvira – '

The interruption came from the small cluster of maids of honour, who sat sewing near the fire – and how much brighter a fire than that in the hearth a few weeks earlier – listening to the conversation.

'What do you wish to say, Francesca?' Elvira said sharply.

'Should the King be too busy to think of our Princess, might he not be resentful, later, that no effort was made by the Spanish suite to see the Queen?'

'I can see no reason why,' Elvira stated coldly. 'You must remember, Francesca, that our Princess is the child of the reigning monarchs of Spain and as such, must be always in the forefront of the King of England's thoughts. He will send for her when it is seemly, I have no doubt.'

Francesca subsided onto her seat with a little sigh. How certain Dona Elvira always was! Yet she contradicted herself without a blink when she told Katherine in one breath that her position was still uncertain, and in the next vowed that her charge was always in the King of England's thoughts. And though Dona Elvira might have complete faith in the importance of the Spanish monarchy, King Henry had shown plainly enough that the fate of Katherine was something which worried him not at all.

Francesca glanced at Maria and catching her eye, pulled a wry mouth and lifted her eyes ceilingwards. Maria smiled primly, but had made no answering moue. She was, after all, seated facing Dona Elvira and anyway, she was much more in awe of the duenna than Francesca was. Maria had been brought up as Queen Isabella's ward, and was as close to Katherine as a shared childhood could make her. Furthermore, as Dona Elvira was not slow to remind her, the Queen had placed the duenna *in loco parentis* over them all. Even the King, who had visited them twice since Christmas, showed himself far from eager to cross swords with Elvira.

Maria sighed, and returned to her sewing. She had grown three inches since last spring, and all her gowns needed false hems, inlets of material across the breasts, and tucks in the waist to be taken out. She had not yet seen much of the court but Katherine had promised them that when the finer weather came, they would all join the Queen at Richmond. To that end, she stitched feverishly.

Katherine took a last look out of the window, towards where the river curled between its winter-hardened banks. That same river flowed past the Tower, where the Queen and her babe lay, warm enough, surely, behind those mighty walls. Katherine thought of Elizabeth's sweet, fair face, and the kindness that the older woman had shown. She wished that she could have overborne Elvira's decision on a visit to the Tower, but remembered sombrely that the duenna was only doing what she believed to be best, advising her as Queen Isabella would have done, had she been present. It was up to her to uphold the older woman, for though they said little enough, Katherine knew that her maids of honour resented Elvira's command.

'Let us ring for the minstrels to play for us as we work,' suggested Katherine, sitting down on a pile of cushions and picking up her embroidery again. 'Francesca, ring for a servant, and shall we invite the fool to entertain us? Spring will soon be here, and then we shall be at court once more.'

Richmond was beautiful in summer, Katherine thought. She sat beneath the cedar tree, enjoying its cool and scented shade, waiting for the arrival of Lady Margaret Pole. With her, a new maid of honour sat, placidly stitching. Another Maria, Maria de Salinas, had joined the Spanish suite, and Katherine had welcomed her friend with open arms.

'You will like the Lady Margaret, Maria,' she said now. She yawned, and stretched. 'She is what one would call a typical Englishwoman in her appearance. Tall, slender, pale-skinned. But she has sympathy and understanding – oh, Maria, she has been the best of friends to me. When I thought that I might lose her in childbirth, I almost despaired!'

'Was she near to death, then, Princess?'

Katherine hesitated. How could she explain to Maria, who knew nothing of her past sufferings, how she was beginning to feel herself to be an unlucky friend? For ever since her arrival in England, she seemed to have loved only those destined to die tragically, and before their time. Arthur had died, and within a few months of her arrival in London she had heard that the only real friend she had left behind her in Ludlow, a certain brother Joseph, had died also. And then the Queen, Elizabeth of York, had died only a week after she had been delivered of her daughter Katherine. The babe, too, had died.

So her nervous fear for Margaret Plantagenet, when her friend had been brought to bed with the child, had been irrational but inescapable. And when she heard that Margaret had borne a daughter, stillborn, and was very ill, she had almost despaired for her friend's life.

But Margaret lived; and what was more, she thrived. And she was coming to see Katherine at Richmond this very afternoon.

So now Katherine said vaguely. 'She *was* ill; I cannot explain it, Maria, but when they told me that Lady Margaret would live, I felt as though I had been relieved of a great burden. I'm afraid you may not understand much of our conversation, since your command of the English language is not yet very good, but that, in a way, is why I chose you to accompany me.' She smiled a trifle apologetically at the other girl. 'You see, Margaret and I have much to discuss. But you will be happy enough to be in the gardens with us, I daresay.'

Maria smiled and nodded, and Katherine thought, already poor Maria is finding Dona Elvira as oppressive and exacting as my other women do. Why cannot the duenna learn the art of compromise, of persuasion? But it seemed almost as though she had to test her power over the Princess and her suite by continually exerting her will against theirs – and as continually, winning.

Maria shaded her eyes against the sun, and said, 'Princess, there is a woman waving. Could it be . . . ?'

She had no need to ask further for Katherine turned, and in a moment was out of her seat and running impetuously across the shaved and tended lawn.

'Margaret, my friend,' she was crying breathlessly, and then the two women, the one tall and the other small, were in each other's arms, laughing and exclaiming.

'Come and sit with me in the cedar's shade,' Katherine urged, pulling Margaret towards the cushions spread out on the needled grass. 'I've a new maid of honour, and she speaks little English as yet. An old friend, you understand, but new to the post in my household and new to this country, of course.'

'She looks charming,' Margaret said, smiling at the thin, dark girl who stitched so diligently.

'Oh, she is. But you, Margaret! I am sorry about the baby, truly, but so *glad*, so relieved, to find you well. You are thinner, I won't deny that, but nothing that some good food and good weather will not cure.'

Margaret glanced down at her flat stomach beneath the smoke-blue taffeta of her gown. She had lost weight, she knew it, and she was glad of the warmer weather for she had felt cold ever since the loss of the babe. But health and vitality, which were still at a low ebb, would return now, she was sure of it.

'I shall eat well with the court, at any rate,' she said, laughing at Katherine's expression.

'Do you jest, Margaret? Or have you not heard?' Then,

as Margaret raised her brows, 'Oh my dear, ever since the Queen's death, the King has acted very strangely about expenditure on food and clothing. We rarely see fresh meat unless there are important visitors, and I believe the pastry-cook has left in disgust, for sweetmeats do not appear frequently at the royal table now. And as for clothes, one would think that all the money for such things had been spent on the Princess Margaret's back, for though she went well prepared to King James, Mary's gowns and kirtles all have false hems and false sleeves, and they say the King himself, and Prince Hal, wear turned doublets. They certainly wear darned hose!'

'And what of you, Katherine? Is it true that King Henry proposed that you should comfort his loneliness by becoming his wife?'

Katherine reddened. 'I know little of it,' she said hurriedly. 'I believe he did propose the match to my parents, but they thought it unsuitable. He did not speak to me of marriage, I can assure you of *that*. And had he done so, I should have realized that he feels it his duty to marry again to protect the succession, and was merely honouring me with the suggestion, situated as I am.'

'Do you not hanker to be Queen of England?' Margaret said teasingly.

The smile left Katherine's face, and her eyes took on a martial light. 'Yes, I do,' she said frankly. 'But I wish to wed Hal, as the King keeps promising me I shall. I do not feel that King Henry would regard me as a mate and consort, but merely as a child-bride, on whom he could beget sons. Let us talk of other things, Margaret, I beg! I own I misliked the whole scheme and would rather forget it had ever been suggested, even idly, as I am convinced was the case.'

'Certainly, my love,' Margaret agreed readily. 'Tell me of Prince Hal. Do you see him often?'

'Not very much,' owned Katherine. 'But he is here for a few days, hunting with the King, so I see him at dinner times. It is difficult for us, you see. There is no official betrothal yet, nor an official denial that there will *be* a betrothal. And the King watches us; we have not exchanged a *word*, Margaret, though we may be in the same room. The Prince eyes me, and I see his father watching us and can only smile, and pass by.'

'And you are in mourning yet again,' Margaret said. 'It is for the good Queen, is it not? Ah, Katherine, I little thought when she promised to be your friend whilst she lived, how short a friendship it would be.'

'I am in mourning for the Queen,' agreed Katherine. 'But the allowance which the King pays me does not allow for new clothes. And I have grown since I came to England, Margaret. Jesu, how we shoot upwards, the maidens and myself! Poor little Francesca is the worst, for she has years of growing still ahead of her! But as a result, our stitchery improves daily. How we make, and mend! I sometimes say that King Henry is training me as wife for his son, for I am sure that poor Hal will be given a pittance for his wife, so that whoever she may be, she will have to turn a doublet prettily, and concoct a gown and kirtle out of nothing at all, or the King will never agree to the marriage!'

'He will certainly demand a good dowry for his son's hand,' agreed Margaret, laughing at the picture Katherine's pretty, accented voice had painted.

'Dowries! Oh, Margaret, don't mention dowries,' Katherine said, casting her work down upon her lap. 'There was trouble over my dowry before ever I left for Ludlow; something about the jewels and plate. I believe that the King said if I used the plate as Arthur's wife, then it was his already, and would not be accepted as part payment of the dowry as had been agreed. I'm not sure. De Ayala made a fuss about it, anyway, and we did not use the plate, which seems so foolish and wasteful, does it not? But now, I am hopeful that a settlement will soon be reached over dowry and betrothal at the same time. My father is bargaining hard, and says that if I am content to renounce once and for all my marriage with Arthur and my widow's portion in his estates, then he will, for his part, pay the remaining half of my dowry to the King upon my marriage with the Prince.'

'And are you willing? To renounce your widow's rights, I mean?'

'And my marriage. Yes, for it has been renounced already, on my behalf,' Katherine said quietly. She took her friend's hand. 'Margaret, you were with us in Ludlow, and you know that I felt . . . the strongest affection, to put it no higher, for Arthur. But he is dead, and I must live. I cannot look back.'

'You are right, of course. I am glad that you want to marry the Prince, for surely it is best for you both, though he is too young yet to think of marriage, is he not?'

'Oh, yes, much too young. But in a couple of years, when he is fifteen, then the marriage would be solemnized.'

Katherine turned towards Maria, smiling fondly at her friend. 'My women are ever loyal, for times are harder for us than we had dreamed when first we set sail for England. We had not thought that we journeyed towards a widower's court, where dancing and parties would be few, and where the heir was still a little lad. Yet they agree with me that we are right to wait, and hope that soon events will justify our faith.'

'So you have put off your blacks at long last, Princess.'

Doctor de Puebla spoke cautiously, aware that the mere sight of his face seemed to irritate his royal mistress. But this morning the glow of happiness which surrounded her had emboldened him to speak.

Katherine inclined her head graciously. 'Yes, doctor. Now that the betrothal between myself and Prince Henry is official, Dona Elvira agreed that I could shed my mourning gowns. The allowance paid by the King does not, alas, extend to my clothing but a friend gave me this,' she flicked the frivolous carnation silk proudly, 'and now I feel free to wear it when I am at court.'

De Puebla bowed, and said in a low voice, 'It is well that you wear it this morning, Princess, for there is one who would speak with you.'

Katherine's eyes held only innocent enquiry, making his role of messenger for Prince Hal seem easier.

'It is the Prince,' de Puebla said in a rush. 'He wishes to see you, Princess, in his study in the palace. He feels that it is right for you to meet thus informally, now that your betrothal is acknowledged.'

'I'll go to him at once, ' Katherine said, getting to her feet with a rustle of many petticoats. She put her hand to her cheek, wishing she had a mirror, but she and her women were in the garden and no one had thought, she knew, to provide themselves with so much as a comb. After all, they had gone out to see the hunt depart, with the King leading on his chestnut stallion, and though it was true that she had dressed carefully, and had hoped to see the Prince, no thought of a meeting had been in her mind.

'Go to him, Princess? You cannot!' Dona Elvira had drawn close on seeing the doctor speaking alone with her charge, and had not scrupled to listen. 'This is not the way in which a meeting between a young man and his betrothed should take place. Where is your dignity, Princess? Your sense of fitness? You must tell him . . .'

Katherine laughed. 'Indeed I must go to him, Elvira,' she said gaily. 'For as you well know, it is only when the King is absent that we may call our lives our own so far as the Prince is concerned. He would never countenance private speech between the Prince and myself, even though I've no doubt that the Prince's tutor will be with him, and a gentleman of his service.'

'But the impropriety!' hissed the duenna. 'I shall accompany you, of course, but to go almost unattended to meet a young man . . .'

'Elvira, he is a child,' Katherine said impatiently. 'Come with me if you must, but let us go at once, without further discussion.'

Dr de Puebla led them through the sunny gardens and into the palace through a side door. Along the passageways they went, the women's skirts whispering over the time-polished floors. Katherine looked in vain for a mirror to tidy her hair and rubbed surreptitiously at her cheeks to bring the blood rushing beneath her skin.

They mounted a short flight of stairs and the doctor thumped on the door, smiling knowingly, it seemed to Katherine, at the man at arms who stood back to allow them to pass.

The door swung inwards and Katherine saw sunshine flooding onto gaily painted walls, a floor strewn with fresh green rushes, and a big, square desk. At the desk, facing them, sat Hal. He was alone.

He stood up as the two women entered, and waved his hand in dismissal to de Puebla. Then he focused his attention upon Katherine.

144

'Why did you bring the bloodhound?' he said furiously. His face had flooded with pink and Katherine saw that his fists were clenched so tightly that the nails dug into the flesh.

Thankful that the duenna's command of the English language was so poor, Katherine said, 'I'm sorry, but Dona Elvira felt it would not be . . . proper . . . for us to converse without a chaperon.'

The colour in the Prince's cheeks faded swiftly, and a look of undoubted gratification stole across his face. Katherine realized that the boy took her words as a compliment to his manhood, and hid her smile.

'Very well, Katherine, since you wish your woman to be present,' he said grandly. 'Be seated, and tell her to sit down also.'

He indicated two chairs drawn up opposite the desk and Dona Elvira, who had marked the exchange closely, sat down at once before Katherine could do so, causing the Prince to direct a baffled glare at the crown of her old-fashioned hood.

'Your chaperon has taken the best chair,' he said crossly, 'so let us repair to the window-seat. It is more comfortable, anyway,' he added, with an impish satisfaction which Katherine thought more suited to his years than his previous haughty tone.

So they settled themselves side by side on the broad window-seat and Katherine turned enquiring eyes on the Prince, who seemed oddly reluctant to speak now that he had her undivided attention.

At last she said gently, 'Did you wish to see me for any particular reason, Hal?'

Hal looked down at his clasped hands, a flush mantling his cheeks. 'I wanted to tell you . . . that is to say, to ask you . . .'

His voice trailed away and Katherine said helpfully, 'You wanted to ask me, perhaps, how I was enjoying myself now that I am at court once more? My woman speaks almost no English, you know.'

'I care nothing for her,' Henry said rudely, but Katherine thought that the tension in him eased a little. 'Yes, I want to know if you are pleased with life at Richmond, and . . . No! It is not what I wanted to say. I wanted to tell you that I think you are very fair, and I'm glad you are to be my wife. And I wanted to ask you whether it is true what my gentlemen say, when they think I am not listening.'

'What do they say, Hal?'

'They say you must be disappointed, to find yourself betrothed to a child,' Hal said. 'But, Katherine, I am tall and strong for my age, as you are small and slight for yours. Soon enough I will be a man, and when I am, I promise that I shall not disappoint you.'

Katherine said equably, 'Of course I am not disappointed. I was betrothed to Arthur before ever I saw him, you know. Our marriage will please our parents, and you and I will be good friends, I trust, as well as good consorts.'

Hal nodded and Katherine, beginning to talk of his studies, his sport and his dogs, studied him closely. He was as he had claimed, well grown for a lad of his years. His skin had the colour and bloom of an apricot, his hair lay like a gold cap on his well shaped head and he was tall and robust enough to be taken for quite fifteen. Beneath his doublet of scarlet satin sewn with pearl drops his chest was broad, and the thin silk of his shirt did not conceal the muscles which rippled when he moved his arms.

'And I can hit the bull at every shot, almost, and throw any lad in the wrestling,' he was saying, whilst Katherine noted his eyes, blue as her own, set beneath the soft blond arch of his brows, the small, straight nose, and the mouth, curved now with pleasure. But surely, one day, when the face was more formed, it would be a sensuous mouth?

Shocked at her own thought, Katherine stood up abruptly, shaking out the soft crushed carnation folds of her skirt. 'I must go back to my women, Hal,' she said lightly, trying to quiet the uncomfortable beating of her heart. 'They will wonder why I am so long away. Your tutor, too, will not think well of me if you banish him and your lessons to perdition so that you may talk with me.'

He rose also, his eyes showing their admiration in a look which brought the colour to Katherine's face once more.

'Very well, Kate,' he said. 'Perhaps you had better go now. But you will come back, and talk to me again?'

'If I am allowed,' Katherine said steadily. 'Goodbye, Hal.' She swept him a curtsy, mockingly deep, smiling up at him to remind herself that he was a child – a child – almost six years younger than herself. But he looked down at her as though she gave him no more than his due, making her confusion more complete.

As she hurried back to the garden, with the duenna panting at her heels, she chided herself for her foolishness. A well-grown boy to be sure, who was going to cross the threshold into manhood sooner than most. But for a woman of her age to blush and feel that heart-hammer when such a one looked at her appraisingly could only be shaming.

Dona Elvira, padding protestingly behind, asked why had the Princess taken fright and flown so suddenly from the Prince. What had he said, the forward young knave? Had he offered her an insult, or was it his too blatant admiration from which she had fled? Lord, but the Princess must remember that she, Elvira, was not as young as she would wish, when she took to her heels and flew across the garden in such a breathless fashion.

Katherine, relenting, slowed her footsteps and answered the duenna's questions as best she might. She had not flown from the Prince, but thought it wiser to leave because, after all, the lad was supposed to be studying with his tutor. No, he had offered her no insults, and his admiration had not offended her. Rather, she had simply decided that the interview had gone on long enough.

Elvira listened, and nodded, and as they neared the group of Katherine's women once more, she said in a low voice, 'Pity, what a pity, that Arthur died. For at seventeen you're a woman grown, and you need a man. The young Prince will not mate with you for many a long month, and in the meantime, you must be patient.'

Katherine turned on her heel, fury and frustration gnawing at her breast. How dared Elvira offer such presumptuous advice to her mistress! Even if it were true, which of course it was not, how dare she voice such sentiments before the Spaniards who sat and stitched in the sunshine.

But they had not heard; no one glanced slyly at her, nor did they mutter amongst themselves. Faces bright with enquiry glanced up, mouths smiled, eyes and voices welcomed her.

It is only within my own heart that Elvira's words burn like fire, Katherine thought grimly. She would say no word of reproach to the woman, who had taken the responsibility of her royal charge so literally, for during the months to come, when her betrothal to Hal would be her only standing at the English court, where else could she turn for advice and guidance but to the duenna?

12 Maria de Rojas

The sun beat down strongly on the whole country, so that masters and men groaned at their tasks, and longed for the evening to cast its shadow on their toils. The heat in the gardens at Richmond was intense, so that few lingered by the long flower borders, to smell the sweet, wicked scent from drowsy poppies, or to crush the hot thyme in sweat-slippery fingers. In the palace, the King and his son worked with windows wide, one at his ledgers, the other at his Latin, and both were glad enough that they had not chosen to take horse in the hunt that day, for surely the heat would have been worse, out under the pitiless brass of the sun?

Yet in the knot garden, Katherine and her closest friends sat on cushions between the neat beds. The faint scent of crushed grass and box hedges, the sweetness of the herbs which grew therein, and the faint perfume from the yew trees all combined to make their retreat into a sweet summer arbour. The heat did not trouble them unduly, though Katherine was careful to keep her skin covered, for she had no wish to freckle.

The five maids had come to the knot garden for privacy rather than for enjoyment of the sunshine, however. They wished to discuss marriage, and it was a subject which they knew instinctively would be vetoed by Dona Elvira. For the marriage in question was that of Maria de Rojas to a member of the English aristocracy, and the duenna had not failed to hide her displeasure at what she obviously considered Maria's defection.

'I wanted particularly to speak to you today, Maria,'

Katherine said. She shifted her position on the cushion, and felt the sweat form even with that slight movement, and slip down between her breasts. She was grateful for the cooler shade of her gabled hood, yet she knew a longing for the feel of a little breeze on her hair, and for the enclosed warmth to leave her neck, so that the air might caress the overheated skin.

The girls moved closer, glad of the thick yew trees which separated them from the open-eyed palace windows.

'I have written once more to the Queen,' Katherine went on. 'When Hernan Duque sailed for Spain, he carried with him a letter to my mother telling her that your hand was sought by none other than young Stanley, grandson by marriage to the Countess of Richmond, King Henry's mother. I am sure that when she reads the letter she will send not only her joyful consent, but money to dower you properly also.'

'Thank you, Princess,' Maria said uncertainly. She hesitated, then added, 'Will . . . can her reply be hoped for soon, do you suppose? My betrothed grows impatient, and . . . '

She bent her head until Katherine could only see her dove-grey headdress, but the movements of her hands in her lap betrayed her agitation.

'What ails you, Maria?' Katherine asked at length.

The other girl raised her head and Katherine saw the flush on her cheeks.

'It is Don Inigo Manrique,' she said reluctantly. 'At first, Princess, when Lord Stanley begged leave to marry me and I was so pleased, Don Inigo was pleased for me, and seemed to share my joy. I have no family save your own, as you know, for I am your mother's ward, so it seemed pleasant to have Inigo telling me to treat him as a brother.'

Francesca gave a muffled snort at these ingenuous words, but subsided into gravity again when Katherine glared reprovingly.

'Then, when no word came from Spain, neither of approval nor disapproval, he began to pity me, to say I had been badly treated,' the small, faltering voice went on. 'He came to me often when I had believed myself to be alone, he pressed my hand, and spoke gravely of the insult Spain was offering to that most powerful lady, the Countess of Richmond. And now that he truly believes Queen Isabella must disapprove of the match, his comfort takes a different tone, and he has made it plain that he thinks I should withdraw from my betrothal to my lord, and become betrothed to *him*, instead.'

'And you do not wish it?'

'Wish it, Princess? Why, no, for I dearly love Lord Stanley. But it is becoming difficult . . . Inigo is with us so much, so constantly, that to turn off his advances without appearing churlish . . . I find I cannot be as forthright as I should be. And Dona Elvira does not appear to notice that her son behaves towards me more warmly than he should. Yet she scolds me for rudeness if I decline Inigo's escort, or refuse to speak to her son apart from my friends.'

Katherine plucked a little leaf from a lavender bush, and rubbed it between her fingers, so that the bruised perfume filled the air. 'It is difficult for you, Maria. I had meant to tell you that you should show less friendship for Inigo, who is a young and hot-blooded man. As it is, I see you desire to show no such friendship.' She frowned, then her brow cleared. 'I had wondered if my requests regarding your dowry were reaching Spain,' she admitted. 'That is why I sent the letter with Duque, instead of by the more usual channels. I am sure that Queen Isabella won't hesitate to make immediate arrangements for your dowry, so it should not be long now before you are safe from such embarrassments; but until then, we will help you to keep Don Manrique at arm's length, even if his mother seems not to understand your plight.'

'Imagine Maria having a suitor too many, when I have none at all,' Francesca said, laughing up at Katherine from where she sprawled at the Princess's feet. 'Would it help if I captured the interest of the unwanted gentleman?' She jumped up and despite the heat, curved her body into the shape affected by the gipsy flamenco dancers. '*Olé!*' she exclaimed, snapping her fingers and wriggling her hips, 'I will dance him into desperate love for me, and then Maria de Rojas need fear him no more.'

'Oh, Francesca, you terrible child,' Katherine said, but she laughed as she spoke, and clapped in time to the wild tune which Francesca chanted as her body whirled in the dance.

Inez was getting to her feet to partner Francesca, when from between two tall yews a small figure approached them. It was one of the out-at-elbow pages of Katherine's suite.

'Princess, you said to warn you if there was need. The King is still writing, and Dona Elvira slumbers on, but Don Inigo has been prowling about the solar. I think he is searching for . . .' he hesitated, his expression wary, 'for one of your women, Princess. Shall you come back to the palace, before you are missed?'

'Thank you, Frederico, you have done well,' Katherine said at once. 'We will come indoors now, but tell me, can we make our way to the Princess Mary's rooms without arousing anyone's suspicion? I am giving her lessons on the lute, and Francesca has been teaching her the songs of our country. No one will think twice if they find us there, singing and playing with the little Princess.'

Frederico considered, his head on one side, great dark

eyes dreamy as he looked inward to his own knowledge of the palace of Richmond.

'Aye, mistress,' he said at length. 'You will come with me, if you please. The other women may return unseen through the stableyard, for even the English are idle in this heat. But should not the Lady Maria come with us, to the Princess Mary's rooms?'

Katherine shook her head at the small boy. 'Frederico, you know everything,' she declared. 'But you are right, of course, it is Maria for whom Manrique searches. Lead on, little man!'

As the three girls followed the shabby little pageboy, Katherine said soothingly, 'Do not fear, Maria. Though it ill becomes me to say so, I do not think Dona Elvira has behaved well towards you and in fact her attitude to us all is far too high-handed. Changes must and will be made.'

'It is the ague. She cannot return to Greenwich with the rest of the court. She must stay here.'

Katherine heard Elvira's pronouncement through the hot waves of fever which engulfed her. She lay in her bed, gazing unseeingly at the faces of those who nursed her, fighting the nausea, the dizzy and unfocused vision, the bands of molten heat which imprisoned her heavy limbs.

Maria de Salina came and brought the news that the King's own physician, Baptiste, was looking after her, but to Katherine, these periodic struggles against ill-health were battles which she fought alone, with such comfort as her women or the doctors could give.

This time, however, it seemed that the King's physician could help, for less than a week after the ague struck, she

153

was well enough to follow the court to Greenwich. But the journey had weakened her, and that very same evening she took to her bed once more.

With a generosity which Katherine altogether failed to appreciate in her weakened state, Henry despatched her to one of his favourite manor houses, still with the faithful Baptiste in attendance, to recover fully in the quiet of the countryside, far from the bustling court.

The Princess was very ill. Dona Elvira scarcely left her side, and during the worst of the sickness, she saw to it that the Princess knew to whom she should be grateful for her recovery. Never a cooling drink was held to her lips, but Elvira's face hovered near; never a damp cloth caressed her burning brow but Elvira's was the hand which laid it in place. By the time the fever began to recede at last, Katherine was tied to the duenna with bonds as soft as silk and as strong as steel. It had become impossible for the Princess to rebel against one who deserved her lifelong gratitude, and the maids of honour saw their hopes of escape from Elvira's iron rule vanishing into the long distance.

They were resigned, however, believing that soon Katherine would begin to plan her wedding to Prince Hal and then once again, the duenna would not rule their Princess, for she would be an independent married woman.

Only Maria de Rojas wept for long hours into the night. For she knew that her chances of escape were narrowing. There had been no word from Queen Isabella, and Katherine had been forced to tell the girl that the King had shown no disposition to yield to her own veiled pleas for financial assistance, which she had directed at him from her bed of sickness. Don Inigo kept up his relentless pursuit, and Maria knew that in any case she had antagonized Dona Elvira by barely concealing her distaste for the young man's advances. Maria was a considerable heiress, and was quite convinced that Inigo loved her money and not her person, for was she not small and shy, especially when compared with an opulent beauty like Inez, or a lively and vivacious creature like Francesca?

So the time passed, and autumn gradually gave way to winter as the hope for her marriage died in Maria's gentle breast, to be replaced by one stubborn thought: she would *not* become betrothed to the importunate Don Inigo Manrique.

Katherine sat before her desk, writing. Her arm curved protectively round the sheet, and her lips moved silently, as she traced the words onto the thick vellum. Now and then, when a word proved difficult, the tip of her tongue emerged between her lips, and her breathing was suspended for a moment whilst she tussled with the spelling.

How best to explain to her mother the fears which she was beginning to harbour? That the dispensation from the Pope would never arrive, so that she herself would never be wed to Prince Henry of England? And poor Maria de Rojas's love life grew daily more tangled. She and young Stanley only waited for the word from Spain that all was well and that the dowry would be paid, to marry. Such a small thing to ask, Katherine thought fretfully. She had heard that her mother was ill, but surely she could have dictated a letter to her daughter, giving the terms of the marriage contract? Maria was her ward, after all.

Katherine added a short sentence to the effect that speed was now of the essence, and reached for the sandpot. She began to sand the wet ink, then blew the surplus off the page and turned towards the door of the ante-room where members of her suite lounged and chatted, whilst the harp players twanged the strings, practising the Christmas melodies which would soon be heard throughout the land.

'Maria,' she called, and as the girl approached, 'I have written once more to the Queen. Soon, surely, we must hear from her, and then you may be easy once more.'

Maria nodded and smiled, but Katherine saw the dark circles around the maid's eyes, the quivering lip, and the nervous start which Maria had given on hearing her name called. She caught Maria's fingers in her own capable hand, and said bracingly, 'Come, read my letter. When the Queen reads it, all *must* be well, despite our fears.'

'Aye, surely,' murmured Maria without much conviction as she bent to peruse the slanting black writing.

Katherine moved away to allow Maria some privacy, towards the brightly lit ante-room, leaving Maria standing in the pool of candlelight which illumined the dark of the study. Inigo had looked up when he heard Maria's name called, and now he came across the room and stood in the doorway, staring at the girl's bent shoulders. Unobserved, Katherine stood in the shadows and took stock of the young man. Handsome enough, with thick black hair and olive skin, his eyes and mouth lacked the determination and firmness clearly seen on his mother's countenance. His expression was dreamy; greedy, almost. He looked, thought Katherine crossly, like a child who believes it has been unfairly refused a request. She saw his tongue nervously moisten his full lips, and the line of his nostril harden and flare. He really *does* desire Maria, she realized with sudden perception. It is not just because she is wealthy, as I had thought.

She watched as the young man straightened his wine-coloured doublet, pulling the jerkin aside to fasten jewelled aglets. He hesitated a moment, then stepped forward, moving across the room like a sleep-walker until he was near enough to touch Maria's shoulder as she bent, absorbed still, over the letter.

Katherine was about to speak so that both young persons were aware of her presence, when Dona Elvira came rustling across the room. She was dressed in black, as always, but her face had a withdrawn and watchful look, and she held a black kerchief to her lips. She glanced at Maria and her son but to Katherine's surprise merely looked away again until her eyes saw Katherine in the gloom.

'Princess,' she said without preamble. 'I have had news from Spain. Will you come with me into your bedchamber, so that we can speak privately? Maria, my dear, perhaps you would like to accompany your mistress?'

It was a command rather than a request and Maria straightened herself at once, and together the three of them entered the bedchamber, shutting the door upon the startled Don Inigo.

Katherine had picked up her letter as she passed the desk, lest it should fall into the wrong hands, and now she stood smoothing it between her fingers, whilst her heart thumped painfully and she waited for the duenna to speak.

Strangely, Elvira seemed reluctant to do so. She made a great play of pressing Katherine into a cushioned chair and then bade Maria sit down also, though she herself stayed on her feet. At last, when the tension threatened to become unbearable, she cleared her throat and began.

'Princess,' she said. 'I have today received a communication from your father, King Ferdinand. My child, you must prepare yourself . . .'

Katherine looked up as she faltered, and then got to her feet.

'I believe I know what you have to tell me, Dona Elvira,' she said evenly. 'My mother is dead. That is why I have had no answer to my letters, and why poor Maria here has not received the Queen's blessing on her wedding. The Queen of Castile is dead.'

Maria, remembering the only mother she had ever known, gave a long, moaning cry and fell across the bed but Katherine showed little emotion.

Her eyes were bright with unshed tears, but only her hands moved, as she tore across and across the letter to her mother, begging for an answer, and her understanding. The letter which Queen Isabella would never see.

Summer had come again, and the gentle rays of the sun struck the great beech tree, turning the edges of the young leaves to gold, and gilding the silvery tone of the bark. A gentle breeze, which stroked the leaves, causing them to turn and move, wrinkled for a moment their reflection in the calm depths of the Thames as it glided slowly between its banks.

The day was all summer; on the river barges were already thick, with Londoners in holiday mood, wearing silk shirts and fine doublets as they pulled their craft across the crowded water. The swans clustered around the boats, hoping for scraps, and as the townsfolk drifted on, with the water smooth beneath them and the sun warm on their backs, they smelt the sun-ripened raspberries on the banks, and saw the drifts of lime pollen as the lazy breeze stirred the laden branches.

Passing the gardens of the rich folk who could afford to live on Thames-side, the passer-by could see the long lawns, gay flower borders, the stiff symmetry of yew and box. The backs of the houses, however, were well screened at this season and kept their secrets.

The most secret of all the gardens was that of Durham House, for against the water grew the great beech trees, with their long branches swaying down towards the river as though they longed to dabble their leaves in the shaded water.

And on this afternoon, the beech trees hid even more than they usually did. For flung down in the shade of the great grey trunks, where the sun did not penetrate and where the grass grew thin amongst the beech mast, lay Maria de Rojas, and she was crying as if her heart would break.

Presently her grief began to spend itself, and she raised her tear-blubbered face to look about her. She saw the beauty of the afternoon and it seemed to mock her, for where, it could have asked, was *her* beauty, now? The lines of her black dress, long outgrown and shabby, did nothing for her burgeoning breasts, keeping them strained back within the too narrow limits of the stiff bodice. Maria stared down with loathing at the tired, dusty black silk; it has not worn well, she thought resentfully, and then her plight came back to her and fresh tears welled. Giving a small wail, she hunched herself into a ball of absolute misery, and proceeded to wish herself dead once more.

It was here, presently, that Inigo Manrique found her.

He had come quietly down the garden, and his sorrow had been almost equal to her own. For his mother had insisted that since Maria was not betrothed to young Stanley, then she must become betrothed to Inigo. And Maria had given a gasp of denial and dismay, and fled from the chamber.

Katherine had seemed annoyed over his mother's pronouncement, yet not angry with him; perhaps she had seen the love in his eyes for little Maria, he thought hopefully. So as soon as he was able to do so, he had come in search of his love. But to find her thus! Weeping with such abandonment, and all because she had been told it was her duty to wed him! Quietly, he lowered himself to the ground beside her and put his hand on her shaking shoulders. He could feel her small bones, like a bird's, and found himself angry with his mother who had caused this unprotected child such distress.

'Maria, if you do not wish it, none can make you wed me,' he said timidly to the crown of her hood. He sighed as she ignored him, and tried to lift her, but she shrugged him off so petulantly that she dislodged her headdress and it rolled onto the ground. Momentarily confused, she sat up, fumbling for the pins which had held her hair close under the cap and failing to find them, let the rich, blue-black locks slide like water through her fingers, to cascade round her shoulders, arms, waist, so that she sat there in a cloak of her hair, eyes swollen and defiant, yet looking unbelievably desirable to his eyes.

In a moment, he was kneeling before her, his eyes hotly raking the lines of her body, never noticing the poor faded gown or the patched kirtle. Maria watched him indifferently, not understanding his sudden silence, his expression, until his hands stretched out slowly, and crept up her arms to the low neck of her dress. Hair caught and clung to his fingers, and she cried out as his sudden lunge at her breasts tore at her hair roots. The sound seemed only to excite him further. He swung her against him, muttering words which Maria only half understood, and pressed his hot lips to the little pulse which beat under her ear.

Her surprise rendered her motionless for a minute, then as his hands continued to grope at her body she clawed blindly at him through the veil of her tears and her thick, fine hair. They rolled onto the beech mast, and Maria heard him groan and felt his weight crush her, so that she seemed to fight, not only Inigo, but her own clothes, which hampered her movements, and her hair, which blinded her and choked her so that the afternoon seemed suddenly dark.

She did not know whether she cried out, or whether she

was silent, but she felt the cool air on her body and re-doubled her efforts to escape. Then, suddenly, his hands were gentle, and his voice soft. She stopped struggling, feeling her limbs heavy as though with a drug, and lay still, waiting for release.

Later, she lay on her bed and wondered if she would die. She felt so ill, so weak, and so unhappy. Katherine came to her, eyeing the little white face without understanding.

'Come, my dear, you are upset,' she said bracingly. 'But you must brush your hair and wash your face, you cannot stay up here for the rest of your life, you know.'

Maria stood up and walked over to the mirror. Her eyes were puffy and there was blood on her chin from a bitten lip. Above the torn gown, the bruises of Inigo's onslaught still stained the white flesh of her breasts.

'I suppose I shall have to marry him, now?' she said in a small voice.

Katherine glanced at the other quickly, her eyes widening as they took in the blood, the bruises, the damaged gown, and Maria's loose hair. 'I . . . see,' she said uncertainly. 'Did he . . . do you mean . . .'

'Tell Dona Elvira,' Maria said with a catch in her voice, 'That I will agree to wed her son.' She turned back to the mirror and began fumblingly to brush her hair. 'I will come down presently, Princess.'

During the course of the evening, Katherine interviewed Inigo, a task which she found both distasteful and embarrassing. To do him credit, the young man seemed distressed, mumbling incoherently when she said he seemed to have pressed his suite with less than decorum, but he smiled with pleasure at the news of Maria's decision to marry him.

It had been a long day, and was not yet over. Katherine, distressed by Maria's unhappiness, was almost more distressed by her own reaction to it. She found herself studying the younger girl, reflecting bitterly that any attentions which Inigo had forced upon Maria had probably been the direct result of lures thrown out by the other maid. Yet she knew, none better, that this was not true.

She lay in the dark, agitating her mind with fruitless imaginings. Had Maria succumbed to seduction, or fought against it? Had she, in fact, been seduced? Or had she managed to fight off Don Inigo successfully?

Finally, she decided that since Maria was still obviously unhappy, she would make one final effort to resolve the *impasse* over young Stanley. She would send a messenger, probably Frederico, a thoroughly reliable lad, to the King of England.

13 Deception

'The King cannot see *anyone*, no matter how important their business. I tell you, he is not available. You must leave the palace at once, for there is much afoot.'

The fat and important chamberlain who had dismissed Frederico could not have made it clearer that there was to be no interview with King Henry *that* day – or any other, judging by his petulant expression. It was plain that of all the days Princess Katherine's representative could have chosen to enter the palace, this day was the least auspicious.

It was enough to make the most complacent person suspicious. Frederico was as cheerful and straightforward as any other lad of his years, but any healthy boy who suspects a mystery must do his best to discover what is happening, and Frederico was determined not to go back to Katherine with a curt message that his Majesty her father-in-law would not receive her representative. At least, the reason should be revealed to her.

So Frederico wormed his way into the kitchens, to see what titbits of news he could pick up.

A cook, used enough to small boys in shabby liveries sneaking down into his domain for a bite of bread and cheese, cuffed him carelessly in passing, and gave him a gooseberry pasty. Frederico bit into the rich pastry eagerly, but did not fail to keep his eyes roving constantly round the big, overwarm room, in an attempt to gauge the temper of the occupants. Around the fire, which roared up hotly casting a devil's glow across the darkened ceiling beams, a knot of scullions toiled to turn the spitted boar without scorching their hands, and Frederico listened to their shouted talk.

'I'd liefer watch a good cock fight, then tussle with one of they,' a small, ill-favoured lad roared, pointing to the boar. 'Why, Master Godbere brought this one low with a thrust from his pike! Not a sport for one as short in the leg as I!'

'Master Godbere has a fine bay stallion, I'll wager he forked that when he did the boar to death,' protested a bigger, pock-marked lad.

Frederico finished off his pasty, losing interest in their talk, which was all of sport. To them, it was a matter of indifference who ate the meal they prepared.

At another table, a fat and buxom matron beat with a wooden spoon at a mess of fruit, adding ever and anon, a liberal helping of honey. Frederico stood close, watching as this prodigal person broke half a dozen eggs into a bowl and began to beat them with vigour, then emptied the bowl into the fruit mixture, and began to beat again.

She looked up, smiling at his interest but threatening, nevertheless, a broken head if he should put so much as the tip of a finger into the concoction.

'Who will eat the dish, then?' Frederico said with assumed indifference. 'Mmm, good mother, but it looks delicious!'

'Them above, the nobles, will eat,' she snapped. 'They say the council will dine here today, but what council, on what business, I neither know nor care. Here, you skinny little fellow, you may lick the spoon, for I've finished with it now.'

Frederico licked, and showered the dish with deserved praise, then made his way out of the kitchens once more. He would learn nothing there, for to work in the King's kitchens was to be utterly remote from the life of the rest of the palace. Why else was it that the tall, grave falconer in the King's service had once been sent to be a scullion in the kitchens? Ah yes, Lambert Simnel had tried to better his lot in life by pretending to be the dead Prince Edward, the Prince who had never reigned. But King Henry had been merciful to the boy, realizing that he was but a tool in the hands of men older and more cunning than himself. He had given him a scullion's job, down amongst the grease and heats of the kitchens, knowing that from there he would be under the eye of the great, yet would know little enough of what went on amongst his betters.

In an ante-room he found half a dozen pages, lads of his own age, playing at backgammon. They seemed bored, and he recognized in their attitude the wary relaxation of those who wait on the great, and are momentarily unwanted by their masters. They were attending on some noble, he reasoned, who was with the Council and who would not hurry to his own place for many hours.

He joined them, sitting on a bench and watching the game, little heeded by the players, all of whom wore the green and white Tudor livery.

'The Prince is with his father,' a tall and gangling youth reported. He sat down on the bench and belched loudly. 'So we shall be mewed up here until his Majesty gives our Hal leave to depart.'

A stocky, ginger-haired boy said curiously, 'Why is the Prince closeted with the Council? What has the Bishop of Winchester to do in the matter?'

'It can be no concern of ours, save that, because of it, we shall be kept from our enjoyment,' the first boy said. He turned to Frederico. 'Hey, you ragged monkey! You are from the Spanish Princess's household, are you not? Do you know why the Prince meets with the Privy Council? Hal frowned and stamped, and is not best pleased, that I *do* know. Is your mistress here, also?'

'I know nothing,' Frederico shrugged, 'and my mistress is at her home of Durham House. I came but to deliver a message. How long will the lords be within the privy chamber?'

'An hour, or ten hours. I know not. But they will bellow loud enough when they want us,' said the red-haired boy. 'If we knew they would be long within, we could find some more profitable amusement.'

'They dine at the palace, that I do know,' Frederico said quickly. 'And I have a new catapult. It can hit the target at a hundred paces.'

'Never!' shouted the ginger one. 'Or not with your muscle behind it, for you're nought but skin and bone. Now with *my* catty, I can outshoot many an archer, I can shoot dead the running hare, I can . . . ' But Frederico had left them to their argument.

Up the passages he ranged, questing here and there, his small, undernourished body whiffling like a moving question mark from one place to the other. He noticed, presently, that the guards were thickest near a certain ante-chamber, and guessed that the Prince and his father were within, and the Privy Council also. He could not get near the room though, and was pondering his chance of hovering outside a door and slipping in unobserved when suddenly, a possible solution sprang into his mind. His catapult! He would go into the gardens, which seemed quiet enough with everyone intent on the business within the palace, and then he could claim that he was but searching for his shot, should any query his presence there.

Luck was with him. Even as he sped along the passages, he heard a noise behind him. It was two of his former companions, the red-haired page and a fat and spotty little fellow. Ginger hailed him.

'Here is the ragged monkey who claims to be able to use his catapult better than I! Come with us, knave, so that we may try our skill one against the other.'

'I will come presently; I am on an errand now,' Frederico said, and was glad when they accepted his excuse without question, used themselves to the strange ways of the nobility they served. He saw that his idle remark had not fallen upon stony ground, and realized that his rendezvous with the two catapult-owning pages would give him an even better reason for prowling the gardens.

Once outside, it was a simple enough matter to melt into a line of ornate yews which marched along the edge of the finely gravelled paths. Within moments, he had almost forgotten the importance of his errand as he bent double, using all the available cover, pretending that he was a fox with the hunt hot on his brush. Pressing close to the ground, he wriggled forward on his stomach to the next patch of bush or long grass which would hide him from prying eyes.

The obstacle which almost confounded him was the terrace. Raised above lawns and flower beds, with only roses set amidst its paving, it was a baking plain exposed in brilliant sunlight, but one which he needs must cross if he was to hear anything which was taking place within the chamber where the Council met.

He glanced, hopeful, at the other windows. But no, his memory was not at fault. The room he sought faced out onto the terrace.

'Perhaps if I am caught they will think me younger than I am, and believe if I say I was but playing at stalking the sparrows with my catty,' muttered Frederico resignedly to himself. But he was determined. He had not come so far nor dared so much, only to turn back now, empty-handed.

Sly and quiet as a grass snake, he slid into the flower bed, wriggling through a patch of marigolds which shed their lambent petals on his dark hose. On his knees now, he could see onto the terrace. Yes, if he could but cross the paving, he could crouch below the level of the windowsill, and since the window was open he should be able to hear the voices of those within.

He filled his lungs with the mild air, and abandoning caution, stood up and stepped, lightfooted, across the terrace. He used the rosebushes as cover where it was possible, and gained the comparative safety of the palace wall in a few strides, to his infinite astonishment. Yet here, he knew, lay his greatest danger. For to be caught spying on the King, and Council, the penalty even for a boy such as himself would be terrible indeed. But he banished uneasy thoughts of bloodstained sawdust and the shriek of the rack from his mind with resolution. He was here to listen, and listen he would.

He dropped to his knees and crawled along until he was beneath the open window. A rumble of voices, and feet; the scrape of chairs, and jovial nothings. The Privy Council meeting was breaking up! He was too late, they were going!

Sick with disappointment, Frederico almost walked away in self-disgust, but then a voice reached his ears, staying him as surely as though a hand had grasped his shoulder.

'Father, I cannot pretend not to understand, but why was it necessary? Why repudiate the betrothal between Katherine and myself? And if it has to be done, why secretly?'

It was Prince Hal's voice, and Frederico listened with all his might, nearly forgetting the thud of his own heart which a moment earlier had been almost deafening him with its drumming.

'My son, we may one day be glad of the gesture. Or it may never be necessary to reveal it to the world. We are but preparing an escape for us both, should it prove necessary.' The King's voice was languid, but Frederico thought he could detect a certain urgency beneath the outward calm.

'But why, Father? Why did you ever agree to our formal betrothal, if you meant to change your mind?'

'With the death of the Queen of Castile, Katherine is less important as a marriage alliance, for her father will have to fight and woo himself friends, to keep the kingdoms of Castile and Aragon together,' Henry said. 'And you, my son, are the best marriage in Europe at present. The wench is here, in our land, living on my bounty; none can gainsay that. But should a better offer present itself – as seems likely – then we do not wish to be tied to an ailing maid, to our country's loss.'

There was a short silence; Frederico could hear the King collecting papers into a bundle, sliding pens along the table. The Prince stood silent for a moment, and Frederico risked a peep above the sill. He saw the King's back view, as the elder man sat at the table, and he saw the Prince in profile, as Hal stood beside his father, looking down at the King's bent head. The expression on the Prince's face was

. . . . enigmatic. A closed, secret look, as though he, too, had formed his own opinion and would now in turn, keep his own counsel. Then the King said, 'And now we will eat, Hal!' and glanced up at his son, an affectionate smile lightening his rather gaunt features.

Immediately the Prince's strange look vanished. His eyes returned the smile, as his lips did, and the momentary constraint was gone from his manner. He gave the King his arm, and together, father and son left the room.

Frederico turned and padded, heedless now of secrecy, across the terrace. He jumped down onto the lawn, his mind seething with speculation. So the Prince had repudiated his betrothal to Katherine, eh? Or had done so at the King's command, rather. He would not tell his Princess, of that he was certain. She had been hurt enough by these blunt Englishmen, and need not, at this juncture, be hurt further. He wondered in whom he should confide. Dona Elvira? Doctor de Puebla? Then he remembered Prince Hal. What *had* he thought? How had he felt, when told that he must swear the marriage contract null and void? The page had said Hal had stamped and frowned, not best pleased.

Very right and proper, thought Frederico. But why had he given his father that strange, unfilial look? As though, had he had a dagger in his hand, he would have plunged it through his father's heart without a moment's compassion. Yet when the King had smiled at him, Hal's answering smile had been that of an angel, no less.

Frederico hurried into the stable where he had left his lean horse, and mounting the animal, turned its head in the direction of Durham House. The Prince was a real man, who would hesitate, and rightly, before so dishonouring a lady. Yet the thought flashed through his mind that there were two sides to young Hal, right enough, and one of them was a mighty strange side, to put it no stronger. On the heels of the first thought came another. Might it not be a better thing for the Princess, if her betrothal to the lad *were* broken off? After all, the father had shown the sort of man he was years since, according to gossip he had listened to when they were lodged in Ludlow Castle. Many of the retainers there believed Henry had killed not only King Richard, but his two nephews also.

His horse slipped on a strip of uneven cobbling and Frederico swore and jerked the reins. That was what came of letting one's thoughts wander when riding! And anyway, it did not do to look too hard at royalty, for both Katherine's parents had behaved in a somewhat ruthless manner as they struggled to gain their crowns.

He sighed, and slowed his mount as Durham House loomed up. He would have to concoct a story for his Princess, now, to account for his long absence and lack of news.

'You call the King a dishonourable man, Princess, because you have discovered his treachery over the matter of your betrothal to his son. I agree that it was bad, certainly. If I can mend matters, I will do so. Yet when I tell you that Dona Elvira could be making mischief by encouraging a meeting between Philip of Burgundy, your brother-in-law, and the English King, you insist that your duenna knows best.'

'Certainly I do, Doctor Puebla,' Katherine said coldly. She could not bring herself to like the little man, with his cold lizard's eyes and his ingratiating manner. 'And why should treachery towards myself be in any way connected with a meeting between Philip and the King?'

De Puebla was too canny a man to say outright what he plainly thought she ought to recognize – that a man who would be treacherous to his daughter-in-law would not hesitate to use the same methods towards her father and brother-in-law if it suited him – but he argued as best he could, nevertheless.

'This is a matter far deeper than you can understand, Princess,' he said, his voice breaking with feeling. 'Don Juan Manuel is not what he seems, he is . . .'

'Don Manuel is Elvira's brother and was my mother's trusted friend and closest adviser,' Katherine said. 'Oh, would that he were by my side now!'

'I cannot force you to listen to me,' Puebla said sadly. 'But there was a time, Princess, when you yourself thought that Dona Elvira ruled your household with too firm a hand. I tell you that Don Juan Manuel, truly though he loved your mother, hated your father. Now that your mother is dead, he works for Philip at the Burgundian court. Do you think he means the King good?'

'You should not speak against Don Manuel in such a fashion,' Katherine said quickly. He is jealous, she thought, because he knows now that I would prefer to have Elvira's brother here in England as the Spanish ambassador, rather than himself.

Puebla sighed. 'I am sorry. And I did not come here to quarrel with you, but to tell you that there is trouble between King Ferdinand and King Henry. Your father has refused to ratify the trade agreement giving England preferable terms in Spain, so that English merchants have been ruined. King Henry is very angry, and though he says he will ruin the Spanish merchants, I fear we have not heard the end of this business.'

Katherine sniffed contemptuously and turned her shoulder to the ambassador. 'Trade agreements! I know naught of them,' she said coldly. 'But the insult to me and my father, contained in the broken betrothal, surely will not go unchallenged by Spain?'

De Puebla shrugged. 'You know best, Princess,' he said, matching her coldness.

She stared at him for a moment, perplexed, then bade him farewell and turned once more to her embroidery.

'Though what the King of England can do to harm the Spanish ruler, I cannot imagine,' she said brightly to Maria de Salinas. She picked up a small pair of scissors and snipped off a length of bright orange silk. 'Against a king as strong as my father, Henry is powerless.'

Within a week she knew what he could do, for she had been told firmly that in future the Spanish ruler must provide for his own. Henry had withdrawn her allowance.

'You are looking very happy this morning, Princess,' Doctor de Puebla remarked almost jovially. 'Where are you hurrying off to? You look as though you were going to a ball!'

Katherine stopped in her tracks, and so great was her excitement that she forgot for a moment her dislike and distrust of the ambassador.

'I am going to seal a letter to send to King Henry,' she said. 'My sister, Queen Juana, has written inviting me to meet her. King Philip wants to meet the King of England as you know, so Juana suggests that I travel in his train, when the two monarchs meet on the Continent.'

A moment earlier, Puebla had been worrying over his lack of means; an outstanding bill for last year's stockfish meant that he feared his own fishmonger, yet though it was still summer he knew that he ought to be ordering new supplies of the fish for the following winter. He had been wondering whether he could find a fishmonger who did not reside in Thames Street, where he was regarded with such distrust by his creditors. He had recently sold a parcel of land in Spain; the money should reach him soon, so that by autumn he would be in funds once more. Relieved of his most immediate worry, he had greeted his Princess with the greatest affability, therefore, and had been totally unprepared for the shock of her announcement.

His hand trembling, he took the letter she held out and read it slowly, whilst the full force of her simple act sank into his mind. She was as good as handing her own father over to his enemies, for if England and Burgundy formed an alliance against Ferdinand, the King of Aragon would speedily be overcome.

But no use to tell her, for she would never believe me, he thought. Instead, he said with hollow cheerfulness, 'Very nicely put, my dear. Very nice. But would it not be more seemly, in view of the importance of the message, if I were to deliver it to King Henry for you?'

Katherine heard the tremor in his voice, and scarcely knowing why, she shook her head and retrieved her letter from his fingers.

'Why, no thank you, Doctor. Dona Elvira has ordered Don Alonzo de Esquival to saddle the fastest horse in our stables, ready to carry my message to the King.'

She smiled again, puzzled at the old man's stillness, and then continued to walk down the corridor to the study, where she would seal her missive. She glanced back once, to see Puebla still standing as though rooted to the oak boards. Then he shook his head, and disappeared at a trot in the direction of the ante-chamber which Katherine had just quitted.

Katherine walked into her Treasurer's study and sat down and watched as he melted wax and affixed her seal. The room was musty and the rushes on the floor were stale, and she thought with pleasure that the letter was her escape from the dirt and disorder which prevailed in Durham

House. When she travelled with the King and his court to France, she would no doubt be expected to dance and to sing, to eat good food and to sleep between clean, soft sheets. She thought that it irked her more than anything that now she could no longer afford the services of laundresses, and was forced to lie in her bedding until the linen was grimed and musty.

She was sure that the King of England would jump at the chance of meeting Philip of Burgundy, and then of course she would see her dear sister Juana, and her position, she was convinced, would change for the better at once. In a rosy dream she left the Treasurer with the sealed letter, and wandered back along the corridor to her own chamber. In the ante-room she disturbed Puebla and Dona Elvira in close conversation. They looked a little conscious when they saw their Princess quizzically regarding them but Katherine only thought that their sudden amity was a good sign for the better life which was soon to be theirs.

The day continued to pass, for Katherine, in a happy dream. She ate more heartily than was her wont at the midday meal, not disdaining the mutton, though it was stuffed with spices and smothered in sauce to hide the sweet smell of incipient putrefaction.

'Maria, let us take our embroidery into the garden,' she said as they returned to their parlour. 'The day is so fine – look at that sunshine, almost like home – that an hour or so spent on the river bank could do us nothing but good.'

The maids of honour were pleased at the thought of a change in the monotony, more particularly as they knew Dona Elvira despised the open air. So they settled themselves in an arbor near the river with the mighty beeches shading them from the sun, and began to sew, whilst the soft lap of the water and the muted sounds of river traffic soothed them almost to sleep.

It was into this idyllic scene that Doctor de Puebla burst. He had hurried all the way from his lodgings in the Strand, through the hot and smelly streets of London, had taken boat on the Thames and then he had run like a schoolboy – only with less agility – all the way to Durham House. Now, sweat-streaked and piteously afraid, he begged Katherine to come immediately into the house so that they might speak privately.

Katherine looked at the old man, and for once she felt real pity for his distress. 'What is it, Doctor?' she said kindly. 'My women will leave us, for there are few places in Durham House as private as the garden.'

As soon as the women had left, Puebla forgot his years of diplomacy and blurted out the whole story.

'When you showed me the letter, I knew that if you sent it, you would condemn your father to battling against the combined force of England and Burgundy,' he said miserably. 'But how could I tell you that, Princess? How could I be the means of distressing you so? I waited, therefore, until you had taken your letter – oh, that fatal, dangerous letter! – into the study to be sealed, and I went to Elvira. She knew, oh yes, she knew what she was asking you to do! As I told you, Princess, her brother loved your mother as deeply as he hates your father. He wishes only to see the King quite undone, and he cares nothing for Spain. Dona Elvira knew this but I explained anyway, as I am explaining to you. I begged her, for the sake of her country, to tell you enough to satisfy you that such a meeting would be fatal. She promised to do so; she promised to see that the letter was not despatched. I believed her, for she is of the old hidalgo blood and, I thought, too proud to lie to one such as I; so I returned home, comforted. Yet I did not altogether trust her, so I left a stable lad outside Durham House, to warn me if anyone left for Richmond. And scarce an hour after I left your duenna, the lad arrived, hotfoot. Don Alonzo had ridden for Richmond and he cried as he passed young Geordie that he was bound for the Palace, with messages for the King, and could not linger.'

He stopped speaking, his tear-filled eyes fixed on Katherine's face.

For a moment, Katherine sat in her chair as one stunned. Then she scrambled to her feet and made for the house.

'Tell me what I must do,' she said without preamble.

They went straight to the study, and Puebla dictated a letter which Katherine wrote. In it, she warned Henry that it had been brought to her notice that the letter she had passed to him in good faith, believing it to be from her sister, might well be a forgery. She said she had been warned that Philip was notoriously unsure of himself, and might well hesitate to take the extreme step of a meeting with the English, so that the court might arrive at St Omer to find only astonished peasants to greet them.

Doctor de Puebla scarcely thanked her as he took the sealed missive from her hand and shambled with all possible speed out of the house.

And Katherine sat at the desk, alone, with the smell of the musty rushes in her nostrils and all her bright hopes crushed in the dust about her. Tears such as she had not cried for many months rose to her eyes, but she would not let them fall. Not yet. First, she must speak to Dona Elvira.

The quarrel lasted all afternoon. From outside the door, Katherine's women could hear the strident, offended caw of Dona Elvira's voice, and the increasing volume of Katherine's normally soft tones. At one stage, Dona Elvira had appeared in the doorway, a wild and somehow splendid figure with her hair falling loose across one shoulder, her headdress torn from her head so that she could run her fingers through her locks. She had cried passionately, 'My husband! My son! Come and hear what this foolish, ill-advised child believes of me, what she thinks of us Manuels. Come to me!' And then she had disappeared into the Princess's chamber once more.

And in due course, Pedro and Inigo had gone into the room, and had slunk out again. Maria de Rojas had gone to Inigo, reluctant still but aware that she should show interest in the man to whom she was betrothed.

'What is happening, Inigo?' she said, but he just shook his head in bewilderment.

'They are very angry, my mother and the Princess,' he said at last. 'I do not know why, but my mother says such things, Maria! I do not think that the Princess will listen to her for much longer.'

And then the sounds of two angry voices suddenly ceased. The listeners heard the small, steady voice of the Princess, speaking quite calmly and coldly. A wail, the sound of quick footsteps, and the door burst open. Elvira rushed out, almost into Francesca's arms, and pulled herself free without a word. Gone was the pale, self-willed aristocrat, born to command. This was a feverish old woman collecting her belongings, clutching piles of gowns and pushing them into boxes whilst she wept and railed at fate.

'We are to leave for Flanders, where my uncle is,' Inigo muttered to Maria. 'I wish that you could come with us, my love, away from this terrible place. But it cannot be. The Princess would never permit such a thing, since we are not yet married.'

The maids of honour, who disliked Dona Elvira heartily, were oppressed by her disintegration and her mouthings against their mistress. They huddled in their own room, only going out into the corridor to report, one to another, on the state of the duenna's packing.

'It is done!' Maria said at last, the relief making her voice sound almost gay. 'The last boxes are being loaded onto a cart, and the horses have been brought round. They are off at last.'

'Yes, they have gone,' agreed Katherine, emerging from her chamber where she had stayed alone since she had dismissed Elvira. 'She has been a hard trial to you, my friends, and a poor adviser to me. But now she and her family will trouble us no more.' She smiled at Maria. 'You have been cheated of another suitor, I fear, Maria,' she said. 'Inigo will never return to these shores. Are you sad?'

She eyed the other girl curiously. *Had* Maria and Inigo been lovers? They had seemed to share an uneasy betrothal, if the truth were told, with Maria seeming almost afraid of Inigo, yet making no effort to break away.

'Do you regret Inigo's leaving us?' Katherine said again, since Maria was still staring at her feet.

The girl roused herself as though from sleep, and a smile grew on her countenance. 'Why, no, I am not sad,' she said. 'I feel as though I had been given a second chance, Princess. As though the slate had been wiped clean, and I can start building up my life again.'

14   Meetings

Despite the gloom of the day, the Old Exchange was crowded with people. A fall of snow had been largely dispersed by the press of the throng, but now a light sleet fell, stinging cheeks, soaking cloaks, turning the road to mud which speedily became a bog near the shop doorways where the press of people was greatest.

The crowds were shabbily dressed but the shops were brighter, for it was here that the goldsmiths plied their trade and in the warm light of candles, lit against the January gloom, the gold gleamed in the form of bracelets, necklaces and brooches. Katherine and Francesca stood in the doorway of the shop, where they had been bargaining with a certain amount of difficulty, and Katherine rubbed her wrist ruefully, where the thick gold bangles would no more softly clash against each other, and catch in her shabby skirt.

'Where is Frederico?' Francesca whispered. 'Why did he not come in with us, Princess? My English is good you say, but his is better; the pawnbroker would have had no difficulty in understanding him.'

'I wanted to manage the transaction by myself, to see whether I could get more money than Frederico,' Katherine explained. She smiled rather bitterly. 'It is now obvious that these pawnbrokers are businessmen, who are not to be swayed by a woman's face.'

They stood in the doorway of the shop for a moment, the warmth from the fire making them reluctant to step out into the chill, until a mutter from the lean-visaged old goldsmith reminded them that the draught was cruel to one who wore only a thin gown over his doublet and hose. Reluctantly, Francesca pulled the little blackened door shut, and they were outside once more, with the cold making them puff smoke into the air, and the mud underfoot sucking at their worn shoes.

Frederico, sheltering in a doorway opposite, saw them, and made his way across the street, weaving with experienced ease between the press of people and the sliding hooves of horses.

'Did you manage all right without me?' he asked anxiously. 'I nearly came in, Princess, to make sure . . .'

'Hush,' whispered Katherine. 'Not "Princess" here, Frederico. I've no desire to be pointed out by the passers-by. Can you lead us to Soper's Lane from here? We wish to buy pepper, and certain other spices, with some of the money the man paid for the bracelets.'

Frederico looked down at the women's feet. 'It is a bitter walk in this weather,' he explained. 'Would it not be better to return to Durham House now, and sally forth another day for spices? You could buy your cloth then, also, for the drapers of Lombard Street are best visited on a decent day, lest you let a roll of silk fall into the mire, or buy the wrong colour by candlelight. It is a foul day, mistresses.'

'All days at this time of the year seem to be foul,' Francesca said gloomily. 'And we must eat. The taste of stockfish grows passing dull, Frederico, and our mistress can wait for her cloth as you suggest until the weather grows more clement. What say you, lady?'

Katherine, starting slightly at the form of address, said stoutly, 'I am with you, mistress. Lead on, lad!'

As Frederico had warned them, it was a bitter walk. By the time they were descending the steps and pushing open the grocer's door, Soper's Lane had lost much of its attraction for them, though the streets signs, depicting stange lands and stranger people plucking exotic fruits, splashed colour above the gloom of the muddy street.

The shop was low-ceilinged and dingy, but the smell of cloves and spices warmed the little party as much as did the heat from a charcoal brazier burning in the middle of the room. The shopkeeper came running out from his backroom, delighted to see two ladies wrapped in their dark cloaks with a little lad to fetch and carry for them, then halted, uncertain. As he drew nearer, he could see the thinness of the material and the shine of much wear across the shoulders of the cloaks.

'What can I get for thee?' he said, peering first at Katherine's small, well muffled figure, and then at Francesca's taller and more willowy frame. 'It is a mortal cold day, good dames, for the like of you to be abroad.'

There was an undoubted question in his tone, but Katherine ignored it. 'The boy has a list of our requirements,' she said, speaking carefully so that her accent would go unnoticed. But she was safe enough; the Spanish Princess who lived in Durham House was not often brought to mind; if they thought about her at all the people assumed that the King looked after her. Certainly no one would have expected to find her wrapped in a cloak which was both darned and dirty, buying pepper in a screw of paper, and haggling over the price of a pinch of saffron and a few nutmegs.

When, finally, their purchases were complete, Katherine gave the parcels to Frederico and they sallied forth into the cold chill of the afternoon once more, to find that the sleet had increased in their absence to something very like a hailstorm. From the slight shelter of the doorway they watched, dismayed, as the hailstones bounced on the cobbles and drove themselves into the soft mud. The weather had thinned the crowds, too, and though people still walked and rode along the streets, they were plainly going about their business, and no one loitered to look at wares, or to buy roast chestnuts from the sellers.

'There is no help for it, I shall have to go back to the house now and bring a litter,' Frederico said firmly. 'You are both mired to the knees already and Jesu, this hail! I will not be long, so stay here, in this doorway.'

He would have darted off into the storm but Katherine caught his arm. 'No, Frederico,' she said urgently. 'The King is insisting that we move from Durham House now that Dona Elvira is no longer present to chaperon us. He thinks it would be better if some noble lady amongst his court performed the duenna's role. Now imagine what would be said – what would be thought – if it became known that the Spanish Princess and her maiden went shopping for food in the London streets? No, I would sooner die from cold and exposure. We must and shall walk home.'

Pulling forward the hood of her cloak, she grasped the arms of her companions and thus linked, they stepped forward into the storm. The wind buffeted them, hurling spiteful hailstones into their faces so that they gasped and closed their eyes against the missiles. And it was thus that the accident happened.

Francesca had closed her eyes against just such stinging hail. She was walking near to the houses, and had bent protectively so that the top of her head, rather than her face, met the worst of the weather. And, suddenly, it met a doorpost, built rather further out over the street than its fellows. The blow made her reel and she released Katherine's arm, staggered, and felt a sharp pain like a knife stab at her ankle. The road rushed up to meet her, melting puddled hail in shining, light-reflecting pools twisted before her vision, and then there was darkness.

She could only have lost consciousness for a few seconds. She swam back to feel the cold of a curved cobble against her cheek, hearing the sound of Katherine's voice, suddenly shrill, demanding assistance of some passing stranger. Then hands lifted her, propped her up against the house, and from within, smells of cooking and a flower scent drifted to her nostrils. Vaguely, she saw that the door was open, and realized that she was being carried over the threshold. A voice she knew was talking to Katherine, and she suddenly recognised Puebla, his narrow ferret-face lined with concern as he spoke urgently to the Princess.

Francesca turned her head slowly, and found that the room no longer swam before her eyes. Her ankle still hurt, and she raised a faltering hand to her brow, where, as she suspected, she could feel a huge lump forming, but already she felt more mistress of herself.

Puebla was still speaking to the Princess, but now she became aware of another man, who leaned against the panelling, watching with some amusement the agitated gesticulations of the ambassador. He was tall and broad-shouldered, with crisply curling grey hair, and from what she could see of his face in the flickering candlelight Francesca judged him to be in his forties.

'Doctor, you are quite right, your Princess must be conducted to Durham House with all speed, and by your good self. But there is no need to drag this little maid with you before she is well enough to be moved. My housekeeper will look after her, bathe her head and tidy her hair, and then I will see that she is brought home in good time, and without scandal.'

The man spoke good English, yet Francesca judged him to be a foreigner. Not Spanish, she knew that. French possibly, or Italian.

De Puebla turned to him, his expression one of profound

relief. 'Signor Grimaldi, I shall be for ever in your debt,' he said. 'If you will take good care of the young lady, I shall go at once with the Princess, and deliver her safely to Durham House and then I will return for the Lady Francesca.'

Francesca leaned back in her chair and said in a small voice, 'I can go right away, Doctor de Puebla, if it is necessary. I am recovering my strength fast.'

'Nonsense,' said Katherine briskly. She came and stood beside Francesca, laying her hand lightly on the other girl's brow. 'You cannot leave whilst your ankle still gives you pain, and that is a nasty bruise on your head. Doctor de Puebla is going to take me home in a litter, and when he returns, the same litter can convey you to Durham House.'

'Very well,' agreed Francesca weakly. She leaned back in her chair once more and closed her eyes. She heard the clatter of departure as the Princess, Frederico and the ambassador left the house, then silence settled on the room once more, and she opened her eyes.

Grimaldi knelt by her side, moving a footstool so that he could lift her foot gently onto it, and a rosy and buxom woman with an enormous white cap stood beside him holding a bowl of steaming liquid.

'Dame Alys will bathe your face and then your ankle,' Grimaldi said softly. He lifted her foot from the stool and peeled off her stocking, dropping it in a soggy heap on the tiles. He touched the swelling gently, pressing his fingers lightly into the puffy, painful flesh. 'You will not be able to walk for a day or two,' he said. 'But bathing will ease the discomfort.'

The woman, clucking, bent and turned back Francesca's skirt and began to press a soaked and herb-scented cloth around the glistening skin of her ankle. Grimaldi stood looking down at the purpling bruise for a moment, then said, 'A stimulant would not come amiss, I think,' and left the room. When he returned with two glasses of mulled wine on a tray, the ankle was bandaged and already feeling more comfortable, and Francesca was tidying her hair into her hood as best she might, with the housekeeper's help.

'Drink up, my child,' Grimaldi said briskly, holding out the steaming glass. 'I have hired a litter, and it awaits you. I shall accompany you to your house myself.'

And despite her half-hearted protests that the boys who carried the litter would be protection enough, he walked beside her, his hand resting lightly on the edge of her conveyance, and talked of her life in the palace, his London lodgings, and his little home in the country where he hunted and relaxed after work in the summertime.

He would not accept Francesca's invitation to accompany her into the house, however.

'You will be safe enough now, Lady,' he said. 'And questions might be asked if you returned at such a time with a bachelor who is unknown to most of your companions. But I trust that we shall meet again?'

'I trust so indeed,' Francesca murmured. She thought that it might be rather fun to see Signor Grimaldi occasionally, for he was undoubtedly an attractive man, and she would enjoy his company. One good thing about the unconventional lives they led in Durham House was the freedom which it offered to those with courage enough to accept the challenge.

Katherine was waiting for her as she was helped into the little parlour, where a fire blazed up in a manner thoroughly foreign to the straitened means of the penniless Spanish suite.

'What a welcoming warmth,' Francesca said, holding out her hands to the heat. 'Are we celebrating something, Princess?'

'In a way, yes,' Katherine said. Her face looked sombre, and she too held out her hands to the fire. 'We have received instructions from the King, Francesca, that we are to move into Richmond the day after tomorrow. So Rojas thought we might as well use our hoard of sea-coal and enjoy good fires for the time that remains to us here.'

'Oh,' said Francesca slowly. 'But that is good, is it not, Princess? We shall be clothed, fed, entertained at the King's expense once we are with the court again, surely? He will not have us under his eye, and yet know us to be without means of support?'

'I don't know; once, I would have thought our lot could only be bettered. Now I am not so sure.' Katherine sat down on a cushioned chair and sighed. 'Lord, but I'm weary! Weary not only in body, but in spirit. Why does my father send neither word nor money? Why does he not either insist on the marriage between the Prince of Wales and myself, or send for me to return to Spain? If only I had taken Elvira's wicked advice and met Juana, our lot would have been immeasurably bettered.' She leaned forward, gazing into the coals as though she could see a brighter future for herself in the burning embers. 'Ah, how different is Juana's life. A Queen in her own right, wife to a man she adores, and mother to beautiful children. How I envy her now!'

The storm had roared out its fury for many hours, and the vessel creaked and groaned, longing to end its resistance and to give in to the tugging, clawing waves and allow itself to be carried down, down, into the silence and stillness of the deep ocean.

Aboard, the worst and best in men had shown itself, as with vows and screamed prayers for promise of life, they fought to save the ship first from the rigours of the storm, and then from the fire which sprang up when an over-turned lantern in the bows spilled its hot oil onto a chest of fine clothes.

The ship, indeed, was laden with fine things, for she carried the Queen of Castile and her husband, Philip of Burgundy, both of whom had to have the best of every-thing. The royal couple had taken ship in January, after weeks of indecision and delay, to sail to Corunna, where Philip would meet his wife's subjects and, hopefully, her father, Ferdinand of Aragon. And now the storm had come upon them, tearing the mast and sails from the ship, scattering the company of vessels carrying other members of their suite, and threatening even now to cast them into the depths where, king or commoner, they would all die the same death.

Philip, in truth, had been glad enough to be occupied with fighting the fire so that he did not have to think about the choking, ignoble death to be met out there in the dark waters. Worse for him than for many, he thought, because he could swim, and therefore his drowning would be more protracted. So he ran with the mariners about the heaving, slippery decks in the devilish glow of the fire, beating at the flames with a long twig broom, dipping the creaking, leaking pail into the sea when the waves ran, phosphorescence topped, higher than the masthead light. And when the fire had slunk out and died, in the face of such opposition, he watched the breakers on the shore of some country – he knew not which – as they clawed in vain for the ship, as if they knew they would yet be the death of her if they could break her back on the rocks in the shallows.

Throughout the forty-two hours of the storm, Juana had been an example to them all. Philip could scarcely spare time, at first, to look into those beautiful haunted eyes with their weird light of obsessional love for himself which filled him with enormous unease. Yet when he did, she seemed to have been washed clean of all her suspicions and jealousies by the very storm which had so nearly claimed them both, for her eyes reflected only a calm and abiding love, and a sort of pleasure that he and she, in this danger, were truly one at last.

True, she had insisted at the height of the storm in being dressed in her finest gown, her costliest jewels, and she had told Philip, 'I wish to be recognized as Queen of Castile if my body is washed ashore.' And by that statement, he had known that her obsession was not dead, but slumbering. For Philip more than any other, knew that Juana thought little of riches, or pomp and ceremony. And he knew, also, that she wished to be known as the Queen so that even in death, she might lie beside himself. She could not bear the thought that a lowly maid of honour might share his bier, whilst her body lay unrecognized.

He had begun to believe the tales of her madness that he himself had whispered, in order to gain control of her kingdom of Castile. For was not such a love as hers, when carried to excess, madness indeed? She had tried to kill one of his fat blonde mistresses, and she had shorn the head of another with her own hands, vowing that she should be shunned by all men in the future for her wanton ways with Philip the handsome.

Her passionate jealousy annoyed and at times disgusted him, for she was even jealous of his dogs, his servants, and their children, if he showed affection towards them. At first, when she had come to him from Spain, the exciting and vivacious daughter of Queen Isabella, he had been happy enough to find her loving and entertaining. But sadly, she was not really his type of woman at all, and though many thought her beautiful, Philip could not agree. She was so dark, with ivory skin where he preferred a complexion of milk and roses, and she was slender and elegant, with long hands and feet and a narrow waist, whilst to Philip, broad hips and full white breasts were beauty. So he resentfully went to her bed, annoyed and peevish with the inadequacies of her slender body, wanting only the comfort of knowing her pregnant so that he could seek elsewhere for sexual satisfaction.

'The only chance for us now, Sire, is to run for harbour.'

The captain of the vessel spoke politely, as though hesitating to interrupt his master's reverie, but it was no request which he made, and he and Philip both knew it.

Philip protested, however, unwilling to put himself into the hands of whoever ruled the cold, rock-girt land. 'I thought the worst was over,' he said.

'It may blow up again at any moment,' the captain told him, 'and we are in no position to withstand another battering. We're near enough to the shore to be able to work our way into this harbour at high water, but if we fail, and are driven past . . .' His eloquent hands showed what a disaster that would be.

'Very well,' Philip said grudgingly. 'I shall go to my cabin for a while.' As the other turned to return to his duties he added, 'What country is it, beyond the breakers?'

The man tried to hide his astonished surprise at the Archduke's ignorance. 'Why, it is England, Sire,' he said.

The rooms set aside for the Princess and her suite were cold and unwelcoming. Katherine stared round the room where she and her ladies would sit that evening, and felt tears of temper and disappointment rise in her eyes. That she should be treated so badly! The floor was bare of rushes, though the velvet dust lay thick, and no one had walked across it to ensure that a fire could be lit in the cold hearth, far less to light one. She walked into the room, stirring up the tickling dust, and turning, said to the servants, 'Make a fire in here, and when you've done that, please do likewise in the other rooms. We must have warmth.'

The nearest servant, a sturdy young man in the King's livery, said blankly, 'What? We wasn't told nothing about *that*! The chamberlain said to bring your boxes in here but you'd got your own servants, he said.'

Katherine pursed her lips and raised her eyes to heaven.

'My servants are tired and cold, and we have brought no firewood with us, nor food either,' she said firmly. 'For tonight, at any rate, you will please light the fires and make the rooms habitable. After that, no doubt the King will arrange for us to be properly attended.'

The servants, muttering, did as they had been bidden, even laying out a supper from the remainders of the King's meal upon her board. As soon as Katherine and her ladies had eaten, they went to bed, tired and discouraged as they had never been before.

Long after the candles had been snuffed and the last ember had died in a heap of white ashes, Katherine lay awake. What is to become of us, if the King will not feed us nor pay us any money? she pondered. What sort of life will we lead, dependent upon the King for a roof over our heads, yet pushed into the lowest places, ignored, and despised?

At last she settled herself for sleep. It was nothing new, after all, to live on the King's meagre bounty. They would have to endure, as it was beginning to seem they had always done. She fell asleep on the wish that someone, somewhere, would hear her prayer for a friendly face and a helping hand in her desperate need.

The wind blew the royal flagship into the little harbour of Melcombe Regis, though others were sent spinning past, unable to take refuge though they tried to do so. And ashore, the frightened countryfolk thought that an invasion fleet was landed, and prepared them a warm reception.

But Sir Thomas Trenchard, who lived near Melcombe Regis when he was not attending on the King at court, convinced the local people that this was the Archduke Philip and his wife, Juana of Castile. Exhausted by their struggles with the storm, Philip and Juana were glad enough to take shelter in the Trenchards' house, and to accept hospitality and help in refitting their ship.

And because there was little alternative, Philip agreed to go to King Henry's castle of Windsor, to be a guest of the royal family until such time as his ship was fit to leave for Spain once more.

Katherine, it seemed, would have her wish.

In the warm candlelight, Katherine's face looked back at her from the mirror, seeming quite as young and carefree as she could desire. Daylight, she reflected, would show Juana the worry lines round her eyes, the new hardness which had changed her; but for tonight, at least, she and her sister could laugh and speak of their childhood. Time enough tomorrow to notice the sad changes which the years had wrought.

'It will be so pleasant, Princess, to see Queen Juana, and to remember our happy times together,' Maria de Rojas said, putting Katherine's thoughts into words. 'But why has she not been here long since? The Archduke Philip has been with the court for many days, yet the Infanta –

that is to say, the Queen – tarried with her ladies in Dorset. I should have thought that the Archduke could have brought your sister with him, as she is so fond of her husband.'

'Yes, but rumour which says Juana is overfond of Philip does not say also that Philip loves Juana with the same devotion,' Katherine said solemnly. 'We must not judge either of them, Maria, but I own it was a disappointment to me when the Archduke arrived without his wife, and seemed reluctant to say when she would join him, if at all.'

'I daresay you will find your sister much changed,' remarked Margaret Plantagenet, who had come to help Katherine to dress. 'Marriage changes a woman, and bearing children deepens her understanding of life and death. You must not expect to see the lighthearted Infanta who said her farewells to Spain so many years ago.'

Katherine stood up, and twisted around in an endeavour to catch a glimpse of her backview in the small metal mirror. 'Am I looking my best?' she enquired anxiously. 'Jesu, but I believe being thin becomes me!' She laughed a trifle bitterly. 'And it is easy enough to remain thin at the King's table,' she added.

Margaret walked over to the Princess and adjusted the narrow chain girdle which hung round Katherine's hips.

'It is all the dancing and singing you have indulged in of late,' she said teasingly. 'You have shown your brother-in-law, at any rate, that you are as bright and happy as can be. He seemed to appreciate your admiration of his skills in the joust and on the tennis courts as well, so he will doubtless report most favourably to his lady wife.'

They moved out of the room, Katherine anxiously adjusting the new hood which framed her face so becomingly. 'The Archduke has not been faithful to my sister,' she said abruptly, in a low voice. 'He is a guest in this land, yet he takes himself a mistress within two days of leaving his wife to recover from her terrible sea voyage. Surely this is not right?'

Margaret patted her arm comfortingly. 'The ways of the great are strange,' she said. 'Philip did not *choose* his wife, had not set eyes on her until their wedding. Your sister, I believe, is black-haired and slender, and the Archduke takes mistresses who are plump and fair; yet this does not mean lack of love, but merely that he is a man who needs more than one woman.'

Katherine sighed. 'Men are so different from us females, are they not, Margaret?' she said. 'But now we shall see my sister for ourselves.'

The doors of the great hall were open and from within, sounds of laughter and music drifted out into the stone corridor. Katherine straightened her shoulders and swept into the hall, whilst Margaret hung back to tweak the train of stammel velvet straight and to check that the Princess was looking her best. They hovered for a moment inside the doorway, whilst Katherine searched for her sister so that she might watch her for a moment, unobserved.

Standing near a fireplace, slightly apart from the rest of the court, Prince Hal was talking to a slender woman whose white and perfect profile was towards Katherine. As she watched, the woman turned slightly, and Katherine saw her face, set with large, dark eyes beneath shapely black brows. The cheekbones were high, the nose straight, the mouth a little sad; in fact, the whole face spoke of melancholy and suffering.

Katherine stared for a moment, unbelieving. Was this Juana? It could not be! Her sister's face had been pale, perhaps, but it had been the healthy pallor of a spring flower, and her mouth had been firm, tilted, quick to smile and tease, loving to talk, to laugh.

The woman looked towards them for a moment, but it was as though she did not see them. Then she turned back and they saw the great, haunted eyes raking the hall, skimming quickly over unregarded strangers, until they came to rest on him she sought. Philip. Yet even in finding him, there was no joy, or repose. Her hands fluttered to her throat, then with a visible effort she lowered them again, gripping her fingers so tightly that her knuckles showed bone white.

Even across the width of the great hall, Katherine could feel her unhappiness, her bewilderment.

She stepped back from the throng, drawing Margaret into a quiet corner. 'It is Juana,' she said blankly. 'But so changed! She was always laughing, Margaret, very emotional, with tears in plenty for sadness to be sure, but with mirth and wit beside. Why is she so quiet and melancholy? She did not recognize me, though she stared for a full minute.'

'You cannot be sure that she even saw you,' protested Margaret. 'And you've grown up since you met last, Princess. Then you were a child, now a woman. Come, you must speak to the Queen, and probably you will find her very little changed beneath her new and queenly dignity.'

They moved amongst the people until they stood before Juana. Prince Hal, apparently unnoticed, still stood nearby. He smiled at Katherine, who smiled briefly in return.

'Juana?' she said tentatively. The older woman brought her gaze to focus on Katherine's small, anxious face.

For a moment she gazed without speaking, then she said, 'Catalina? Can it really be you? Ah, it seems a lifetime since I saw you last, and then I was happy. Yes, I was happy, in Spain.'

'And I was happy too, sister,' Katherine said fervently.

'To think how I longed to be a woman grown so that I, too, could leave Spain and become the Queen of a foreign land. I meant to do so much for my country!'

Juana looked at her sister with more attention. 'You are not happy.'

It was a statement, not a question, but Katherine shook her head. 'No, Juana, I am not happy. My first husband died, you know, and since then . . . but I forget my manners. Prince Hal is my betrothed, dear Juana! Hal, have you met my sister?'

The Prince glanced from one face to the other, and a blush, deep and fierce, swept up from the neck of his doublet and dyed his face scarlet. 'We have met, Katherine,' he said. 'Queen Isabella has daughters more fair than most.' The compliment had an agonized sincerity, and his voice broke and squeaked with adolescence, so that the colour already staining his fair skin darkened.

Juana swept him with her unsettling, indifferent gaze, and then her eyes were far from them once more, searching, searching.

Katherine noticed with pain that Philip had seized the long, yellow locks of the maid of honour on whom he had lavished his attentions earlier. He was pulling her towards him, joking, pretending to capture her as a fisher draws in his net. Katherine thought that it was all in play, probably a gesture of friendship towards King Henry, for the handsome and slow-witted Philip probably believed that to please another man, one should admire his women. But the look of naked agony on Juana's face was more than she could bear.

'Shall we go to your apartments and talk a while, sister?' she said timidly. 'I would ask you to my rooms, but they are small and at this hour the fires will not be lit.'

Juana wrenched her attention from her husband and

blinked like a sleepwalker roughly roused. 'My apartments? Yes, yes, of course,' she said. She took the hand which Katherine held out and together they set off across the hall. Prince Hal, forgotten once more, watched them go.

Katherine and Juana walked without speaking along the corridors until they reached Juana's apartments. They entered, and some Spanish women standing by the window watching the courtyard below, turned, smiling uncertainly at their mistress.

'Leave us,' Juana said. The women rustled from the room, and Juana sat down on a chair near the fire, indicating another to Katherine. 'Now, little sister, tell me about your life in England,' she said gently. 'Your betrothed seems a handsome young man; is he kind, and attentive?'

'Oh, Juana, I am so unhappy here,' Katherine burst out impulsively. 'The King will not give me an allowance, my women have not been paid for years, nor the rest of my suite, and we are hard put to it, sometimes, to find sufficient food, let alone clothing. And our father will not send! Not one *maravedi* has come to me from Spain. No attempt has been made to send the rest of my dowry, yet the marriage date between myself and the Prince is less than six months distant.' She sighed. 'He will not wed me, I know, unless my dowry has been paid, and even then . . .' Her voice trailed into silence.

'I, too, have known unhappiness and little else, since I left Spain,' Juana said quietly. 'Philip is the best of husbands, but he is sometimes unfaithful. You may find it difficult to believe, Catalina, but he has strayed from my bed more than once.'

Katherine, who had heard the gossip that Philip kept numerous mistresses and only slept with Juana when his women were not available or when he wished his wife to become pregnant, was silent. What could she say? Did Juana really think that the stories of the Archduke's notorious infidelity had not reached the English court long since?

But Juana spoke without waiting for an answer. 'I can give you a little money, to relieve some of your hardships,' she said. 'I, too, have always to ask Philip for money for my personal use.'

'This is not money for personal things, it is for food,' Katherine murmured.

But Juana did not appear to have heard her sister. 'They say I'm mad,' she remarked, her voice low and pensive. 'My own husband tells folk I am mad, unfit to rule. That is why he takes me to Castile, so that he and my father can meet and agree that Philip must rule my people for me, since I cannot be queen in more than name.'

Katherine was shocked into angry speech. 'Then Philip lies,' she said hotly. 'You are not mad, Juana! Unhappy, perhaps. Lonely and neglected, yes. But never mad.'

'You must not speak against the Archduke like that,' Juana said. 'He does not lie. It is his lust to rule Castile; because of that he would do anything, say anything. But what care I who rules Castile? If I could but have Philip's love, whole and entire, what difference would it make to me who ruled Spain?'

'What of your children, Juana?' Katherine said. 'What of little Charles, and Eleanor? They must love you.'

'The children?' Juana said vaguely. 'Ah, yes, they are fine children, for they are like Philip. Have you talked much with Philip whilst he has been at the court?'

'I have seen him, and spoken to him occasionally,' Katherine admitted. 'Though he and the King have so much in common that they spent most of their time talking only to each other.'

'He admires golden-haired women,' Juana said. Her eyes scanned Katherine's face and neck closely, their expression suddenly wild and strange. 'You have golden hair beneath that hood, Katherine, and you have a pale and creamy skin, where mine is sallow. Does Philip admire you, little sister? Does he draw you apart so that he can tell you of your beauty, and stroke your silky hair?'

Katherine coloured, and tried to check the startled exclamation which rose to her lips. 'No, sister,' she said. 'Your husband hardly notices me.'

'No, for you are small and slender, and he likes his women to be buxom and jolly,' Juana said. She sank back in her chair, and laid the back of her hand against her brow. 'Jesu, I am tired! But what of him? Will he want to dance? I should be there, in the great hall, or he may dance with another. Come!'

She had risen to her feet and stood impatiently, her hand held out to her sister. Katherine rose also, and together the two women made their way back to the hall. Katherine half wished she could be alone, to think about her sister's words, but another part of her mind cried out against solitude, for alone, she would dwell too much on what had passed between her and Juana. 'Does he draw you apart so that he can tell you of your beauty?' *Why* had Juana said such a thing? Her whole attitude when they discussed Philip had been strange. Remembering their upbringing, Katherine could only marvel that Juana was willing to see herself pushed from the throne of Castile without a struggle.

She is not mad, Katherine told herself loyally, and thinking, believed it. Her sister was not mad. She was torn apart by her love for Philip and by his continuous infidelity, but she was sane enough. Sane enough for what? her thoughts continued. To rule Castile? Surely for that, except that her obsessional devotion to Philip might cause her to neglect important duties. Sighing, Katherine had to admit that she did not know how far the strange behaviour which Juana displayed towards Philip might go. One day, Juana might be mad indeed, and perhaps if she were made to rule Castile now the additional interest and responsibility might keep her sane. But even Katherine, divorced from the politics and policies of Spain for so long, had to admit that it was unlikely Juana would ever be given the chance to rule.

I will see her tomorrow, and find out more, Katherine vowed. But the next day saw her accompanying the Princess Mary and most of the younger members of the court back to Richmond, and by the time the rest of the royal party joined them there, Juana had been sent off towards Plymouth, in a litter. The sisters would not meet again.

Katherine caught one more glimpse of her sister, through the eyes of Maria de Rojas, and that disturbed her most of all. Maria had stayed behind at Windsor for an extra day, since she and the older woman had once been friends when they lived at the Spanish court together.

The two women were before the mirror in Katherine's bare little room. Maria was brushing the other's hair and preparing to coil it into its night-time net for bed. As she worked, she told Katherine more of her sister.

'She loves her children, and it has probably upset her being parted from them,' she said comfortingly. 'No doubt it will do her good to see once again the country where she was brought up. I thought that she seemed better, truth to tell, once Philip had left her, and she did not have to watch over him continually. Only one thing was – unusual – about her, after you had left.'

'What was that?' Katherine asked. She picked up a ruby clip and held it against the thick swathe of her red-gold hair, then shuddered and returned it to her jewel box.

'Well, I wished her good fortune and a good voyage to Spain, and she thanked me, though, poor lady, she seemed distressed at the thought of further sea travel. And then,' she hesitated, then plunged on. 'Then I said to comfort her, that she would soon set foot on Spanish soil again, God willing, and Juana whispered, "If there be a God, to will or otherwise." '

'I wonder if you heard aright,' Katherine said. 'Surely Juana would not allow blasphemy to pass her lips?'

Maria shrugged. 'She has changed,' she said, 'but maybe I misheard her.'

They left the subject then, to talk of other things, but Katherine was uneasily aware that Maria believed she had heard Juana's words correctly. And on thinking it over, she, too, became convinced that Juana's faith in God might well be wavering. For she looked on Philip as a man might look on a god, and he failed her, continually and repeatedly.

If there is madness there, it lies at his door, Katherine found herself thinking angrily, and was glad that she had seen her sister for those brief hours, for Juana had changed, and would change more.

The maid who had played about the halls of the Alhambra had gone, and the woman who had taken her place was a stranger to gaiety. No more than that, Katherine told herself firmly. No more than that, yet.

15 Conspiracy

The writing straggled across the parchment, as it had straggled across so many parchments for so many years. Sometimes the page had to be torn across, because the daughter of Spain would not allow her tear-stains to be carried across the seas to her father's kingdom, and sometimes the sheer uselessness of her task overcame her, so that the letter was destroyed.

But today, the words which she wrote must reach her father, however badly she was expressing herself.

'This man, Fuensalida, whom you sent to help me and to further your interests with King Henry, is worse, far worse, even than Doctor de Puebla was,' she wrote, her hand trembling with indignation as she remembered how much worse. 'He is so overbearing, so conceited, above all, so tactless, that every man's hand is against him. The English King hates him, with reason, and scarcely ever gives him an audience, and when he does I live in fear, for Fuensalida will then insult the King in some way, so that my lot becomes even harder.' Katherine nibbled the end of her pen, and considered the many petty annoyances which the new envoy had caused the King to heap upon her head.

'You made me your ambassadress, when I told you that de Puebla was not managing the business of Spain at all well,' she wrote. 'And now I can only assure you that I speak as your daughter, as your country's representative, and as the betrothed of the Prince of Wales. Our lot can only be worsened by this dreadful man. Recall him, if you value our reputation, and send some more reliable envoy.'

Her plea seemed forcefully written, and she wondered what else she should tell King Ferdinand. Once again, she and her suite were lodged over the stables at Richmond, and the rooms, though bare and scented by things less pleasant than the straw which was, today, the strongest aroma, were respectable enough. The King fed them once a day when he dined in the great hall, and at the appointed hour Katherine, her women, and many of her poor, unpaid servants, put on the least frayed of the garments left to them, sat as inconspicuously as possible at the long board and filled their empty bellies.

The food was not what it had been, however. As the King grew older, his appetite grew less, for his interest in the dishes set before him was aroused only when he pondered on how much or how little each had cost. His praise for a cheap and filling dish would be unstinted, as would his censure for rich viands or elaborate confectionery. The other nobles who lived at court grumbled over the King's parsimony, but they could go back to their own homes and eat well at other times; she and her people could not.

A scratch on the door made her raise her head, and the face that peeped round the corner at her brought a smile to her lips.

'Margaret!' she cried joyfully. 'How good it is to see you. You often come to me when I am worried and unhappy, and you always make me feel that life is not so bad, after all.'

'And why are you unhappy this afternoon?' Margaret asked, crossing the floor and sitting on the stool near Katherine's desk. 'You look very busy,' she added.

'Yes, I'm writing to my father,' Katherine admitted. 'Oh, Margaret, isn't Fuensalida the most trying man! I had to apply to the King of Aragon for help, because Puebla is old and ill, even if he is honest, which I doubt. When my father sent a true Castilian nobleman, Don Gutierre Gomez de Fuensalida, Knight Commander of the Order of Membrilla, I was delighted! But what a liability he has turned out to be. He cannot keep peace with the Council and instead of talking to them, argues with them.'

'Yes, one way and another your household are none too popular at the moment,' agreed Margaret, a smile tugging at the corners of her lips. 'Your confessor, the Franciscan friar, is even unpopular with your women, I understand.'

'They think Frey Diego upholds me in my determination to stay in England until either myself or another is wed to the Prince,' Katherine said cheerfully. 'He *does* so uphold me, but his feelings could not make one jot of difference to how I shall behave. I believe myself to be betrothed to the Prince whatever anyone may say, and shall stay in this country, unless my father orders me to leave.'

'And what does he think of Fuensalida?'

Katherine chuckled. 'You should say, rather, what does Fuensalida think of my confessor? He thinks him too young to be anyone's confessor, and much too forceful and peremptory for a royal household. Frey Diego thought Fuensalida a very great man at first, because Fuensalida championed my cause with such spirit and cried out to the King, the Council, everyone, over my wrongs. But now he sees how the envoy can only make enemies for me, and is too stupid ever to trust with an important mission, and we both work to see Fuensalida called back to Spain.'

'And is it true that most of the plate and jewels, which were to have made up the dowry payment, have been sold in the pawnshops of London?'

'Not most of it,' protested Katherine. 'Some, yes. We had to eat, Margaret; what would you have had us do? I suppose the story is all round the court?'

'Yes, I'm afraid it is. But, Katherine, it is not the worst story which is whispered about your ménage.'

Rather to her surprise, the Princess did not look interested, but gave her an indulgent smile. 'Don't say you listen to such things, Margaret,' she chided. 'I take it that you've heard I am the good friar's mistress? What evil, foolish things the minds of men can invent, when they are idle! Frey Diego is handsome, for a friar, and as I've said, he is young. Enough to start tongues wagging.'

'I'm glad you take it so calmly,' Margaret said, smiling at her friend. 'I was afraid you would be shocked and horrified.'

'I was, at first,' Katherine admitted. 'Words could not describe my sick despair when I realized I was the object of the most vile slander, and helpless to give it the lie, for the most part. But Frey Diego taught me to despise such malicious tongues as those which pass on these evil rumours, and I have seen for myself that those who believe are not worth my pain. My friends, despite my pitiful situation, are many.'

'Have you told your father again that you are living from hand to mouth, and have been these three years, to my knowledge?'

Katherine picked up the pen and signed her name with a flourish. 'No, for what use is it?' she said tiredly. She sanded the letter and jerked the handbell on the desk. 'I say to my women, we will endure, and if only Fuensalida was not such a bungler something should have been arranged by now, for he has brought the rest of my dowry money, you know. All that is lacking now is agreement over the missing plate and jewels. Well, almost all,' she added, remembering that King Henry had been negotiating for the hand of several European princesses for his son, and that no word had been mentioned regarding her own marriage to the Prince.

The door was opened rather abruptly, and Frederico came into the room at a run and skidded to a halt before the Princess.

'Here is a letter . . .' began Katherine, then stopped, for the page was plainly agitated. 'What has happened, Frederico?'

'I was searching for you, Princess,' the boy gasped, his chest heaving. 'Something strange has happened. Frey Diego had been out to buy some books, and was returning through the streets with a pile of them under his arm. I had accompanied Lady Francesca and Maria, who went into the city to buy some sweet grapes for your table, and some plums too, since one of the palace servants said they were cheap today. Frey Diego was ahead of us, hurrying along, avoiding the kennel, which is always bad in summer in the Strand. As we watched, he seemed to slip. He went half down on one knee and then, as I thought, two passers-by helped him to his feet. But it was not so, Princess! The men had him by the arms and hurried him into a nearby house. We ran to the door, and I would have beat upon it, but the ladies forbade such a thing. Lady Francesca ran to get help, and Lady Maria waits, watching the house. I came back here and your treasurer and other men servants have gone to the house, but I wanted you to know about it.'

'Whatever can have happened?' Katherine cried. She turned to the door, so abruptly that she knocked the forgotten letter down amongst the rushes. 'I must go to him!'

'No, Princess,' Frederico said sharply. 'The day is hot, and there are no horses to spare. You wait here, whilst I return to the place. I will come straight back when we have broken the door down, and pray heaven, the friar will be with me.'

Francesca ran along the street with the summer stenches thick in her nostrils, as her breath was thick in her throat. Her one thought was to get to the house of the only man she knew and trusted in this part of London. She had been unable to take up Grimaldi's invitation to visit him again after the Princess had moved from Durham House, but she had met him, nevertheless. He was a banker, and came to see both the King of England and her own mistress on business. So now she ran to his house, knowing that if he could help her, he would.

He liked her, she knew. He brought her small gifts; lengths of silk, dainties for the table, and once a girdle, fashioned from links of silver leaves.

Reaching the remembered door she banged upon it, reflecting that since Fuensalida now lodged with Grimaldi, she had a double chance of assistance. If the banker was out then surely the envoy would be at home?

She heard the soft flutter of steps on the further side of the door and stood back, nursing a stitch in her side which pricked and tore like a knife-stab.

A servant opened the door and upon her gasping out her errand, beckoned her into the hall. She collapsed gladly onto a hard chair and even as she began to feel the pounding of her heart slowing to normality, a door opened and Grimaldi crossed the tiles and stood before her, his face enquiring.

Francesca explained the friar's plight, unconsciously stressing the fact that only dire necessity had brought her to Grimaldi's door, begging for his aid.

'So you come to my house only when events force you to do so,' he said, with a touch of sarcasm in his tone. 'But never fear, child. I will go at once to this place you mention and free the friar from the clutches of the rogues who fell upon him. Your ambassador will be back shortly, and I will leave a message for him so that he can see you safely back to the palace.'

'I am sorry to cause you so much trouble,' Francesca said stiffly, feeling the blush rise to her cheeks. She wished she could explain that visiting an unmarried man who lived in the city would never be countenanced by her mistress; but he should understand without being told, she thought angrily.

Grimaldi glanced at her swiftly, but only said, 'Not at all. You did right to come to me. Did you journey to the city by water?'

Francesca nodded, her eyes on his face. He was old, of course, and his hair was grey. But his vigorous movements were those of a young man. And his eyes were shrewd enough to have read that Francesca was fascinated and attracted by him, even whilst horrified by her own imprudence.

'Then I will advise Fuensalida to take you home by the same route, when he returns,' Grimaldi said, scribbling on a sheet of paper. 'I shall leave you now with my housekeeper, and will ride at once to the Strand with my menservants, in case of further trouble.'

A servant opened the front door and Francesca saw a horse, already saddled and bridled, waiting by the mounting-block. She watched Grimaldi stride out into the street and saw him mount, landing in the saddle with only the slightest heaviness. He has a very good seat, she thought as she saw him swing the cloak round his broad shoulders and urge the horse into movement. Then she leaned back and closed her eyes, allowing her thoughts to go with Grimaldi, to the house where so much must be happening.

'Lady Francesca! A servant of Signor Grimaldi came to

me where I was working for your mistress, and bade me return to this house, for you had need of me. What is wrong, my dear? And why are you here?'

Francesca opened her eyes, to find Fuensalida's worried face close to her own. He is like a well-bred camel, she thought disdainfully, disliking the long, arrogant upper lip and the liquid black eyes, half hidden by lids which folded over the irises.

Francesca forced a smile to her lips. 'Why, Don Fuensalida,' she said. 'It was good of you to come; the Princess will be grateful too, if you will escort me back to Greenwich. I came out with the Lady Maria de Salinas to buy fresh grapes for our Princess – one of the servants told us that they were both plentiful and cheap in the city today – when we came upon Frey Diego, set upon by ruffians. I came here, for help.'

The ambassador drew back, the look of alarm upon his countenance strengthening his likeness to a camel.

'Frey Diego? And you tried to rescue him? I suppose that even now Signor Grimaldi is accompanying him back to the palace. Lady, how could you be so blind? You have no more love for that wicked man than have I! You should have turned your head away, pretended to have noticed nothing.'

Francesca eyed the ambassador narrowly. His eyes refused to meet hers, and the long lip twitched, so that a bead of spittle ran down the cleft beside his mouth, to be dashed away impatiently as Fuensalida drew his hand across his chin.

'Don Fuensalida, you had a hand in the friar's downfall,' Francesca said accusingly, and before the other could answer, 'You should have trusted me, told me what was afoot. I would have given you every assistance, and certainly would not have tried to stop your bullies doing

208

their work. Why, I swear that if he did not constantly bolster up Katherine's confidence in the English marriage, we should have left this country, long since.'

'My men would have taken him, bound, aboard a ship which is even now anchored in the Thames, though it sails for Africa tomorrow,' Fuensalida said gloomily. 'Then, perhaps, Katherine would have listened to reason. But sometimes, when I've been struggling with the thick-witted monarch of this country, or when I've striven to make the Council see some sense, I truly believe that my only course should be to use force on the Princess. Get her aboard a vessel by some means, and sail away with her to Spain! Thus we could all of us be rid of this treasonous island for ever!'

'Very good, Don Gutierre,' Francesca said, and he smiled at her use of his first name with stiff-necked grati-fication, so she did not point out the impracticabilities of his scheme. He would not only have to capture the Princess, she mused, but her household, consisting as it did of some fifty Spaniards. And then someone would have to provide a fleet of ships, fully provisioned, for the long sea voyage.

As though he could read her thoughts, Fuensalida said, 'I've the money to make up the rest of the girl's dowry; what better use could be found for it, if there is to be no marriage, than to spend it in taking the Princess and her retinue back home to her father, to Spain, where we all belong?'

'It would be good to see Granada again,' said Francesca slowly. Her mind was filled with the pleasant picture of her garden at home, with her little sister, another Catalina, reaching up to pluck a glowing orange from the branch where it nestled amidst dark green leaves. Then, against that picture, another took its place. A middle-aged banker from Genoa, whose body was virile and well made, so that his great deep chest and broad, well-muscled shoulders seemed to threaten to burst from the confines of the finely pleated white linen shirts he affected. She saw his dark face with the jutting brows, the big, masterful nose and the determined chin. His lips, she remembered, could feel softly sensual, for once at the palace he had pressed them into the palm of Francesca's hand on parting, and she had felt a deep and uneasy thrill out of all proportion to the gesture.

In her mind his eyes mocked her; dark, hooded, knowing. I have yet to ask you anything, he seemed to be saying. Why should you think I am in love with you, you chit of a wench? I have known many beautiful women, and I have resisted them all.

Yet Francesca was sure that he was attracted by her, and knew also that the virility which drew her to this unlikely suitor would be difficult to find in the orange groves of Granada, where a suitable match would be chosen for her by her parents.

'My lady,' Fuensalida's voice was high-pitched, impatience blending with nervousness. 'We should return to Greenwich or our mistress may wonder what has delayed us. She has a suspicious nature I have noticed, which makes me dislike the friar the more. For why should an innocent maid suspect, unless she, also, has been taught something of intrigue?'

Francesca wrinkled her nose with distaste for suspicions which she knew to be unworthy, but stood up nevertheless, and followed the envoy out into the street. After all, she mused, life in Spain was a known and familiar quality; life with Grimaldi was not. He might believe that a wife should be repressed, living only to give birth to children. He might beat me, Francesca thought, remembering the strength which had picked her up as though she weighed no more than a kitten when she had hurt her ankle. And, shame-fully, the thought made her heart beat with something very like enjoyable anticipation.

'Someone shall suffer for this, Princess!'

Frey Diego, released, was striding the parlour in front of Katherine, shouting, the bruises on his face already beginning to show. 'Whoever did this deed shall be punished! I am a man of the church, my cloth should have protected me against a scurrilous attack of this nature. I will find out who paid those men to attack me, never fear. I will make trouble for someone, I will . . .'

Katherine listened patiently enough, though she said nothing. Francesca had confessed ignorance of any who might have attacked the friar, but Maria de Salinas had recognized one of the assailants as a horse boy employed by Fuensalida. Katherine, however, knew better than to tell the friar of their suspicions. Manlike, he was enjoying his threats, his shouting, his great strides across the rushes. But he could do nothing against Fuensalida. The ambas-sador was in the prime of life, rich and influential. Back in Spain, he could no doubt have made life very difficult for a humble friar, not that Frey Diego had ever shown him-self in the least degree humble. But in England, though Fuensalida's hands were to some extent tied, so were those of Frey Diego, a young and friendless man who was regarded with suspicion by his own countrymen and some doubt by those of his Order who had met him, because like Fuensalida, they thought him too young – and too hand-some – to be confessor to a young and impressionable Princess. So Katherine held her tongue, and sympathized with Diego whenever he paused for breath.

When at last he left them, she turned to de Salinas, a

smile on her lips. 'Maria, forgive me for not speaking of Fuensalida,' she begged. 'But it would not have helped the friar; indeed, it would probably have made much mischief. The best we can hope for is that the envoy has now wreaked his spite, and will leave my confessor alone in future. But I shall speak to him privately, of course.'

Francesca, standing attentively nearby, bit her lip with vexation. If Katherine spoke to Fuensalida, then the man would assume that she had betrayed his confidence. She would have to see him, and assure him that no word of his activities had left her lips.

As soon as she was able, she slipped quietly out of the room. She must find him now, and tell him that his boy had been recognized. And she would tell him, also, that she had some business to see to in the city, so that he would escort her to and from the palace. For one thing she had determined. Grimaldi wished to know her better, and it would take several meetings before she knew whether or not she desired his advances.

To that end, therefore, she would have to stay on good terms with Fuensalida, for Katherine would not countenance her maid of honour leaving the palace constantly without an escort.

Grimaldi was planning another present for the little wench with the big dark eyes. A gown, this time, he thought. He disliked seeing so fair a maid, with so fair a body, dressed always in dull and dusty black. He had wondered whether she would accept such an intimate gift from his hands until the Spanish envoy had returned from the palace, with some garbled tale of the little lady having business to attend to in the city, so that she needed his escort.

He had preened himself, had Fuensalida, apparently convinced that it was his spare and aristocratic frame which attracted the wench. But he, Grimaldi, knew better. He had seen the glances she had sent him, out of the corners of those big, velvety blue eyes when she thought that he was not looking at her. Glances as though she were puzzled because she found him attractive.

He laughed softly, and stroked the bale of dark blue branched velvet which lay on the table before him. It would suit her, this fine, soft stuff; it would match her eyes, too, which always pleased a woman. He conjured up a mental image of her, dressed in a low-cut gown of his velvet, with her black hair curling loose around her shoulders and the dark colour making whiter than snow the whiteness of her breasts. Jesu, but the thought of her beauty made him want her! He tried to bring to mind the other women he had wooed and won over the years, though he had never married any of them, but beside the sparkling and intelligent beauty which was Francesca's, they seemed but poor, pale ghosts.

If you want her, which you do, you will have to marry her, for she is no light woman to come to your bed, he told himself, and knew that to possess her he would marry her tomorrow, and forswear all other women.

His mind made up, he picked the material for lining the gown, and then went over to the fire and sat down in a comfortable chair, with a mug of wine to hand.

Coolly, he planned her capture.

16 Flight

It looked, Francesca thought, like the beginning of a hard winter. Already the strong and blustering gales had torn the last leaves from the trees, so that the orchard which grew between Richmond Palace and the Thames was a skeleton forest, holding out beseeching branches towards the spires and minarets of the building.

It seemed almost that as the illness of the King of England tightened its grip upon him, so the land itself was entering into the grip of winter; but God alone knew whether King Henry could throw off his ailment when spring returned.

Francesca was making herself a new kirtle, to wear with the gown which Grimaldi had given her, and the effort of stitching innumerable pleats round the wrists brought her tongue pointing out in concentration. The kirtle was nearly finished, and she would wear it that evening to dine with the court, in the great hall of Richmond. That was why she sat alone in the bedchamber shared by Katherine's maids of honour, and stitched by the window.

But whatever the state of the King's health, she thought, would life in England ever be any better for the Princess and her women than this? She knew there would be no royal marriage, for the Prince's name was bandied about by one and all, being linked first to one princess and then another. But Katherine was never even mentioned, neither in the taverns nor on the wharves where the foreign ships sailed in from the Continent, packed with goods and rumour alike. And the return to Spain, once longed for and plotted over, had somehow lost its attraction. Her uneasy friendship with Fuensalida had strengthened since the day she had discovered his plot against Frey Diego. She did not like the man, but he was useful, a mine of misinformation she sometimes believed, but he kept the channel of communication open between herself and Grimaldi.

He did not know, of course, that Francesca was in a fair way to losing her heart and her head over the Italian. He believed, as did Katherine, that Francesca had been befriended by a member of the envoy's household, whom she visited whenever possible.

But of late, Fuensalida had been an uneasy companion. He believed that rumours of war between England and Spain were true, and that if they did not leave the country soon, they would be unable to escape at all. According to the ambassador, Henry had demanded – and been granted – permission by the Pope to act as guardian to Juana's son, Charles, now that Philip of Burgundy was dead. In the name of little Charles, Fuensalida hissed, the King of England would attack Spain, and then where would they be?

No doubt the guardianship of her son had strengthened the King's attempts to win Juana's hand in marriage, now that they were both widower and widow, Fuensalida believed.

Mature reflection had not convinced Francesca that any of Fuensalida's fears were about to be realized. The King, devious though he undoubtedly was, would do better, in Francesca's opinion, to take the dowry money, marry his son elsewhere, and then ship the Spaniards off to their own country. The very fact that the King continued to allow Katherine and her suite to live in his palaces, close by the court, seemed to prove that for the moment at any rate, war was not of paramount importance in his mind.

The kirtle was progressing, and Francesca held it against herself. She had found it impossible to admit to the strait-laced Katherine that she was accepting gifts of such an intimate nature as clothing from Grimaldi, so she allowed her mistress to believe that the gowns came from an English lady of the court who had no more use for them. And Katherine, enviously gazing at the glowing materials and delicate ruffles, said wistfully that she wished *she* had a friend whose proportions so perfectly matched her own.

Francesca had felt pangs over deceiving the Princess, but these had gradually disappeared, due to Katherine's own attitude to Grimaldi. She persisted in being apparently impervious to his charms, and besides saying with a little grimace of distaste that there was something disgusting in a man over forty who wore such skin-tight hose, she appeared not to notice the banker at all. Francesca, who rather enjoyed hearing the maids of honour, and other women at the palace, saying what a fascinating man her lover was, found Katherine's attitude hurtful.

She admitted to herself now that she knew where her heart lay. She wanted to marry Grimaldi, and was happy to think that though his money might have attracted her at first, she had speedily reached the point where she would have wanted to marry him had he possessed nothing but debts. But she knew that such a marriage would immeasurably hurt her parents, and alienate her mistress, who believed firmly that one should marry within one's class; and the banker was not a member of the nobility by any means.

Yet though she knew Grimaldi could not be considered a suitable match for her, to hear him despised and spoken of slightingly hurt her as much as a slap in the face would have done.

Francesca lay the now completed garment down on her

bed and began to remove her worn velvet gown and the patched and darned kirtle. She was in her petticoat, brushing out her hair, when the door opened without warning and Katherine walked into the room. Her mouth was tight with annoyance and her cheeks flamed.

'Francesca,' she said crisply, before the other could speak, 'what is this I've been hearing? My confessor tells me that you have been gossiping about him to Grimaldi, of all people. Have you no loyalty, woman? The man is a commoner, and however fascinating he may seem, you are of noble blood! I had thought that you visited his house to mingle with persons of the ambassador's entourage, but now Frey Diego tells me that you sit at the feet of Grimaldi, have even allowed him to give you gifts. I will not tell you all we spoke of, for fear of offending you, for surely, such things cannot be true? What have you to say?'

'I have done nothing wrong, Princess,' Francesca said with assumed coolness. 'Though I *cannot* like Frey Diego, and must own to liking Grimaldi.'

'Such liking does you no credit,' Katherine said coldly. 'You have deceived me. You went to Grimaldi's house and had a secret liaison with the man, knowing full well that I believed you to be visiting the sewing woman employed by Fuensalida. Well now, thanks to my confessor, I know the truth. And I tell you that these visits must cease. You will have no further dealings with Fuensalida except under my eye, and you will never see Grimaldi again. Is that clear?'

'Princess, Signor Grimaldi wishes to marry me, he is not merely enjoying a light affair,' Francesca said desperately. 'And whatever the friar may have told you, we have done nothing wrong, nor have I deliberately deceived you. A few presents of which I knew you would not approve; yes, I took them, and now I am sorry. But little harm has been done, surely? Can I not keep the gentleman's friendship?'

'No doubt he offers marriage. No doubt, in order to lure the highly born members of my suite to visit his little house,' Katherine said, with something closely akin to a sneer. 'But he must have known that you would not marry him! A de Carceres, wed to a merchant banker! It is laughable. No, my dear, you have been foolish, but Grimaldi has been too cunning for you, and we must end his plotting. I will send a note to his house tomorrow, by Fuensalida, telling him that you have realized the gravity of your offence, and will not visit him again.'

'And if I love him?'

Katherine turned in the doorway, her expression unreadable. 'You sound like a kitchenmaid,' she said witheringly, and left the room.

For a moment, Francesca felt herself gripped by panic. It was too soon to decide, she thought wildly, too soon! She had in truth not decided to accept or reject Grimaldi's offer of marriage. She loved him, yes; but to wed would mean to lose her family for ever, and her hopes of returning to Spain. To lose the respect of her friends, and to bring her mistress's wrath about her ears. Worse, she would have been disloyal to Katherine, for to marry and leave the Princess's service when affairs in England were proving so difficult for the Spaniards was almost treacherous.

And yet . . . never to see Grimaldi again? To stay with the Princess, basking in her approval, with the love of all her friends, would be a poor substitute for the enrichment of her life which she believed marriage to the man she loved would bring.

She knew that she must decide at once, and keep to her decision steadfastly; for once Katherine's message had been sent, she would be unable to meet her lover.

Francesca did not go down to dine with the court. She stayed in her room and bent her mind upon her problem.

By the time the early winter dusk had given way to darkness and candlelight, she had made up her mind. She donned the new kirtle, and over its shimmering satin, she drew on the gown of dark blue velvet which had been Grimaldi's first really personal gift to her. She took her time over brushing her hair and pinning it back, then she covered it with a jewelled hairnet. Her cloak was old and worn, but it boasted a hood which could be pulled well over the face so she chose to wear it instead of the newer and warmer garment which had been another gift from her lover. She hesitated a long time over packing a bag with the rest of her things, then decided against it. She would have to walk from the river to her lover's home, and a bag would hamper her.

At last she was ready. She snuffed the candle with wetted thumb and forefinger and looked round her in the pale moonlight at the room she was to leave behind for ever. There were three beds beside her own, for all the maidens of the Spanish suite slept together in here. She hesitated for a moment, gazing at the comfortless straw mattresses and the thin coverings. Her friends would go on living here or in some other mean place in some other palace, once she had gone. They would be forbidden to see her, she was sure, so despite her own more affluent circumstances she would not be able to help them. They would say she had deserted the Princess, and they would be right. But she had made her decision.

She sighed, and lingered still in the doorway, a small, forlorn fugitive, who would be unhappy to stay, unhappy to go. Then she conjured up a picture of Grimaldi, as she had last seen him. Wearing a pearl-grey doublet and hose, with a white silken shirt, its many pleats emphasizing the muscular strength of those broad shoulders. She saw his face, dark

219

and slightly smiling; not handsome, perhaps, but the face of the man she loved.

Without another thought, she closed the door softly and stole down the corridor.

Sounds of music from the parlour showed her where the Princess was sitting with her women. A shadow amongst shadows, she crept down into the inner courtyard and heard the soft whicker of resting horses, and smelled the warm odours from the stable. She paused in the shelter of the half open door as the cold hit her, but it was no good now, to think of taking one of the animals. The royal grooms would never allow her to use one of their horses unless she had permission.

She crept quietly past the inviting light and noise where the King's household servants ate and made merry now that their working day was finished. She crossed the outer court-yard, not bothering to hug the shadows now, for gallants going to see their ladies, and ladies visiting friends, would be crossing freely at this time of night.

As she passed out of the palace the gatekeeper merely gave her a reminder, in a bored croak, that she must be within the gates again by ten of the clock or she would find herself benighted.

As she began to walk away from the palace, she found herself thinking that she should have walked first down to the river within the palace walls; there, she might have been able to beg a lift with some other person going towards the city. But it was too late now; she would investigate the marshes in the hope that some late boatman would be willing to take her to Blackfriars, and if she could find no one, then she must think again about the possibility of using one of the royal boats.

The biting cold was beginning to penetrate around the wrists and neck of Francesca's cloak, and her thin-soled shoes were little protection against the iron in the frosty ground. At least it was better than sinking into the marsh, Francesca told herself grimly. She beat her hands together, then gave up and pushed them up her sleeves, hurrying to where a lighter streak ahead showed the river.

But there was no one on the bank; no late boatman waited for a hiring. Francesca walked a short way along the river path, then stopped abruptly. A small rowboat, a cockleshell craft, was pushed in amongst the reeds, close to the bank. The oars rested within. Francesca did not give herself time to think. She clambered into the boat, refusing to give way to alarm at the way it rocked and tipped, even encradled in the reeds. She pushed off from the shore, glad now that she had taken her turn with the oars when the Princess had rowed on the river for pleasure.

Soon enough, though, she discovered that it was quite different to her summer pastime, to row a small boat on such an icy-cold night. The moon was out, fortunately, but its white light, whilst lighting her progress, seemed to make the inky shadows impenetrable, so that she rowed on blindly. She clutched the oars with numbed fingers and her hands, soft despite the work she was forced to do now that money was so limited, pained her greatly at first as the rough wood of the oars pierced her cushioned palms. But soon she could not even feel her hands. She struck her knuckles sharply against the boat's edge, and saw the whiteness of her skin gradually darken as blood formed in the vicious graze and welled out, to run down her fingers, but she felt nothing.

She had not rowed far, but already her breathing was laboured, and she had splashed badly with the oars once, so that the front of her skirt was wet and heavy against her knees. She saw the lights of a landing stage, and would have avoided the golden circle if she could, but she did not seem able to control the boat properly and she rested on her oars not because she wished to, but because she must. She heard voices, some concerned, some angry, as her little craft bobbed on the ripples, just out of reach of the bank. Then someone reached out with a boathook and brought her boat alongside.

'Madam, the river is no place for a lady, when . . .' a voice began, then broke off with an exclamation. 'Lady Francesca! What are you doing here, at this time of night?'

The relief which flooded her was warm and sweet. Fuensalida! He, surely, would help her?

'I want to visit the city,' Francesca tried to explain. 'I have to go to the house of Signor Grimaldi.' But her voice did not come out strongly and confidently, as she had meant it to. Instead, a reedy whisper emerged from her throat.

Fuensalida, helped by another man whose face was only vaguely familiar to Francesca, helped her out of the boat, and propped her, like a wooden doll, against the mounting block.

'The poor wench is all but frozen,' Fuensalida remarked to his companion. 'She wants to visit a lady of my household about some work which is being done. Can you sit in my barge, lady?'

'Yes, if you would be good enough to convey me to Blackfriars,' Francesca said.

Someone sniggered, and a voice suggested coarsely that it was a strange time to see one's seamstress, but Fuensalida contented himself with giving the unknown speaker an offensive look.

'Come, Miguel, Pietro, help me to get the lady aboard,' he said briskly, and sooner than she had believed possible, Francesca found herself in the small, lamp-lit cabin, with a rug draped round her shoulders and cushions at her back. She was so cold that she could not hold the rug round her, and was grateful, in a hazy and distant sort of way, when

Fuensalida came down into the cabin as the barge began to move, and tucked the rug securely round her, eyeing her as he did so with bright curiosity.

'Now, lady, you may tell me why you were on the river, alone, in that peasant's craft,' Fuensalida said. 'If you wished to travel to the city at such an hour, why did you not ask for my escort?'

'The Princess has forbidden me to consort with either yourself or Signor Grimaldi,' Francesca said with an effort. 'She is sending a message to his house tomorrow, saying that my head was turned by his gifts but that I have come to my senses at last. Once she has sent the message, I shall be watched constantly. I might never have the chance to escape. I have to explain to the gentleman myself that it is no message of mine.'

'I see,' Fuensalida said thoughtfully. 'But this means that if the Princess discovers you have left the palace, there will be trouble. You will be disgraced for ever, lady.'

'I have to see Signor Grimaldi,' Francesca said stubbornly. 'I will risk discovery, disgrace.' She smiled slightly. 'The Princess might even send me back to Spain!'

Fuensalida looked at her doubtfully, not knowing whether she was serious, then turned from her with elaborate unconcern, and began fiddling with the edge of the rug. 'I shall be disgraced, too, if it becomes known that I assisted you in this escapade,' he pointed out. He glanced at Francesca, his eyes running over her features furtively. 'But that would not matter, if only . . .'

Francesca, misunderstanding him completely, began to assure him that he might disclaim all knowledge of her, when he slid along the seat and put his arm round her, pulling her close to his thin chest.

'Oh my lady, Francesca, if only you will allow me to express the passion I feel for you,' he exclaimed. He pushed the velvet hood away from her face and nuzzled the side of her cheek.

Francesca, considerably startled, wriggled in an attempt to remove herself from his half affectionate, half amorous embrace without causing either of them embarrassment. Then, perhaps because of the sudden quickening of her heartbeats, the feeling began to slowly tingle its way back into her numbed limbs.

She uttered a low moan, followed by another. It no longer seemed to matter that Fuensalida was making fumbling attempts to get inside the rug which he had tucked, so thoughtlessly, round her person barely five minutes earlier. She doubled up, holding her agonized hands, feeling nothing but the return of the hot blood as it forced its way through to her bursting fingertips.

'Do not pull away, my little flower,' Fuensalida beseeched, wondering why the woman seemed suddenly to have become possessed of St Vitus dance. She was wagging her hands now, uttering small shrieks, not attempting to dispossess his groping fingers but showing no interest in his movements whatsoever. Such indifference was almost insulting, but Fuensalida, his normally cold and calculating soul warmed by passion, did not stop to consider the question.

It was unfortunate, for Fuensalida at any rate, that the feeling began to return to Francesca's feet just as the envoy dropped on his knees before her, intending to announce his devotion even as he tried to pull the rug away from her body. The pain bit and tore like a wolf at her ankles, instep and toes, and her foot shot out seeming, to the dazed envoy, to have suddenly become iron-shod. She caught him squarely in the doublet, and he gave a snort as the air shot out of his lungs in a woof! and he found himself being kicked furiously and aimlessly every time Francesca strove by movement to ease the agony of her throbbing toes.

The envoy tried to recover his dignity, tried to imprison the desperately pounding feet, but it was no use. Francesca, with tears running down her face as her small feet seemed to swell to huge puffballs of pain, was in no mood to listen to speeches of passion, far less to submit to seduction.

Fuensalida found himself rubbing her hands, covering her with the rug which he had thrown off so eagerly, and behaving, in fact, like a perfect gentleman.

And he realized, as he helped her off the barge and supported her wavering footsteps towards his lodgings, that so far as Francesca was concerned, he had behaved in an exemplary fashion all evening. Her pain, and the shock of her predicament in the small boat, had blotted out every other thought from her mind.

He banged loudly on the front door of Grimaldi's house, telling himself that he should be thankful things had turned out the way they had done, but half regretful that he had missed such an opportunity of arousing Francesca's passion, which he was sure was only hidden by her maiden modesty.

The door opened, and Fuensalida began, 'Tell your master . . .' when he realized that Grimaldi himself stood in the doorway. The impatience in Grimaldi's glance melted as he took in the situation and he gathered Francesca's cold, shuddering body up in his arms and strode into the parlour with her as though she weighed no more than a child.

Fuensalida, who had found that supporting Francesca from the riverside had caused his chest to heave uncomfortably, thought, unreasonably, the man's a rogue.

'Thank you for bringing her to me,' Grimaldi said curtly, and then to Fuensalida's alarm, he shut the parlour door firmly in the envoy's face. But before he had deposited his burden on the couch, Fuensalida had seen Francesca's arms curl confidingly around Grimaldi's neck.

So that was how the land lay, Fuensalida reflected. Poor, foolish wench, to waste her love upon an Italian merchant banker when he, the cream of the Spanish nobility, would have been glad to favour her with his attentions. He hesitated. Should he knock on the door and demand admittance? After all, he had not realized that he was assisting in an elopement. He could tell Grimaldi that after he had talked to the lady, he, Fuensalida, felt honour bound to return her to her mistress at the palace. But on the other hand, he had noted the ease with which Grimaldi had lifted Francesca in his arms, the way his muscles had rippled when he moved. It was possible that Grimaldi would strongly resent any interference in his affairs.

One was certainly not afraid of violence – but perhaps a compromise? He left a boy sprawling in the hall, with instructions to wake him the moment that the Lady Francesca left the parlour, and desired to be conveyed back to Richmond.

Then he retired to his bed, where he enjoyed an undisturbed night's sleep.

They were married next morning. Fuensalida was an uneasy witness, and in fact it was he who brought the priest, at Grimaldi's request.

'You will be married within the hour – but only if you desire it,' the envoy said nervously, and, 'We both desire it,' Francesca said demurely, with mischief in the slanting glance which she sent to Fuensalida, though the submissive adoration in the expression which she turned on Grimaldi told its own story.

She wore the blue velvet gown which her lover had given her, with a wreath of snowdrops in her dark hair. It was a hurried wedding, and not before time, Fuensalida found himself thinking accusingly, every time he caught the swooning look of love in Francesca's eyes.

'Princess, I believe that Francesca is *happy*,' Maria de Salinas said timidly. 'She truly loves the man, and though she has given up much to be with him, I do not think she will regret it.'

Katherine closed her lips firmly, hemming a shift with quick jabs whilst she gazed unseeingly at her work.

'I have not seen her, of course,' Maria explained hastily, 'but I have spoken to Fuensalida. Francesca desires only that she be with her love. Surely, it is better that they are happily wed, than that Francesca should have stayed here, fretting but dutiful?'

Katherine lifted her eyes to her friend's face, and Maria saw them tormented.

'I am becoming bitter and envious,' Katherine said slowly. 'I feel no pleasure over Francesca's happiness. Indeed, I find it difficult to believe that she *wanted* to marry Grimaldi. Oh, he's a lusty man enough, I daresay,' she went on, over Maria's murmur of protest, 'and no doubt he knows how to treat a woman when he woos. But to marry an Italian nobody! Well, she has chosen her bed, and now she must lie on it, however uncomfortable it may prove to be.'

But it was not the thought of Francesca's foolishness which gave her lips their bleak line, nor made her eyes so cold. It was the thought of Francesca's happiness, Francesca's state of married bliss. Katherine had not been indifferent to Grimaldi's mocking and audacious glance, nor to the heavy-lidded eyes and the lips with their sensual curve. She had been able to see why Francesca found him desirable. But for years, now, she had not allowed herself the indulgence of considering a man as anything but either a friend, who would help her cause, or an enemy, who would destroy her if he could. She did not wish to be tormented by useless bodily desires once more, which she had believed had mercifully ceased to visit her, years since.

And now, because of Francesca, she knew once more a stirring in her blood which she had not felt since Arthur died. The slow, aching tingle, the yearning, the surges of emotion, which she had forced herself to despise. And worst and most tormenting of all was the knowledge that Francesca had forsaken her and instead of being punished, she would know all the natural sweetness of such desires, coupled with their fruition and fulfilment.

All my women will know more of men than I, she thought, as she stitched. All of them will marry before I do, and they will be happier than I. The coldness spread from her mind to her body, so that she shivered, then, straightening her shoulders, she made a vow.

I will not admit defeat. I will not become a dried-up old spinster, full of my own failings, eyeing every passing full-grown man with frustrated desire. I will not let the King forget my claim on his son. I will marry Prince Henry! Yet even as she made the resolve, she knew that more than mere determination would be needed before ever she was married to the heir to the throne of England.

17 An End and a Beginning

The birds sang sweetly in the orchard, down by the river. The pale blue sky overhead was reflected again in the gently flowing water, and Katherine watched a flotilla of great white swans floating along on the current, and thought about the story that swans only sing as they die.

Back in the palace, a man was dying. The King of England. The man who had contributed so generously to her misery and unhappiness these past seven years. Somewhere within those newly built walls of smooth, creamy stone, somewhere near the dying King, his son must be. That son who had been betrothed to her and who should have been her husband now, for quite two years. Yet she scarcely saw him, except briefly across the crowded court. And he scarcely noticed her.

She had seen him this morning, as he hurried towards his father's chamber, for King Henry had ailed for weeks. Young Hal had been preoccupied, his smooth forehead creased in a frown, his blue eyes gazing ahead of him, his mind already with his father. Yet for one brief instant, as she curtsied and stood against the wall to allow him and the councillors with him to pass, those eyes had rested on her, and had certainly not had indifference in their depths. Could it have been embarrassment? Or annoyance even? More likely a vague stirring of recollection; a feeling that he *ought* to know the young woman who curtsied so deeply, that once he had known her very well indeed. It could be, she knew, little more than that.

So Katherine stood alone by the river, and tried to dispel bitterness towards the dying man from her heart and to welcome into it, instead, the realization that once the Prince had named his bride, there would be no place for her here. She could go home, indeed, with no one to reproach her. For it could scarcely be thought her fault if the young Prince refused to abide by his father's half-hearted and oft-rescinded promise that his son would wed Ferdinand's daughter.

She acknowledged now, in the forgiving light of one who is about to quit the place, that England was fair, and that she had been happy here before her father and King Henry had begun to quarrel. She admitted too, that her father had not done rightly by her. Faults there had certainly been, faults on both sides, but it should have been Ferdinand rather than Henry who thought about his daughter's feelings, marooned in a foreign land without a penny to bless herself with. He had been too busy with his foreign policies, his plots, his dreams, his plans, to spare a thought for his child. He had had no time for a youngest daughter whose first husband had died, and who seemed foolishly unable to win herself a second.

Katherine lifted her face to the morning and for the first time for longer than she cared to remember, she felt young again, and carefree – desirable, even. This was not the end, but the beginning, she told herself. Henry the King would die, and go to his heavenly existence, and the Dowager Princess of Wales would die too, and Katherine would begin *her* new existence, which surely would be heavenly compared with the poverty and degradation of the past seven years.

She turned from the promise of the hard young buds burgeoning on the chestnut trees, and went back into Richmond Palace.

Outside the chamber of the dying King, Fuensalida made his last desperate attempts to persuade the Council to agree to Prince Henry's immediate marriage to his mistress. He was scarcely noticed by the men already busy with details of the new reign. From one to another he bustled, pleading Katherine's cause, but others had causes also, and less need to persuade. Eleanor of Aquitaine was favoured by some, though she was only nine and could not be wed for a time, and yet another party favoured a marriage with Marguerite d'Alençon, the sister of the heir to the French throne. She was a pretty, lively girl, and would bring a rich dowry from Louis of France, eager to secure the English alliance.

Another suggestion was the daughter of Duke Albert of Bavaria, a wench ripe for the marriage bed, who would bring the friendship of Flanders, Burgundy, and other important European states.

No one mentioned Katherine. Though the second half of her dowry money was in England, it had not been handed over and was, because of the Princess's inroads on her jewels and plate, not intact. The first half of the dowry money had been spent, long since. It seemed also that Ferdinand was in eclipse. He was surrounded by enemies and even within Castile, his regency was questioned by his own subjects.

Fuensalida tired of prowling around the palace, and took himself off to the city, to visit Puebla, the hated, the despised. But Puebla could tell the envoy nothing. He had not seen the King himself for several weeks and as he pointed out, the decision would now seem to rest more with the Council than with the dying King.

'I am dying, too,' he said, his watery eyes not sad at the prospect, but twinkling with amusement. 'No one will make much fuss when I am dead, save my creditors. Yet my son looks after me with most tender care, and I think that I am more fortunate in that respect than the King of England, for my son will mourn me truly. And will the Prince mourn for his father?' He shook his head, repeating himself as the old are apt to do. 'Will Henry mourn for Henry? Will Hal sorrow because his father is dead? The King is dead, long live the King, they say, and young Hal will shout it louder than any. For he has been kept too close, that one. None of his subjects know him – what a situation, eh? Ridiculous! They see him stride through a crowd, lift a hand at a window, pass them in the street with a quiet countenance. They do not *know* him.' He shook his head again, musing at his thoughts.

Suddenly he seemed to recall that Fuensalida had called on him for his advice, and not merely for his speculations.

'I cannot help you this time, my friend,' he said simply. 'It is true what I said, that no one knows this Prince. We shall have to wait and see.'

Francesca and her husband heard that the King was dying, and Francesca was sad, for Katherine.

'She has longed for her marriage,' she said sorrowfully. 'Indeed, hope for it has kept her spirit strong. Oh, I know I've thought her stubborn and foolish, to stay in this cold land from pride alone when it would have been the sensible thing to give in and return to Spain. But now! To see her humiliated, either to bend the knee to young Hal's choice, or to scuttle aboard the first ship for Spain! I almost wish I was back at Richmond, by her side.'

'Almost?' Grimaldi said softly. He caught her by the hips, drawing her close to him so that they stood pressed against each other, breathless at their nearness, their warm-ing love.

Francesca felt her bones melt at his touch as they always did, and raised drowned, adoring eyes to his face.

'Oh my dear love, not even almost,' she whispered.

Young Henry stood by the window, looking into the palace gardens. Behind him, the dying man in the big bed breathed . . . stopped . . . breathed again. Each breath was hoarse, slow, painful. Each breath, in fact, seemed as though it must be his last. Yet somehow, from somewhere, it seemed that he found the strength for . . . just . . . one . . . more.

Hal did not grudge his father the time he took a-dying, though the thought passed fleetingly through his head that it was a fine day for hunting. But he banished the reflection easily enough; there would be time for that.

Then he saw a woman come into the gardens, waving her attendants back to the palace. He watched her as she strolled, pensive, by the Thames, ducking under the apple tree boughs, bending to pull a primrose down by the water. Idly, he wondered who she was. He thought her fair, her very smallness and the frail quality of her arms in the skimpy black dress attracted him. As he watched, she ducked under a branch too low for her, and her hood was pulled from her head. He saw her put up a hand to pat the loose strands into place, then hesitate and with a shrug, shake loose the copper-gold burden of her hair. He gasped as it fell around her, thick and soft, rippling like a cloak of some faery metal.

The man on the bed muttered, and the lad turned obediently towards his father. But the maid in the garden was a warmth in the pit of his stomach, and a new idea came to him as he stood, remembering her.

Marriage.

He had long known it was his duty but now he realized it was more than that; it was a matter of the first importance. What little he knew of women – and it was little, indeed – he had heard from the talk of other men. Now, he would learn for himself and it would be a pleasant task, if all he had heard was true. His father had muttered of brides, pressed the importance of the marriage alliance, suggested many different princesses. Eleanor of Aquitaine, he remembered. But she was a little schoolgirl. His newly discovered manhood was repelled by the idea. Marguerite d'Alençon had been suggested; a pretty young woman with a lively wit. But the negotiations would take months, and he wanted a bride now, now! He considered mistresses and dismissed the idea, still-born. He wanted someone he could share everything with, and he would soon lose the respect of his subjects if he took himself a mistress; besides, he would not be eighteen for another six weeks.

The man on the bed sighed, and moved his head with infinite labour an inch on the pillow. To him, it had been a mighty task, but the watcher scarcely heeded it.

'My son.'

The little, dried-up whisper was yet still a command and the Prince bent, with a certain reluctance, close to the worn grey features and the mouth which dribbled spittle from its slackness.

'Yes, father? Shall I call my sister? Your Council?'

'No. Henry, you must have a wife. Do not act hastily, I beg. Do not take the Spaniard, for all their screechings. She is worth nothing, now. Wed a good alliance, my son.'

'Yes, father,' Henry said obediently, and then something in the face on the pillow made him hurry to the door.

The men waiting in the ante-chamber crowded into the room. Priests moved nearer the bed with all the paraphernalia for the last rites. Old, grey-bearded councillors formed an outer ring, some with tears on their cheeks for the reign which was about to end. The Prince stepped back, stood with his shoulders leaning against the window frame, content to watch others assemble round the figure which was the centre of attention.

He sensed, instinctively, that this was the last time. He could afford to wait, for in a few short hours, it would be he who was watched by everyone, it would be his word which would sway all these men to act as he wished.

He smoothed his hand over his red-gold hair self-consciously, then as the muttering of the priests trailed into silence he raised his eyes to the group around the bed.

A man detached himself from the others, and approaching the Prince, bent his knee.

'The King is dead,' he said in a ringing yet solemn tone, and then, louder, 'God save King Henry!'

18   A New Life

'The new King – King Hal – has sent for me. He wishes to speak to me – God knows why – and so I must look my best. He is at the Tower of London.'

Katherine did not know whether she should be excited or apprehensive, but in any event, she must look her best. She wore the last remaining black gown with some pile still on the material, and rubbed her cheeks to pink with her finger-tips. Her hair could not be loose at a time of national mourning, but it was brushed smooth as satin before the hood was set on her head. Her women were as nervous as she, clustered in the bows of the barge when they set off from Richmond by water. They believed that the new King meant to tell their Princess himself that she must leave the land, and thought it kind of him, on the whole. There was very little hope in their hearts as they waited in an ante-room at the tower, and only the mildest curiosity.

Henry heard the noise of her arrival and hurried to the window to look down on the landing-place, but he could see nothing of her except for the top of a black hood. He wondered whether she was still as fair as he had thought her when they had first become betrothed. He remembered her quite clearly as she had been then; a small creature, with lovely skin and eyes, and a gentle mouth. But since then, he had only seen her amongst her women when they dined with the court; a figure dressed always, it seemed, in shabby black, with her face pale and worry lines round her eyes. How would she look now?

An abrupt rattle on the door heralded her entrance and they faced each other across the small room. Henry thought with a shock of surprise, why, it is the maid who lost her headdress in the garden when my father lay dying, and then felt he had always known it, in his heart. He held out his hands to her, smiling his charming smile, and said re-assuringly, 'Katherine, I would prefer a quiet and speedy marriage, so that you may share my coronation. But you must decide. Would you rather wait a while, and be married before all the people, with full pomp?'

Katherine stared, her blue eyes wide, a flush gradually

bathing her face in rose. 'Do you wish to marry me?' she said, her voice rising to a squeak.

Henry laughed, more at ease because of her obvious confusion.

'It was agreed, was it not?' he said lightly. 'I told you, when we became betrothed all those years ago, that I thought you fair, and wished to marry you.' He gestured impatiently. 'Yes, I know my father had changed his mind, he thought it better to marry into the Flanders or the French alliance. But I am King now, and I must choose for myself. Katherine, do you *want* to marry me?'

This brought her head up with a jerk. The blue eyes fastened with painful intensity onto his, and he saw her lower lip tremble. Then she said, 'Want to? Oh yes, indeed, Henry!' and he laughed triumphantly, crossed the distance between them in two strides, and took her in his arms.

For a moment she stood, small and astonished, not moving. He felt her sob, just once, then her arms reached up to his shoulders and she relaxed against him, warm and soft and supple. He swung her off her feet and sat down, holding her on his lap. She seemed so young now, with her face shining with triumph and excitement, that it was impossible to believe she was five years the older. With trembling fingers he pulled off her headdress and pushed impatient, square-tipped fingers through her hair, so that it fell, warm and sweet, upon his hands. He bent his head and tasted her lips, feeling them tremble and soften beneath his own. Then, sighing, he allowed her to scramble to her feet, so that they might confront the Council together.

Later, he congratulated himself upon his decision. He wanted her now, as he had wanted her when he had watched her from his father's deathbed. And he would marry her, he told himself virtuously, as much because it was his duty so to do as his pleasure.

He wondered what she was thinking, and felt a rush of pride that in bestowing himself, he had bestowed so much. She would be Queen of England because he loved her. He knew himself to be tall and strong, and had seen admiration in many eyes since he grew to his full strength. Yes, little Kate was a fortunate woman, he thought; then he remembered the cascade of bright hair, the straightforward gaze of clear blue eyes, and the rounded curves he had felt when he hugged her.

I, too, am fortunate, he thought complacently.

They were married. England waxed sentimental over their love, and the Council beamed and winked at the speed of Henry's decision. And now, the two Marias and Inez were preparing Katherine for the marriage bed. They had bathed and scented her, unbound her gleaming hair and brushed it until it shone again, laughed with her, and envied her loudly.

'He is like a sun god,' de Salinas said. 'His thighs are powerful from the hunt, yet he has never known a woman!'

'Soon enough we shall leave you to enjoy your bedsport,' Inez reminded her, 'and when we come to dress you tomorrow morning, you will be Queen indeed!'

A murmuring outside the door sent them flying across to the bed to pull back the sheets and ease Katherine between them. Henry entered with an abruptness which led Katherine to suspect that he had been pushed. She saw a glimpse of laughing faces over his shoulder, then her view was obstructed by the breadth of him as he squeezed past the door, and shut it in the gleeful, affectionate faces of his friends.

For a moment he leaned against the oak, his chest heaving, the smile he had worn for those outside slow to die from his lips. Then he crossed the room and knelt beside the bed, so that his head was on a level with Katherine's.

'Don't be afraid, Kate,' he said, his voice tender. 'For there is nothing to be afraid of.'

In the palace, the dancing and feasting were over at last. The minstrels had played to the point of exhaustion and now they slept, as did the Spanish maidens, who had danced the soles out of their shoes with joy. Even the dogs who had snuffled for scraps in the rushes, slept before the dead fires, their stomachs well-lined, their dreams contented.

But in the royal bedchamber, the King and Queen were wakeful still. The fire had died to a mound of white ash, and the stars outside grew pale, yet the newly married pair lay talking, enraptured by their tenderness, and by the new life which was opening up before them.

Henry rolled over in the bed and kissed Katherine's shoulder, marvelling at the silk of her skin. 'We will have a fair court,' he whispered. 'The best in Europe, Kate! No more turned doublets, or pease pudding at banquets, or hard bargains driven against our subjects. It will be a good life, my heart's darling.'

Katherine remembered the sad seven years of her widowhood as though it had been a bad dream, and her brief happiness with Arthur as though it had happened to another woman, in another life. She could see so clearly, now, the golden future which Henry sketched for her, made the more glorious because she would enter it beside him, safe in his love.

His lips moved warmly from her shoulder to her neck, and she turned her head, kissing the soft, damp hair which fell across his brow.

'A good life,' she murmured. 'Ah, but I love you, Hal.'

They sank into love once more, with hunger and with

tenderness, and his hands reached out for her, drawing her close. In the garden, the dull limbo light of dawn stole across the sky, stealing shadows and changing the world to grey.

'Oh Kate, I love you too,' he muttered fervently. 'We will love one another always, until death.'

Outside the window, as though in answer, a blackbird gave its shrill warning shriek, and like an echo, a thrush piped mockingly.